EMBRACE the *Desire*

Spring Stevens
author of *Embrace the Fire*

CRIMSON
ROMANCE

F+W Media, Inc.

This edition published by
Crimson Romance
an imprint of F+W Media, Inc.
10151 Carver Road, Suite 200
Blue Ash, Ohio 45242
www.crimsonromance.com

ISBN 10: 1-4405-7974-1
ISBN 13: 978-1-4405-7974-5
eISBN 10: 1-4405-7975-X
eISBN 13: 978-1-4405-7975-2

Chapter 1

"Damn you!"

Lying in a bed of white silk and fur, Payne jerked hard on the chains anchoring him to the bed. The crippling pain that he endured still lingered in his muscles and deep within his bones. "Damn you to fucking hell! I will never break."

He could survive pain; pain was something he was very accustomed to.

But this?

He was a Destroyer! He was a fighting, killing machine, damn it!

And he was chained like a dog, a beast! Expected and commanded to be subservient!

"Well, screw you!"

Flat on his back, straining against the enchanted chains, and with nothing else to do, he gave in to the thoughts running through his mind. Gyth, Lord of the Heavens and master of the Destroyers, leaned more toward torture and control than simple persuasion. No doubt, that was reason enough for the god to have enlisted Payne into his little army of immortal warriors whose chief purpose was to defeat his bitter enemy Damon, Lord of the Underworld.

Ironic really.

A virulent laugh echoed around him. Gyth threw the Destroyers to the proverbial wolves, not caring who survived as long as the enemy did not. Yeah, the enemy—Gyth's enemies.

In reality, the Destroyers were just a tool, Gyth's fighting force against the Underworld's offspring, even though they had been led to believe that the sole reason for their existence was to protect the One Race, the descendants of the gods that lived on earth.

Yeah, right. The age-old battle between the Heavens and the Underworld, or in truth, the battle between Gyth and Damon, which in turn had wrought the rise of the Destroyers, otherwise known as Gyth's lapdogs.

Damon! The Serpent Lord of the Underworld, *a.k.a.* dear old dad.

The name ripped through Payne like shards of steel and ice. The day would come when that bastard would have to stand toe to toe with him and it was a day Payne would wait a hundred thousand lifetimes for. After he almost died when his mother-dearest and those foul-breathed witches practically flayed him alive just to make points with that scum, Damon, all he wanted to do was to cut everything of Damon's out of his soul and have his revenge. Afterwards, he had been adopted by humans and had determined to hone his fighting skills. The only thing that kept him sane was his lust for revenge. So, when Gyth came to him and offered a means to that end, he didn't refuse.

Now, almost two thousand years later, the plan was still the same as ever. Damon would die by his hands.

Burning rage festered in his black eyes. Every Destroyer had his reasons for accepting Gyth's offer to become one of his lapdogs and Payne sure as hell had his.

"Bastilla."

The name was a whisper on his tongue, an endless torment in his cold heart.

Her image surfaced in his mind transporting him back to a time when he had loved—the only time in his existence he had known such a thing. The only time he thought he was loved in return. He had memorized every detail of her face—her long black silky hair, large dark innocent eyes, and the creamiest olive skin. She was perfection with a beauty that defied the natural world.

She had been the only good thing in his entire world.

Until Damon.

Until he realized the truth.

The soft rustle of silk brought Payne's attention back to the predicament at hand. Gyth stood in front of the bed, his eerie topaz eyes clearly expressing his agitation. Like Payne really cared! After all, what could the bastard in white do to him that had not already been done countless times before?

His sarcastic laugh brought fury to Gyth's face. "Have you changed your mind Destroyer?"

"No," Payne grunted softly. He wouldn't be so easily broken.

"You'll take the female known as Chanta Timbers through her Burning," Gyth ordered with a haunting laugh. "She'll need a strong Destroyer to assist her transformation to the One Race."

A female's face, one he knew, appeared in Payne's mind. Her skin was fair, her hair blonde, and her eyes the color of steel. His heart skipped a beat as her lips stretched into a blinding smile. She was light in the darkness, goodness personified. She was the exact opposite of Bastilla.

"Two words, Gyth: screw and you."

Topaz eyes met Payne's. "You'll do as I command."

The order tugged at every ounce of Payne's willpower.

As a Destroyer, he had to follow Gyth's commands, and never disobey, like a dog on a leash, trained and obedient. But Payne was ever the disobedient one, so why mess with success?

With heavily dripping defiance, he replied, "I won't take her through the Burning! I enlisted in this shit-fest against Damon for one purpose and only one, so screw you!"

"Hmm, well so be it Payne." Gyth's eyes swirled, turned white. "You shall endure the tortures of The Algea once again until your mind has changed."

Chanta Timbers' face appeared again in his mind, her large eyes full of excitement and wonder as she read from a book in her lap. She was beautiful, enchanting, and full of vitality. And he cursed under his breath. Her face had plagued his dreams for eight years. Shutting his black eyes and forcing her image from his mind, a growl ripped from his chest in anger.

"Get out of my head!" Payne roared. "I won't take her through the Burning!"

With a flick of his wrist, a mammoth of a male god dressed in black leather appeared beside Gyth holding a set of manacles. "You summoned me my lord?"

"What are we waiting for?" Payne laughed as his feet were manacled. "Can't wait to see the bastards again!"

The leather bound brainless slave of Akhos, the spirit of pain, grinned. Through his razor sharp yellow teeth, he gurgled. "The Algea await your return. They so enjoy the company your body and mind provide."

"I want him completely broken this time, spare no mercy, spare no pain. He is to be completely obedient." Gyth frowned as he looked down at Payne. "You'll do as I command or you'll suffer the consequences again and again. Learn from your mistakes Destroyer or I shall put you down myself."

"What's stopping you?" Payne spit out. "Two thousand years and I have yet to face Damon as you swore I would! Hold up your end of the bargain and I'll uphold mine!"

"The bargain was set, the deal between you and me was written in stone. One day, after you have served your purpose in my war against the evil of the Underworld, you'll have your heart's desire."

"Two thousand years! How much longer do you expect me to wait?" Payne jerked on the chains again.

Gyth paused, his pristine white robes swirling round his feet as his eyes swirled and glowed white. "Time will lead you to the path that you must walk. Your destiny is before you Payne, choose very carefully when you face the crossroads ahead."

A scream ripped through Payne's soul as the enchanted chains dug into his flesh. His back arched, the pain twisting inside his muscles, winding a path to every nerve ending in his body.

Refusing to break, he stared straight into Gyth's eyes with venom dripping from his lips. "I only walk one path and it will lead me to vengeance!"

• • • •

Payne reappeared suspended over a bed of wooden stakes. If he fell, he wouldn't die. He would be in a lot of pain but he could handle that. A laugh escaped his lips. All this for a woman going through the Burning. It was ridiculous.

Chanta's face came to his thoughts again. She had one of those faces that you never forgot, and he hadn't forgotten He didn't have to rack his brain when it came to her. He remembered. Eight years ago, he met her. Gyth had ordered a new sanctuary to be built in Kentucky and Payne had been placed there as a precautionary measure to ensure none of Damon's minions attacked. They hadn't, and Payne had gotten really bored, really fast.

He ran into her on a clear night. She was sitting under a green apple tree staring at the stars. As the memory resurfaced, the details of that night were crystal clear.

• • •

Lexington, Kentucky—eight years ago

Payne took his nightly walk around the sanctuary and paused as he looked across the rolling hillside. Alone under a tree, a woman was sitting, staring into the stars. She was out of the protective shroud Gyth had placed around the sanctuary.

Wondering if she was a member of the One Race, he made his way to her. First, something rumbled from deep inside of him that sent goose bumps along his flesh. Second, every feral instinct he had sprang to life. And before he came to his senses, one word bounced around his thoughts: *Mine.*

To announce his arrival, he stepped on a dead branch. She jumped to her feet, her face a mixture of surprise and fear. It wasn't the reaction he had hoped for, but it was for the best.

"Who are you?" She stepped back looking around. "No one is supposed to be out here this time of night."

He nodded, gave her a look he surmised would make her shake in her——he looked down——bare feet. "Are you from the sanctuary?"

Her mistrust pierced him for reasons he didn't understand. "Who are you?" she demanded.

She was wearing red and pink plaid pajamas, barefoot, and her blonde hair was braided. And she was pretty, too pretty to be on the outskirts of the shroud. She would make an easy target, an easy kill.

"Payne."

"You're the Destroyer Gyth has protecting us?" She attempted a half smile.

"Yes." He stepped closer, and could smell her lemon and honeysuckle scent. "Why are you out here? Gyth ordered everyone to stay on sanctuary grounds."

She looked up. "Watching the stars. And I'm not everyone. I play by my own rules."

"Really?"

"Yes, really."

"Well, you just haul your star-gazing ass back to the sanctuary, okay?"

She squared her shoulders, bracing her hands on her hips, her eyes narrowing. "Don't talk down to me. Get off your high horse and stop trying to order me around."

"I will repeat myself just one more time. Haul your ass back to the sanctuary." Payne took two steps and looked down at her. He could see, too, that beneath the challenge in her grey eyes, there was an undercurrent of fear, and it unsettled him. "Or I'll take you back myself."

"Excuse me?" She sputtered and stepped back. "I don't know who you think you are, but I don't take orders from you or from Gyth."

Narrowing his eyes, he grinned devilishly. "Over my shoulder or on your feet. Which way is it going to be?"

She turned on her heel, took a few brisk steps, and then started to run. Instincts fired in his brain, commanding him to chase. She made it a few more feet before he scooped her up, twisted her, and threw her over his shoulder.

"My way." He laughed as her fists beat at his back. "Such a pretty little girl out here all by her lonesome. If Damon's minions didn't get you, any number of horrible creatures could have."

Again, the word "mine" screamed at him from every corner of his mind but he refused to acknowledge it. He didn't have time for such silly notions or feelings. There was simply no place in his life for it. End of story.

"Let me go, you over-sized fool!" She kicked hard and he swatted her backside. "How dare you?"

"Oh, little lady, I dare." She was light as a feather and much too thin. Despite her fight, he could feel her fear cascading down his shoulders. "As a member of the One Race, you know better than to let yourself be unprotected."

"Who's going to protect me from you?" Her fingernails cut into his shoulder, her words cutting far deeper.

"Ouch! That hurt!"

She immediately relaxed her grip. "Sorry. But you brought it on yourself."

"Point taken."

"Look, I only work at the sanctuary, I'm not living there. Will you please put me down?"

He shifted her and planted her feet on the ground in front of him. He stared her down. She didn't shrink. *Interesting*.

"No one can protect you from me." He grabbed her wrists, pulled her to his chest. "You only work there?"

"Yes," She tried to arch her back away from him, but he only pulled her closer, taking a deep breath as he did. "You're a member of the One Race. I can smell it on you."

Even though her entire body was shaking, she looked up defiantly with a snarl on her lips. "Get your hands off me! How dare you touch me. Gyth will hear about this."

The woman was infuriating, maddening. . . and sexy, especially when she was pissed. He hadn't wanted to kiss a woman in a long time. Now seemed like a good time.

Payne laughed and flashed a bitter smile. "Tell him I did this, too."

He backed her up to the black fence that ran around the sanctuary. Leaning in tight, he stared at her full pink lips. When her mouth opened to protest, he took advantage of the moment, pulled her into his arms and kissed her. It wasn't right, for him to take this from her. He knew it.

"Bastard!"

Payne blinked, the stinging impact of her hand and her curse burning straight into his heart. "What makes you think for a second that I want your lips on mine?"

Catching her hands, he stared into her eyes, a fighter's eyes. She didn't even quiver, just simply stared back at him, one eyebrow cocked slightly.

"Well? Don't you think you should let me go now that you've had your fun trying to scare me?"

"I wasn't trying." He smiled devilishly as he easily manipulated her hands and brought her body flush to his leaning down to capture her lips.

She struggled in this embrace.

She was afraid; he could sense it, but she wasn't about to let on. That aroused him; everything about her did—her smell, the way she tasted of honey and sweet wine. The damnable word "mine" started ping ponging inside his brain, and he stopped dead in his tracks, his lips hovering a scant inch above hers.

With a growl of disapproval he pointed at the sanctuary. "Get out of my sight. Don't ever come out here again. Stay within the shroud."

She sank to her knees. Her emotions lighting up the air around him. "Oh God, you … you demon. How dare you! You had no right to touch me." She touched her lips.

"A kiss is the least of your worries." And he meant it on every level possible. He didn't understand what was going on inside his body but he knew without a doubt that this female, this woman, was the cause of it.

Payne crouched on his hunches and looked her dead in the eyes. He was taken by surprise when she returned his look with that cocky little eyebrow raised again. Perplexed by her spunk, he let his eyes devour her. Instead of her shaking in fear, she blatantly copied his action.

Whatever the attraction was that he was feeling, it had to be destroyed, annihilated. He didn't need or want any weaknesses and even though his body was demanding hers, he had to let her go. He couldn't afford to get absorbed into emotions he didn't know how to deal with, he had a mission to fulfill and she wasn't part of it. It was entirely too dangerous for someone like her, someone as good as she was, to get involved with the likes of him.

Compelling her to watch, he let his eyes change. Allowing the "demon," aka his Destroyer that lay under his skin to come out to play, he let his black irises expand devouring the white part of his eyes. Slowly, he let his double-edged fangs unsheathe, a gift from his father. As they slid down over his bottom lip, she scrambled backwards, her eyes wide with terror.

"What are you?"

His voice warped, twisted, a hissing sound hanging on every *s*. "Didn't Gyth tell you why Destroyers are so good at killing? We're all demons under our skin." She rolled under the fence and was on her feet before he could count to three. He wanted to chase her, wanted to get her in his arms again, and wanted to kiss those lips. Without looking back, she ran to the sanctuary, ran from the demon that lurked under his skin. And he could only remain as he was, crouched low to the ground, fighting every instinct in his entire body.

Chapter 2

As Akhos' slave disappeared with Payne, Gyth gritted his teeth. Cracking the muscles in his neck, he dematerialized sending himself to earth. Knowing that if Payne did not break soon, the world would have bigger problems to deal with, he sent a summons across the earth. He needed players in this game and he had to take the necessary precautions.

Determination raced through his heart. The oncoming events had to be played with precise control and like chess, the king had to be protected at all costs. The queen and her rooks would have to rule the board and corner the opponent's men.

From time to time, Gyth had to take these little excursions with a fair amount of patience, even when they involved the throne of the Heavens. Knowing what future lay ahead, he had to turn the tables. He wasn't going to allow Damon to rise from the Underworld, nor was he going to lose the throne any time soon.

Materializing in front of the Tortured Souls, the bar that served as a sanctuary for his Destroyers, his eyes darkened. If the game was to be played and for his team to have a fighting chance, he would have to make sure that he chose the best of the best to be Chanta's rooks. The bishops and the knights, although important, would have to be probable forfeits in the game as well as the pawns.

His nostrils flared. As much as it dismayed him, Payne was the king in this game and he had to be protected at any cost. True, Chanta was the priceless asset; however, in order to achieve the desired outcome, Payne would have to survive. And the best protection he could give him was sitting at the bar drinking vodka. Gyth's own son, Varick Ta Farg, was the best of the best.

Given the recent events in Varick's life, he may not be a willing participant in the game. With a low grunt, Gyth walked into the bar and met Varick's eyes. No matter how defiant his newly transformed son was, he knew that Varick would never allow any serious harm to come to Payne.

Varick was a god now, his powers restored. Gyth got his eyes full of Varick's appearance. Black trench coat, black cowboy boots, and a black button up silk shirt graced his muscular body. He and Gyth shared common traits. They had the same gold eyes and the same white hair. They both flexed their jaws when angry or upset. Gyth's gaze flickered over the red braid hanging from his son's temple.

The braid was the same as Terror Sky's, the elemental god that served Isten with a faith that defied logic. Gyth had no idea what the braid meant, but he was sure it did not bode well. Nevertheless, Varick would serve the purpose at hand simply because of Payne and their friendship.

Across the empty bar, Varick set his glass down, small sparks of purple flames jumping from his fingers. "Where the hell is Payne?"

"In the realm of the Algea." Gyth replied, "Either he'll do as I command or he'll be ruined."

In a flash, Varick was in Gyth's face, his hand wrapping around his neck. "Father or not, if you harm Payne, I'll destroy you!"

"Before you take me on, you'd better learn how to control those god powers. Your threats are empty until you do," Gyth reminded him. "Remove your hands or I'll have that bastard son of Damon's neutered and skinned alive."

Varick stared hard at his father and slowly dropped his hand. "What do you want from me? That's why you're here isn't it? To make a bargain in return for Payne's freedom."

Straightening his robes and trying to keep his anger intact, Gyth followed Varick to the bar. "The female, Chanta Timbers, is entering her Burning. Her destiny is to be protected at all costs." Gyth gritted his teeth. "You'll make sure that Payne takes her through it and that she survives."

Varick shook his head. "Payne won't touch a woman. There isn't a woman alive that holds a flame next to Bastilla."

"That concubine from his past? He still holds that wench in such high regard?"

Varick shrugged. "To each his own. But I'm telling you right now, Payne won't take any female through the Burning. Just isn't going to happen."

"Granted, Payne wouldn't have been my first choice, but he's the only one strong enough to do this. Your job is to make sure he does his duty and that she lives." Gyth walked around the bar and poured himself a shot of vodka. "Chanta's destiny and her life is of great importance in the Heavens. *They* will try to take her down as she enters the Burning and her presence is revealed."

"Then hide her presence." Varick paused. "You can't, can you? And who are 'they'?"

"The Angels, an ever-loving thorn in my backside." Gyth shook his head. "I have very little control over her life. I cannot hide her, I cannot force her against her will, and I cannot interfere with the Burning."

Suspicious, Varick stared hard at Gyth. "Why?"

For a moment, Gyth wasn't sure he wanted to answer that question. "Because she is an enigma, part angel, part goddess. I cannot interfere with angel affairs, no matter how great or small. Angels are literally another pantheon of their own, one that I do not and cannot control. I can at best only make bargains with them. Its part of the gods-be-damned laws."

There was a lot more at stake than just Payne's destiny. Not that he cared about what happened to Payne, but Chanta's future was another matter. She had to survive, especially now that her original destiny had been unwritten.

The Angels were always and forever after the throne, especially Chanta's mother. She was the biggest thorn in Gyth's backside and unfortunately, it was of his own doing.

If Chanta didn't survive the Burning, there would be consequences in the Heavens. And Gyth wasn't about to lose the throne. He had forfeited too much and fought too damn hard to simply let Chanta's mother take it.

Gyth swallowed the shot. The bitter, sweet burn lingered in the back of his throat. "I had a deal with the Angels and that bargain cannot be broken. I agreed to let Chanta live as normally as possible on earth—to live as a human, until she turned twenty one."

"Does Chanta know she's part angel?"

Gyth slowly shook his head. "She understands that she is descended from the gods but she has no idea that her mother is an angel."

"That doesn't explain why you can't protect her now or hide her here on earth."

"Chanta Timbers isn't just part Angel." He watched Varick uneasily as he made his way around to the front of the bar. "She's your sister."

Varick slammed his fists on the bar. "Then why in the nine hells is she on earth?"

"Angels aren't gods." Gyth grimaced as Varick grabbed the bottle of vodka from the bar and tipped it to his lips. "When angels are born, they are sent to earth to reside here and learn human nature. And as you know, only full-blooded gods and full-blooded angels can reside in the Heavens."

"There's more to this, isn't there?"

Gyth nodded and stared into his son's eyes. "Gods make mistakes and meddle in things that they shouldn't regardless of the consequences."

"What mistake did you make?"

"Chanta was my mistake. I wanted a daughter at any cost. Her mother offered me a bargain and I took it. The bottom line is if she dies, I will lose the throne and the Heavens will fall to the

Angels. If I lose the throne there will be nothing to stop Damon from rising from the Underworld and unleashing hell on Earth."

Varick tipped the bottle to his lips, swallowed, and leaned against the bar. "Does Damon know about her?"

Gyth sat down on a barstool, his legs suddenly feeling like Jell-O. "Damon does have an interest in her. He could have killed her, but at the time he didn't know she was my daughter. Now that she is entering the Burning, all bets are off that he won't figure it out." For the first time in his long life, Gyth's heart felt heavy. "There's something about her that Damon found irresistible. I was lucky to have found her when I did."

"Damon? Did she know who and what he was?" Varick slowly sat down beside of him at the bar, his jaw slack. "Where does that leave her?"

Gyth shook his head as disgust rolled around his stomach. "No, she didn't know, not until Damon was one step from slicing her throat."

Silence hung between them for seconds, mere seconds that felt like eons.

"But Damon didn't harm her; he couldn't for some reason." Gyth closed his eyes. "That's the night I found her, naked and in his arms in a dark alley. Her terror was heart shattering. Not until after Damon vanished did I realize just what had been wrought between them. My own flesh and blood was in love with my bitter enemy. I have been protecting her ever since that night because she allows me to, but now, I cannot protect her from the Burning. It is her time."

"Because she is part angel, you have to have her permission to protect her and I can only assume, she doesn't want your protection."

Gyth could only nod. His voice lodged in his throat.

"Has Damon made any move against her?"

Gyth shook his head. "She is a member of the One Race because my blood runs through her veins, but that also means that only someone with the truest strength of the gods can save her. That leaves her in desperate need to have a Destroyer take her through the Burning." Gyth reached for the bottle in Varick's hand and added. "That leaves her in desperate need of Payne."

Varick stood, his topaz eyes swirling with power. "And Payne is Damon's son. The chances of him doing this are zero to none especially if he finds out that she was once Damon's lover."

"He must or Chanta will die." For added measure, Gyth stood and grabbed Varick's shoulder. "Your sister, my daughter, will die."

Chapter 3

Mounds of books lay scattered across the granite coffee table, littered the floor, and obscured any pathway through the small living room. In these pages, Chanta Timbers had found so many ways to leave the planes of reality. They were her escape. They offered her silence in the wake of so many storms.

Today, escape seemed impossible. Her thirtieth birthday was just around the corner. Being a member of the One Race had plenty of advantages, if you survived the Burning. And that was a big *if*.

The Burning would start on her birthday, last a week, maybe two. She would be consumed with confusion, weakness, muscle cramps, headaches, and lust. The drive to have sex would push her right over the edge and send her straight into the Burning. It was biology, simple and complicated.

Because she was descended from the gods, on her thirtieth birthday, her life as a human would come to an end, literally. Biology would demand her body to undergo major changes, her genetic makeup, which was dormant, would awaken and force the change, the transformation, to take place. Only the strongest descendants survived the Burning because it was an overwhelming physical and mental challenge.

And if that wasn't enough, the need and desire to have sex would consume her. If she refused to have sex with another member of the One Race or a Destroyer, she would die. End of game. It was the consequence of being a descendant of the gods. Too bad she didn't know who or even which one of her parents had passed on the god genes. She had been left at an orphanage, had no memory of either of her parents.

If she survived, she would be granted special powers—a unique gift, a special ability that was hers and hers alone, as distinct as a fingerprint, and long-lasting life. Chanta could live for hundreds or thousands of years. She would not die of old age, her body would restore itself, never wearing down or causing her demise by natural causes.

However, she was not immortal. She could die by another's hand. Even the gods could die.

The problem was that during the Burning, many members felt the urge to mark their sexual partner as theirs ... for the rest of eternity. It was a bond that was unbreakable, and if one died, the other would slowly go insane. She didn't want to be marked and belong to anyone, especially not for the rest of her conceivably very long life. And she didn't want to mark a man either. If he was not a member of the One Race or a Destroyer, but a regular mortal, his life span would be short, and she damn sure didn't want to go insane.

Insane with godly powers sure didn't sound like a good combination.

And a Destroyer? They harbored demons under their skin, were ruthless killers, and from the stories she had heard, they were emotionally brutal. Male members of the One Race were few and far between, most already bonded with someone that had taken them through the Burning.

And if she were to be marked, then what? She had a job she loved, she had devoted herself to helping children of the One Race, and she wasn't about to give that up. Not to mention, she was just turning thirty and had already been through enough rocky relationships to last her several lifetimes.

If she had a choice she would just stay human and not go through the Burning.

But she did not.

She breathed in through her lips, the fragrance of the old books calming her nerves. Shoving those thoughts aside, she looked down at the pile of papers to her right and groaned. Shoving her thoughts of the Burning aside, as well, she turned to the stack of reports by her side.

Chanta ran her slight fingers through her thick cotton-blonde hair. What exactly had she been thinking when she told her students to do reports on the creation myth? And why had she not picked just one for them. Oh no, she had let them choose their own. Twenty research papers and almost all of them were on a different myth.

There were just so many gods and so many myths. She should have simply assigned the One Race creation myth, which would have been much easier. And because she knew she wouldn't be able to sleep until she graded each one, she gave in and grabbed another book.

A rattling noise jerked her from her thoughts. She sat up and went to her knees peering over the couch. Her heart was in her throat, terror only inches from claiming her. Straining, she listened, watched.

"I'm safe here." She whispered as her eyes darted around the room. "I'm safe."

A faint smile spread cross her lips as a small black cat jumped on the back of the couch and purred at her. Her body relaxed, a sigh escaping her lips. She was safe; she knew that, but still, sometimes an odd feeling of fear crept up her spine and beat at the base of her skull, like a warning bell going off.

Instantly, she thought of Damon and the night he had revealed to her what and who he truly was. Anger crept over her terror. She was just another member of the One Race, just another plaything in the ongoing war he had with Gyth. And he had used her in the foulest of ways. He seduced her, made her feel things that she had never felt and still hadn't felt to this day.

Members of the One Race had to be careful, fearful. They never knew when or where they would be attacked or even how it would happen. Under Damon's rule, the minions of the Underworld were constantly trying to eradicate the race. And there were so very few of them that survived. If you were descended from a god, the safest place to be was at a sanctuary.

A sanctuary like the one where she was a teacher. One Race Academy, a private boarding school for One Race children, was one of the safest places on earth. Secluded and hidden behind the guise of a horse farm on the outskirts of Lexington, Kentucky, the academy protected those children. It was the kind of protection she had needed when she was a child.

She had dedicated the last nine years of her life to the academy, making sure it was stocked, staffed, and protected at all times. The children there were orphans in one way or another and needed the protection the academy offered. With her dying breath, she would see to it that those children were not harmed.

With the profits from her diner, After Midnight, she managed to stay afloat and one step ahead of her bills. Quietly nestled in the hubbub of the city, the diner offered her an escape from the academy. The paychecks she received from the academy were safely nestled away in a fund to help support the children she cared about so very much.

If she could make a single difference in any of the One Race children's lives, she would do it, no matter how much she had to give.

Groaning rather loudly, Chanta reached for an old tattered and yellow stained book, the only thing that had survived her childhood, other than the emotional scars. How she had managed to keep it was beyond her. Being tossed from one human home to the next, from one orphanage to the next, it was simply a miracle it had not been lost.

She vaguely wondered about her parents. Were they dead? Why did they leave her at a human orphanage? She had so many questions and not nearly enough answers.

Slowly, she opened the cover and for the millionth time, she read the words written by the mother she had never known.

"To my precious daughter, my heart, my soul, and the light of all things good—in your possession I leave this book. One day it will lead you to your destiny and all will be as it should be. With love, your blood-born mother, Elena."

She stared with steel gray eyes at the words for a long time before turning the page and taking a deep, ragged breath. The title page was empty, save one inscription in ancient Sanskrit. "As Above so it will be Below. Herein reads the *Book of Light*."

Her Sanskrit was not the best, but she read it anyway.

"All life sprouted forth from the hands of the eight gods of creation. This is the telling of one of these accounts, written and sealed for all time by the eyes of Isten, the eldest and most grand of the eight gods."

Her phone rang stirring her from the familiar trance the words seemed to always put her in. Numbly, she reached for the phone, her eyes falling to the next paragraph and her mind burning the words hard into her heart. *"Isten saw what would come, saw man stepping out from the ground and procreating. He saw the race grow, spread. But they were unprotected. Holding his hand out, he manifested a ball of white light. Within the light, a being grew. And that being was called an Angel. Henceforth, Angels became guardians of mankind."*

"Hello?"

"Chanta?" The familiar velvet male voice made her smile. "What troubles you child?"

She snorted. "These research papers! I'm telling you Gyth, they're going to be the death of me."

He laughed. "Nonsense. Your teaching skills are excellent. I'm sure you'll get them graded before the weekend is over."

"Well, one thing is for sure, next time I'm going to be a little more specific about the subject." Wondering why he had called, she gently laid her book on the couch behind her. "Is there something wrong?"

"It's time." His voice sent a cold chill down her spine. "In less than six months, your Burning will begin."

She swallowed hard. "I know."

"For your benefit, I have hand-picked a Destroyer for you." He paused. "He's strong and his powers are exceptional. I chose him because I believe he'll successfully take you through the Burning."

"But . . ." Her voice faltered. Destroyers were demons. Cold, calculating demons who killed without mercy and without pause.

"Chanta, when I found you, I swore to you that I would do everything in my power to make sure you would survive and others like you would have more than a fighting chance."

"I know. And you've helped me so much." Memories of the day she had met Gyth swamped her. "I owe you my life."

"Nonsense. What Damon did to you was because of me; it was a shameless and cowardly thing. There is nothing I can do to make those things up to you, so allow me to assist you in this."

Tears came to her eyes, her heart breaking all over again. She didn't dare mention that somehow, Damon, in human form had made her fall hard for him. "I can never pay you back enough for saving me."

"Let me help you again." His voice was almost pleading. "Allow me to send him to you so you'll have a better chance of surviving."

She leaned her head back and closed her eyes.

"And if I can't go through with it?"

"You must. If you can't do it for yourself, do it for me. Do it for the children at the academy. Just make sure you survive."

Survive? He made it sound like an invitation to a death match, but then that's what it was. With a ragged breath, she answered, "Okay."

Chapter 4

In the pit of the Algea's lair, Payne succumbed to the betrayal of his mind to his tortured body. He screamed viciously as steel spikes fell upon his limbs pinning him to the marble slat beneath him. In the darkened recesses of his mind, he heard Gyth's personal hounds of misery, the Algea, taunting him. Akhos and Lupe laughed as Ania begged them to let her have a turn.

The spikes vanished and his wounds started to heal, his bones mending as his shattered mind slowly gathering tidbits of information about his surroundings. A need for retribution slithered through his soul as his numb body refused to move. It was times like these that he was grateful for his ability to heal so well. Being the son of Damon had its advantages.

Ania, a black-haired slender wisp of a goddess, crossed the black marbled floor and stood in front of Payne's mangled, but healing body. Her hair was swept up on top of her head with a golden tiara firmly nestled in its curls. She wore a short white silk chiton that came just above her knees, gold sandals were on her tiny feet laced up her legs just under her knees. Gold bracelets dangled on her arms and gold earrings dangled from her ears down to her shoulders.

She was devastatingly beautiful in a dark, sultry, maddening kind of way. Maddening to the point that Payne would gladly gouge out her eyes or his own for that matter. He felt the urge to laugh, but his throat wasn't working properly.

She pouted. "Come on Payne. Hurry and heal so we can play."

He wanted to choke the babbling witch until her black eyes popped out of her head. Of the three spirits of pain, she was his least favorite. Being the most abhorrent of the menacing trio, she was the most worthy of his hatred. The goddess of sorrow, grief, and mental distress, she could, with a single, slight touch, take a man to his knees and turn his hand on himself, causing him to take his own life.

His psychotic laughter filled the dark chamber. But he was no man, he was Payne! Let her do her worst.

Before his body had healed enough to allow him movement, Ania reached down and ever so gently ran her fingertips over his brow. Her hysterically gloomy chuckle split through his hard exterior and despair clutched his entire being. Dangerous and volatile emotions tore through his mind like red-hot daggers, sending him back through time.

Ania's voice echoed softly, her words scorching his thoughts. "Deeper inside than ever before. Let me see your pain, your suffering, your heart's torture."

No matter how hard he tried, the images and memories surfaced like oil from water. His earliest memory took over, drowned out the male that he was and took him down the venomous path to self-destruction.

His mother, head witch of the coven he was raised in, lifted her hand, and with a howl of anger beat him until he passed out. When he woke, she was kneeling over him, his blood dripping from the dagger in her hand. Naked and afraid to move, to breathe, to cry, he watched as his mother carved into his skin over his heart the star that claimed him as property of the god Damon.

But he wasn't just property; he was Damon's son.

The beatings and the bloodlettings at the hands of his flesh and blood mother tumbled around in his unforgiving mind. Years of nothing but pain and fear cascaded over him, fueled his desire to die. But he wasn't even allowed that option. He was a god's son and in his mother's unmerciful care.

Then Bastilla had appeared and his heart rejoiced, finding something other than fear. She was his everything, but her treachery and fearful love of Damon sliced through his soul. With one look, she had ripped out his heart and served it to him on a gold platter. Her love was pledged to his father, bound to him in ways that even Payne could not describe. She had refused him and betrayed him to his mother and father.

Twisting violently as Ania's will compelled him deeper still into himself, images of his father flashed through his mind. The evil acts and sinister deeds he had been obliged to observe while chained at his father's feet drove his soul to the brink of insanity. Innocent people tortured, maimed, and flayed alive for Damon's viewing pleasure, all the while he was compelled to watch, never blinking, never trying to help.

And then there were the deviant sexual acts that plagued him. Countless times he had witnessed orgies and intense bondage ceremonies, all in the name of his father. So many naked twisting bodies, tied up, flayed, and beaten that their faces and names blurred into a mass of anger in his brain. Before the age of fifteen, he had witnessed the most extreme sexual acts known to man, and some only known to the gods.

It was his death and rebirth as a Destroyer that magnified his lust for revenge. For Bastilla's betrayal, nightmares that knew no end, and his lost childhood, he would kill Damon, and Gyth had offered him a means to that end. For the unnecessary beatings, he would kill his mother. But Gyth had not held up his end of the bargain. Years and years of being Gyth's lapdog, not fulfilling his need for revenge, and all the betrayals he had endured, forced his thoughts and emotions together ripping the despair and gut-wrenching sorrow from his chest.

But he would not be broken!

He welcomed the sorrow, the pain, the humiliation, and the truth of who and what he was. Each action he had taken, every second of torment he had endured fed his inner beast, fired the desire and lust for Damon's blood. To kill the one true evil in the world, that was his one and only purpose.

Tears burned his eyes, yet he refused to cry. So much pain cascaded through him, threatened his sanity, and manifested into rage as he defied his emotions. With all that was Payne, he jerked on the chains and sat up.

When he spoke through blood, aching, and unshed tears, his roar was deafening. "Pain is and always has been my ally!"

• • •

Ania stood as still as stone, Akhos, with his blood red hair tied at the nape of his neck, bowed his head, and Lupe caught his breath. Never had they heard such a splendid sound. Not once in all their existence had they witnessed such infinite and all-consuming strength.

The Algea nodded in unison, silently agreeing that their torments were useless. Akhos stood from his seat, his long white chiton splattered red with Payne's blood, and held out his hand to Ania as Lupe spoke in his gravel biting tone.

"Someone has committed a great injustice and it must be righted." Lupe floated to Payne's side. "Gyth has no idea of the strength he has barely contained in this one's soul."

Ania's black tears ran down her cheeks as Lupe grabbed Payne by the throat and held him up, his body dangling in his grasp. "We must consult Isten. Pain that runs as deep as this breeds revenge and will break the chains of command. If indeed he succeeds in his desire to kill Damon, the hierarchy of this world will fall."

Payne's despair brought a soft moan to Ania lips as Akhos nodded.

"He won't be pleased with us for complying to Gyth's wishes where this one is concerned." Ania groaned again as Payne's memories leapt like fire through her heart. "His destiny has been unwritten."

Running his other hand through his dark blue hair, Lupe nodded. "The destruction of this universe hangs on a teetering edge!"

Ania took Lupe's hand. "But do we dare consult Isten?"

"We must." Lupe jerked away from Ania, throwing Payne across the marble chamber. "Isten will be angered that we have not come sooner."

Akhos disagreed. "No, he will understand. We were born to serve and cohere to whatever god rules this universe. Before he went into dormancy, Isten declared us free from his service and to serve the uprising gods. We have only done as we were born to do."

Ania nodded hesitantly. Her brothers did not know the things she did, and she was wary to consult them. "And what of Gyth?"

Lupe snorted. "He must follow Isten's command. He would not be sitting on the throne if Isten had not made it so. Remember, we chose to follow him and to serve him." He smiled. "And now, we choose not to."

Akhos chuckled. "Free will, sister mine. We, like all things before the creation of this universe, truly do have free will and none can dictate our lives or our destinies."

"Why would someone erase Payne's destiny?" Ania asked, even though she knew the why of it full well. "Of all the beings in this universe, why him?"

Akhos held his hand up, silencing her questions. "Regardless of why or who, we must consult Isten. If this universe is on a one way path to destruction, we must warn him that it draws near."

Ania nodded. Akhos was right in this. The course had to be taken and she knew that. She vaguely thought of her friends on earth and knew she could not stand by and let the future fall as it was going. She would intervene.

"Yes, of course, brother mine. Under no circumstance can we allow destruction."

Lupe took Ania's hands in his large ones. "And if destruction is inevitable, what of all the innocent lives in this realm? And exactly where would you feed your need for sorrow? Where would any of us feed?"

Ania thought of Jaiden and his precious books. "With Jaiden gone, perhaps it's best for us to deliver Payne to Isten and let him decide the next course of action." Of course, she completely disagreed with that, but she didn't know exactly where her brothers stood on the matter. "Perhaps, Isten, being the oldest and grandest of all gods, would better know how to handle the situation."

With deep breaths and with slight agreeing smiles, Akhos and Lupe nodded and looked at Payne. His body, once bloody, broken and unidentifiable, now twisted, mended, and rose above the marble floor.

"We'll take him to Isten's sanctum and once more pledge ourselves to our king."

Chapter 5

The Isle of the Blessed and the Condemned grew dark as Isten took a deep breath and awoke from his slumber. His thoughts troubled him as he turned his senses outward, into the vast universe he and the other seven gods had created so very long ago.

His nose flared as he felt the *Book of Light* open. The words rumbled inside of him, the past crashing into the here and now. The universe groaned, crackled, and roared in defiance. Isten's eyes glowed softly as he wondered what had caused such unrest.

He searched deeper. All he had created, all he had envisioned was out of balance. Somewhere, somehow things had gone utterly awry. He considered all the possibilities and yet none of them made sense.

He had taken things into his own hands with the aide of two trusted allies, Terror Sky and Charon. A year ago he had rewritten one of his descendant's DNA, Varick Ta Farg. And in doing so, had set things back on track, but yet he still felt the onslaught of destruction, a twisting rip in time and space. There was simply no answer coming to him for this traitorous act and he could not find the culprit behind it.

He had been pulled out of dormancy after thousands of years of sleep. And what he had found was beyond reason. He was trapped by an unseen force on the isle, and yet, he still had his power. His ability to leave, however, evaded him. He was the most powerful being in this universe—or at least he had been.

His spine tingled as the words from the *Book of Light* crashed around his presence. A god-born female was reading the words from the book, a book that explained the need for angels. Anger stirred his contemplation as he recalled the birth of the books and the god-child he had used to create them: Jaiden. The name should have been stricken from history upon his demise, but yet his name and books had survived … somehow.

The *Book of Destruction*, the *Book of Creation*, and the twelve books of knowledge were precautionary measures, and most had been lost since he had been in dormancy. Charon was now on a mission to retrieve all of those books. Someone was using them to change destiny, change the future.

The question was who and why?

For the thousandth time, he raised his hand and tried to leave the isle, but still he could not. Fury marred his white brow. What god, what being could have banished him from the universe he had created? And what of the other gods of his pantheon? Why did they not heed his call?

Raising his eyes to the sky, a purple flash announced Terror Sky's arrival. The Elemental god, in dragon form, landed at Isten's side. Seconds passed as the red dragon's form twisted and melted. Isten waited as Terror Sky shook off the last effects of the transformation into human form.

"What news do you bring me?" Isten's voice boomed, echoing down the rust colored valleys and canyons. "What is this unrest I feel in the universe?"

"A Destroyer, one called Payne." Terror Sky shook his head. "The Algea are here and they have him. They have advised his future has been unwritten."

"What? Unwritten?" Isten couldn't believe his ears. "The only one allowed to interfere with those books was Jaiden, and he is dead."

"The Algea cannot explain it and neither can Charon. But they do know that Gyth doesn't have the books, but some of them are in the Heavens."

Isten turned and stared hard at the elemental god. "Are you sure of this?"

"Yes." Terror Sky ran his hand through his black hair. "Charon and I went to see Gyth. I could feel the books' presence, but could not locate them."

"There are nine layers in the Heavens. Could you at least tell what layer they were on?"

Terror Sky shook his head. "There is more. Gyth has enlisted Varick's aid with Chanta Timbers. She is entering the Burning."

Isten stood as stone, felt his gray eyes blazing. "It cannot be. Her birth is too soon. Has someone altered her destiny as well?"

"I don't fathom to understand how this universe or fate works. She was born as you intended, but from there, her life has not been as it should have been." Terror Sky looked up and watched as the sky grew darker, casting long shadows across the desert of the isle. "From what I can gather, her destiny has been integrated with the Angels and with the Destroyers."

"And Damon? If her destiny has been changed, then his, too, must have been."

Terror sky remained silent, his brows pulled together in thought.

"We must find the one behind these changes. And do our best to correct the balance." Isten curled his hands into fists. He was Isten, the most grand of the eight original gods of creation and he was not going to stand by and let his universe be destroyed. "And find a way to get me out of this prison!"

Terror Sky nodded, his body twisting and rising into the air as he transformed back into dragon. Isten waited patiently for Terror Sky to leave, then he turned his attention to the floating castle barely within sight.

Thunder rolled as Isten roared in anger. Red horns twisted out of his head as his body lifted and twisted in the air. He was Isten, father of this universe, king of his pantheon, and his very creation was falling apart at the seams!

Lightning streaked across the sky as his fury rose. Someone would pay for the treachery and the meddling! With a violent burst of energy, his body transformed into dragon as fire spewed from his mouth. His red and black scales glittering under the lightning that danced in the sky.

His great eyes latched onto the black castle that sat nestled in storm clouds above a barren mountainside. Payne was inside with the Algea. The Destroyer was in for an awakening and Isten wanted answers.

Answers that he would have one way or the other!

•••

Chanta Timbers was oblivious to the male that sat in the back of the teacher's lounge. He was cloaked and invisible. He watched her carefully, took in her facial features, her actions, and her small structure. She was indeed a daughter of Gyth. He suddenly pitied her. Then laughed and scowled at himself; after all, he was a son of Gyth.

Hours passed before Varick uncloaked himself and then waited for her to see him. When she did, he held his breath as he looked into her eyes. His stomach flipped, knowing that he would have to introduce her to a world of terror and sacrifice, of pain and treachery.

"Can I help you?" Her voice was soft, compelling, and warm.

"It isn't what you can help me with. It's what I can help you with." He tried to smile, but failed to manifest it on his face.

She laughed and eagerly looked around the small room. "Where is he?"

"He who?" Varick questioned.

"Gyth." She answered as if she had known him her entire life. "Isn't he with you?"

Varick shook his head as his skin crawled. He had never witnessed a soul giddy to see Gyth. It almost made him physically ill. He swallowed hard. If he had been human, he was sure he would have vomited. Or worse.

He stood and went to her table. Taking her hands into his. Her eyebrows knitted together making her look even more like Gyth. A female version, shorter and sweeter.

Varick smiled and managed to spit out. "I am related to Gyth, his son, in fact."

"His son?" Chanta laughed. "He never told me about a son." Suddenly her face flushed. "You're a Destroyer, aren't you?"

"No. I used to be." He watched as relief washed over her face.

Varick ran his thumb over her fingers. Instantly, he felt the bond of blood, thick and true, running through her veins. This was his sister.

"Good genes." Varick laughed, suddenly feeling at ease.

She look confused. "So, what exactly are you doing here?"

"Payne." Varick stretched his legs out under the table. "Gyth chose him to take you through the Burning. Unfortunately, he is missing."

Chanta stood, her hands fisting. "What did you say?"

"Payne is the one Gyth has chosen to help you."

She took a step back.

"Payne . . .? Why does it have to be him?"

"Because he's the best and the strongest."

Varick waited for a reaction, watched her lift her hand slowly to her lips.

Varick shrugged. "But it seems he's gone AWOL."

"Good. Maybe he'll stay that way."

"He obviously already made an impression."

"You could say that … and it left a lot to be desired."

Seeing the apprehension in her gray eyes, he continued slowly and with as much soft compulsion as he could muster. "Payne may not exactly be Mr. Charm and Personality, but he's a good guy ... and more importantly, he's strong. Now sit and listen."

She shook her head. "No. I made up my mind." Taking another step back, she darted out of his reach. "Gyth can't do that to me. I won't let him. And why would he send you to tell me Payne was missing? Why can't you take me through the Burning?"

She stumbled backwards, her breath catching in her throat as she turned to the door. Her face was pale, her eyes suddenly appearing much too large for her face. With a quick step, he grabbed her wrist and pulled her into his arms.

"Because I am Varick Ta Farg, I'm descended from Isten, one of the eight gods of creation and so are you." He swallowed the curse. "You're Gyth's daughter, just as I'm his son."

Her face paled, her jaw going slack. A second passed and she laughed, rather hysterically. "You're kidding me?"

"No, I don't kid with anyone. He is your father."

•••

Chanta's body went still and Varick slowly released her. She followed his lead as he pulled out a chair for her to sit. Without a word or an expression, she sat as he explained in every detail how she was Gyth's daughter and how her mother was an Angel.

For an hour, she listened.

For an hour, she denied everything he was saying.

For an hour, she sat numb to her core as the words from her mother's book came pouring out of a man's mouth who claimed to be her brother. The same man who was claiming Gyth was her father. She wondered silently if she had lost touch with reality and was hallucinating.

Without thinking, she reached across the table and pinched Varick. He knitted his brows together and stopped talking. He felt real.

"I am real." He laughed as his eyes sparkled.

"I have lost my mind." She stood. "If you'll excuse me, I think I need some fresh air."

Varick stood as well and walked with her to the door. "Perhaps what you need is a reality check."

She turned to him as he took her elbow. Her gasp was lost as purple sparks sucked her into a vortex and spun her straight into time and space. Just as suddenly as she had disappeared, she reappeared inside her small apartment, her books still laying scattered everywhere in her living room.

Varick's voice bounced around the room. "I'll find Payne. He'll take you through your transformation. If you ever have need of me, just say my name."

"I don't want Payne to help me. I don't want that monster near me." Chanta screamed as she spun around the room. "Why would I have need of you?"

Varick appeared in the middle of the room facing her. She dropped to her knees.

"You're the daughter of Gyth who rules the Heavens and he has enemies. That means you're going to need protection and lots of it."

She laughed hysterically. "If he's my father and Payne is the one chosen, I'll need a dagger or a sword. Payne is a demon, a monster."

"Like I said, he's not going to win a popularity contest any time soon, but he's the best choice." He started to wonder how she knew of Payne.

"Best choice?" She walked around the room, looked behind the curtains. "Why is my best choice my worst nightmare?"

"Because sister mine, as part of the One Race, you'll have enemies and being Gyth's daughter means you have to let someone who holds the power of the gods in the palm of his hand to take you through the Burning. Payne is the best choice and the strongest of the Destroyers. Not only will I protect what is mine, Payne will too."

"Sister?" She croaked as tears burned her eyes. "If I'm your sister, where the hell were you when I needed protection? Where the hell were you when I needed someone, when I was all alone? Where the hell was my father and my mother?"

As he vanished, he whispered. "You'll never be alone again."

Chapter 6

In the depths of the Underworld, Charon appeared in Damon's bedroom. His black robes swirling about his booted feet as the sound of dead crunching leaves followed him. Damon sat crosslegged in the floor in front of two mirrors that cast a green light around the room. It was an ordinary scene in the Underworld.

Taking a closer look, Charon saw that Damon sat in the middle of a five-pointed star drawn with blood on the marble floor. A glass bowl was sitting at each point. Charon didn't bother asking what Damon was doing, he already knew.

Each bowl held a *shade*, the spirit of a dead person from when Hades had ruled the Underworld. Damon was using the shades' miseries and woes to feed himself. With the lack of ambrosia, the food that fed god powers, all the gods in the Underworld, had to turn elsewhere for nourishment.

It was the same with the One Race; they, too, had to find nourishment where they could, or over time, a form of psychoses took place. A burning rage would consume them until eventually death was the only option.

Damon smiled, his black lips glistening in the green glow. "I see you have returned."

"You and I have business to discuss." Charon lifted the hood of his robe, his face nothing more than a skull with red eyes. "As before, there are bargains to be made."

Damon raised an eyebrow. "We do have much to discuss. The last time we spoke, you said Varick was Gyth's weakness." He paused as Charon looked at the woman tied to Damon's bed.

Damon tapped his long fingers on his chin as he narrowed his eyes. When he spoke, the woman groaned, sounded eager. "I have done my research. Why didn't you tell me about Chanta Timbers?"

Charon remained silent as he studied the woman on the bed. She was compliant to Charon's chagrin. Dressed in black leather, she appeared to be perfectly at ease waiting for her master. Charon laughed.

"You asked me to reveal Gyth's weakness." Charon continued as he watched anger flash across Damon's face, "You didn't specify which one."

"She's his daughter," Damon hissed, shattering the large glass bowl at his side. Wails of pain erupted from the shards as he picked up the largest piece and slung it across the black marbled floor. "If I had known she was his daughter, I could have used her to bring Gyth to his knees! I tire of these games."

Charon's cold laughter echoed around the room, the misery in his tone causing the woman on the bed to groan. "You didn't know and yet you fed from her misery and glorified yourself in her pain."

A cruel smile lifted the corners of Damon's mouth. "To this day I have not found one such as she. The challenge she gave me was thrilling."

Damon stood, his long black hair dragging the floor. He went to the mirror. "What happens if I shatter these portals?"

Charon grinned. "Do it, break the mirrors. Once they are broken, you won't have a way to travel to earth and you'll be confined here once more."

Damon stilled. "Perhaps." He turned ninety degrees and uncovered another mirror. "Perhaps not."

The portal Damon uncovered wasn't to earth. It was a one-way ticket straight into the lowest layer of the Heavens.

"Do you desire to speak to the Angels?"

"Who is Chanta's mother?" Damon's question lingered in the air like oil in fire.

Charon turned on his heel. "The information you seek will cost you."

"She is descended from an Angel, isn't she?" Damon laughed, his eyes glowing red as blood. "Her pure heart is what attracted me to begin with. Her infallible courage and strength beckons me to break her. I want Chanta Timbers."

Charon paused. So, the snake god desired something. Turning to face Damon, he watched as Damon waved his hand and Chanta's face appeared.

From the folds of his robes, Damon withdrew a soft leather pouch. "I found her when she was eighteen. Alone and scared. She had no idea who or what she was. And neither did I, at first. But the more I became smitten with her, the more I realized just how unique she truly was."

Remaining quiet as Damon continued, Charon watched as Chanta walked down a dirt path. "I wonder if Gyth thinks about me being with his daughter. Do you think it plagues him to no end that I defiled her with every inch of my body, that I know every inch of hers with the most intimate knowledge?"

Charon stiffened. The books called out to him from the isle, their sudden summon catching him off-guard. "What did you do to her?"

Damon laughed, the sound bloodcurdling to say the least. "Let's just say she'll never forget my face." A sigh escaped him. "She has such wonderful long nightmares and such heartbreak and loneliness."

"Why would you do that to her if you were smitten with her?"

Damon looked straight into Charon's eyes. "I realized she was more than just any ordinary member of the One Race. Even that damning emotion that was threatening my insanity didn't stop what had to be done." Damon's snakes, the ones that crawled out from under his skin, rushed out of his fingers and slithered up his arms dancing wildly to his words. "I won her trust, I won her delicious body, and most of all, I won her heart. And as she was falling in love with me, I revealed my true self." He threw his head back and slashed his hand through her image. "Love. What a sickening emotion."

"Love is what makes the world go around. Humans are especially fond of the emotion."

"It's a weakness. It's a disease that worms through and destroys all sane senses."

Damon was a monster, a pure bred monster with too many powers and no compassion. His legendary hatred and evil knew no bounds and was the reason he had eventually won the place as king of the Underworld. No matter the species, Damon satisfied himself with the pain of others; he enjoyed it. He especially enjoyed Chanta Timber's pain.

A glint of steel caught Charon's eye as Damon turned back to the mirror. Lodged in his shoulder was a dagger of some sort. It was buried to the hilt and Charon could make out the stain of blood running down the length of his robe. He found another sticking out of Damon's thigh.

Each of the daggers had a five-pointed star, Damon's symbol, etched on the hilts. He wondered. Who had lodged them so deep? Better still, who would want to get that close to him? Why had he allowed someone to do such a thing? And why had he left the daggers where they were?

Damon's voice brought him back to the conversation at hand. "Come now Charon, really, we need to work on your view of the world."

The demon god waved his black-clawed hand and a female in chains, bound and gagged, appeared at his feet. "This is Lena. She has come to beg for her life. What say you Charon, how would you rather she die?"

Charon narrowed his eyes. The girl's muffled cries pulled his eyes to her face. She was young, less than thirty and very beautiful.

On her bare left shoulder, a five-pointed star tattoo glowed in the red haze of the chambers.

"She is one of your witches." She was also a member of the One Race, but Charon kept that to himself. "She no doubt would give her life to you in a heartbeat."

"Really? Do you think so?" Damon grinned. "Let us see, shall we?"

He pulled the dagger from his shoulder and cut the strip of cloth from her mouth. She screamed, her terror escalating as Damon took her chin in his clawed fingertips. A hiss of pleasure wilted across the chamber as he bent to one knee and kissed the girl on her still screaming lips.

The woman on the bed remained calm, waiting.

Charon watched as one of Damon's snakes slithered out of his mouth and forced its way down the girl's throat. Her body jerked, her eyes rolling back into her head. Damon took the woman's head in his large hands and pulled the snake out of her mouth. The snake curled around his bicep hissing with blood dripping from its fangs.

Damon stood as the slumped body of the woman hit the floor. He turned on his heel and made his way across the room to a chair that sat by his bed. "Tell me, what kind of bargain do you want to make this time?"

Charon's scythe appeared in his hand as the books on the isle called to him once more. "Oh, I think you're the one who wants something Damon. What will you give me to get what you want?"

Damon's smile slithered across his lips as he leaned back and crossed his legs. "I want Chanta Timbers to fall back in love with me."

"I cannot give that to you. Emotions are off limits." Charon laughed. "But you knew that already."

"Yes." Damon held out his hand and a long silver chain appeared. "Allow Bastilla, my wife, to travel through one of your portals. Let her believe she has escaped the Underworld and escaped me."

"Why would you release her?" Charon knew he was asking too many questions yet he was curious. "Especially seeing as how you have no idea just what it is that I'll want in return."

"Because, she'll bring me what I want." Damon's eyes swirled from red to black to red. "I knew one day, she would be of use to me. You see, Charon, I own her soul. And if you do this, I'll give it to you."

The books summoning grew louder, creating tiny pinpricks of pain in Charon's mind. They wanted the soul that Damon was offering. He didn't understand why, but knew he could not deny their demands.

And they wanted, demanded more than just her soul, they wanted others. Souls, he would need to collect as he collected the remaining books.

A trickle of sadness crept down his spine. He, of course, had no free will and had to do as the books commanded, that was his calling. It had been that way since Jaiden had been slaughtered over two thousand years ago. And yet, in the heartbeat of time that the thoughts had manifested themselves, he yearned for the free will to do as he pleased.

Charon bowed slightly to Damon as his emotions played havoc with his mind. "So it shall be, another bargain between us."

Chapter 7

Isten grunted loudly as Gyth, in his dragon form, landed on his black marble terrace. Gods were notorious for hiding their true forms. And that was a pity in itself. The dragon form was one of many forms, but it was Isten's favorite and Gyth's as well. Dragons, were amazing, powerful, and majestic creatures.

Already awoken from slumber by Terror Sky and the Algea, Isten was in no mood for Gyth. Rolling his silver eyes, he twisted his heavily muscled neck, his bones popping and cracking.

He knew the reason for Gyth's visit after speaking to Akhos. Disgust rippled through his body. Gyth had used Payne when the Destroyer had been at his weakest, and all because of the hatred he had for Damon.

A layer of dust stirred as he moved slowly across the empty chamber leading out to the terrace. His mind opened, seeking, searching, and seeing. Lightning flashed as he stretched his six foot eight inch frame, his heartbeat growing stronger with each passing second.

As Gyth transformed from dragon into human form, Isten stopped time with a slight wave of his hand. He gritted his teeth as he circled Gyth and touched his temple. He threw his head back letting the eons of knowledge flow from Gyth into himself. All the while, disgust and fury dug at his soul. And in the center of all the knowledge, he felt chaos. Chaos in the world he and the other seven gods had created.

Digging deeper in Gyth's mind, he found that Gyth had no knowledge of who or what had trapped him on the isle or that he was even trapped here.

The very air surrounding the Isle trembled, time warped and bled with the sorrow and pain manifesting itself in his mind.

Blood red tears fell from Gyth's eyes as he dug deeper into Gyth's mind. Isten found the sacrifices, misery, and longing that filled Gyth's heart, but did not find any treachery.

Isten stood, the dust disappearing, the blackness creeping out of the corners. His dingy and tattered robes replaced with a black one that fell to his feet. The folds of the robe gave way revealing the silver and black armor beneath them. His gray, sharp eyes went to Gyth and he grunted in annoyance as time once again resumed normally.

It was, for the lack of a better way of putting it, time to get back into the game. He had stood-he glanced over his shoulder at the throne-he had sat for an eternity too long being silent and sightless.

As Gyth blinked, Isten announced loudly. "Gyth. I sent Terror Sky to aid you in taking the throne over two thousand years ago and it seems you have failed to do as I commanded. Chanta was to mate with Damon, those orders were specific." Isten gave him a chilling look. "This war with Damon has placed you on the borderline of treason."

"She is my daughter."

With a roar, Isten slammed Gyth into the wall, watched him fall to his knees. "It was a direct command! And with Jaiden dead, it was imperative that those orders were to be followed through."

"At the time, I wasn't aware she would be connected to me, I didn't know she was going to be my daughter. She doesn't deserve to be mated to that abomination!"

"Abomination? What right do you have to call him such? His presence in this world was predetermined, his destiny intertwined with Chanta's." Isten turned on his heel, his fists at his sides. "It is with great reserve that I don't blast you into oblivion."

"As you said, Jaiden is dead. How was I to know? I did what had to be done or he would have killed her out of his hatred for me." Gyth bowed his head. "I come only to consult with you."

"A hatred that you created." Isten slammed his fist into the wall, the stones cracking under the force. "He never would have harmed her. His destiny was to father a child with her and that child would keep the balance. If that balance isn't maintained, the world will fall."

"Damon is true evil, he doesn't know the meaning of being a father. Look what he did to Payne!" Gyth stood, dusted off his robes. "I refuse to allow my daughter to go through a living hell with that demon."

"This is an act of betrayal. My own blood-born descendant defying orders." Isten whirled around, his eyes meeting Gyth's with more rage than he intended. "You would give me more pleasure being staked to my mantle than pissing in the wind on my terrace."

Gyth's lips formed a thin hard line across his face. "I cannot undo what has been done, nor would I if I could. Treason or not, I won't condemn my daughter to the confines of the Underworld, nor will I let that bastard ruin her."

Isten laughed. Gyth was a fool. "That bastard, as you so lovingly refer to him, was to father the angel that was to take Elena's place. And now, look at what you have done—meddled with fate and led Chanta straight into Payne's arms. The odds of Payne fathering an angel are slim to none. If he gets Chanta pregnant during her Burning, the consequences could be disastrous."

The grimace on Gyth's face didn't go unnoticed. "I took precautions. Payne is no longer a god, I stripped him of his powers long ago. There's no chance of Damon's evil taking over his soul." Isten watched the tight smile form on Gyth's face. "He's nothing, but one of my Destroyers."

"Really? Your Destroyers? You, of course, realize that Varick's godhood has been returned and his destiny was to be leader of the Destroyers. You no longer control them or harness the powers you took from them. They are in Varick's hands now." Isten leaned onto the bannister surrounding the terrace. "If Payne wants his god powers back, do you honestly think that Varick won't return them to him? And with Payne's destiny unwritten, I fear he'll destroy his father and the Underworld will lay claim to him."

"Varick isn't a fool. Even if he figures out how to return Payne's powers to him, he won't do it, he'll realize just how evil his powers can be."

"He damn well better." Isten slammed his fists onto the black marble bannister sending debris flying across the dark sky. "I see two paths before Payne. If he chooses the wrong one, a war like nothing you've ever seen will come. A war with destruction of this universe at its end."

. . .

Varick staggered and landed into the stonewall outside of Tortured Souls. His entire world was off-kilter and his new powers that be were throwing him for a loop. His white brows were knitted together as he tried to concentrate. A curse echoed around him as he looked down at his shaking hands.

Physically, he was in a lot of pain and mentally he was somewhere in fucksville. His six foot six frame, hard as steel and full of powers he still did not understand, was on a slow burn to exhaustion. His muscles ached, his face was bloody, and his lips cracked. He ran his hands through his long white hair, his index finger tangling in the red braid that now hung from his temple.

He turned, pressing his back to the cool stone wall. One deep breath after another, his body relaxed as he turned over the latest situation in his mind.

He had a sister and she was innocent. Gyth had agreed to release Payne, but now would only confirm that he was missing. And on top of that, his body was not tolerating his new powers very well. He could not control them very long at a time and damn sure didn't understand them. Every time he used them, he crashed hard.

It was as if they were rejecting him, as if they truly didn't belong to him.

Sweat beaded his forehead as visions swamped his mind. Images of Payne being tortured, broken, and bleeding flashed before his eyes. Payne being chained and humiliated and his most inner secrets revealed.

Something inside his mind popped, careened around his skull, and came to a skidding halt before his eyes. Payne's godhood, Payne's powers were inside him demanding to be set free, were punching his eyes out of his skull screaming in utter rage. The power was refusing to be controlled, refusing anyone's demands except for Payne's.

Varick's fangs punched out of his gums, his rage boiling his blood by degrees. A scream, a curse ripped out of his throat as he looked upward to the star filled sky. Gyth had taken Payne's powers as well as countless other Destroyers when he converted them. And they were all inside Varick now, all of them swirling faster and faster out of control.

All this power, all this rage and he could do nothing!

Black smoke misted from nowhere, surrounding Varick. He crouched as the smoke grew darker and the smell of sandalwood and vanilla filled his lungs. From out of the obsidian depths, a female stepped forward. Her solid black eyes boring into his, she cocked her head to the side and pointed at him.

When she spoke, Varick wanted to shield his ears from the toxicity in her voice "I am Ania, an envoy from Lord Isten. If you want Payne, come with me."

Turning her hand over, palm up, she offered her hand with an evil grin. "I must warn you Varick Ta Farg, my touch won't be pleasant, at least not for you."

His guts twisted as he recognized her face from the visions he had of Payne. She was one of his torturers. One of the Algea, she was one of Gyth's hounds of misery.

Lunging forward, he grabbed her hand and a vicious roar left his mouth as his past slammed into his backbone. As she pulled him into the smoke, her unmistakable laughter brought a chill to his bones.

She was misery personified.

Even though seconds passed, it felt like an eternity in his mind as the years of his life whipped through his thoughts. He clung to her hand, refusing to give in to the over whelming emotions.

"Such strength," she whispered on a sigh. "I would love to spend more time with you, but alas, we are here."

Varick winced as her voice filled his mind. "You must learn how to control yourself Varick Ta Farg. There are so many lives dependent on you and so many enemies equally dependent on your not controlling yourself."

Varick stepped from the smoke and swallowed hard. What did she mean? Things were already bad and what he was seeing before him could only mean it had gotten worse.

In the dark chamber, seated on a throne of black marble and silver, Isten stared straight at him. Gyth was to his left and Charon was to his right. Clenching his teeth, Varick listened in silence as they spoke unemotionally about the oncoming destruction if things weren't righted. They spoke of Payne and of Damon's rule of the Underworld. And they spoke of the books of knowledge and their power over the universe.

Their voices rattled his bones. Like dinosaurs feasting on the weaker ones, they spoke of sacrifice dend the impending disasters ahead. All the while, Isten sat staring at Varick.

His patience was wearing thin, their chatter blurring into nonsense.

He stepped forward, his mouth open to insist on the subject of Payne's location.

"Tread carefully." Isten warned. "I would take great offense if vampire god blood were dripping on my marble should you open your mouth and piss me off."

His fangs slid from their sheaths as his eyes burned white. "Where. Is. Payne?"

Gyth turned to Varick. "Silence!"

Varick's shoulders rolled, his neck cracking. "Where is he?"

Isten stood, his armor catching a stream of light. "You cannot even control your god-born powers. Like a pup still suckling its mother, yet you would offend me in my own walls?"

Varick didn't stop until he stood toe to toe with the silver-eyed god. "Where is Payne?"

"Do you have a death wish? Do you wish Angelica to no longer have her mate by her side?" Isten grinned slightly as Varick growled and Gyth stepped forward. "You're in my domain Varick and you will play my game. Or have you forgotten who gave your powers back to you?" He looked at Gyth. "And who took them from you to begin with?"

"Varick is yet new to godhood, forgive him for his insolence." Gyth gritted his teeth, his jaw flexing. "He does not know the protocol of the ancients."

"He will learn protocol and he will abide by my rules and you will, too." Isten nostrils flared. "Or you will have one less son."

Gyth tightened his fists, but said nothing.

Turning to Varick, Isten stated loudly. "Payne, the son of Damon is here."

"You'll find those books and they will be returned to me." Isten stood, stepped down from the throne. "And I want to know who has them and how they are changing the future."

"And you're sure they are in the Heavens?" Gyth asked.

Isten cracked his neck. "There are seven books in your domain. Find them or it will cost you the throne just as it did your father."

Varick stepped back. Isten wore the power of time like a gods be damned shield. It was unmistakable, unbreakable. His entire presence harnessed raw blinding power. From the top of his head to the tip of his war boots, he was the god of all gods. But he was undaunted, perhaps suicidal at this point.

"Nothing charming about you. And your lack of humility is disgusting," Varick stated dangerously as Gyth disappeared. "All that power and you strut around cocked and loaded."

Isten's eerie eyes met Varick's. "All this power and yet I have not taken control of this universe, even though I could do so without so much as a snap of my fingers."

Varick noticed the apprehensive expression on Isten's face.

"Then why don't you? Why don't you use all that power and fix the universe, erase the evil, and right all the wrongs?" Varick didn't hesitate to add, "Why not take control of the Heavens? Why not take the throne from Gyth?"

Isten laughed. "You have balls, son of Gyth." He raised his eyebrow. "Truth is, I don't want the throne even though I did create it. I want the books of knowledge, every single one of them."

"Why?"

Isten turned on his heel. "As it is with every creation, destruction will always be a lingering, hanging possibility. It's the reason that everything has to have balance in this universe. If that precious balance is not maintained, destruction is but a single heartbeat away. Those books keep the balance."

"What's that got to do with Payne?"

"Straight to the point." Isten sat down on his throne. "Someone erased his destiny."

"And?" Varick asked, "What does that even mean?"

"It means Payne holds the destruction of this universe in the palm of his hand." Isten leaned forward. "Prepare yourself Varick because if you want him back, you'll do as I say."

"And if I don't?"

"I will send your remains to your mate in very small pieces over the next thousand years and the Algea will feast upon her pain and misery all the while." The Algea appeared to Isten's right as he continued. "And Payne will live in a tortured state of mental arrest the entirety of his long life."

Varick said nothing, just looked down at his shaking hands.

Isten took a deep breath through his nostrils. "You and I have much to discuss Varick; time is on our sides. You must learn to use it wisely and for the right purposes. Pledge yourself to me and I'll release Payne to you."

Varick laughed. "Another pact with a god? Seems I already have one of those with Gyth and one with Charon."

"It wasn't a pact with you and Gyth. He did it so that his only son would be safe from his grandmother and would not have to endure the torments of being a god. And so that no one would know that you're one of his weaknesses." Isten ran his hand down the front of his armor. "He took your god powers from you and used them to create the Destroyers. He can't create another Destroyer, but you can. You, Varick, are the true lord of the Destroyers."

Silence hung in the dark room as Varick nodded slowly. His knees suddenly felt weak with the knowledge that his own father had stripped him of his powers and had used them for his own purposes. He looked down at his hands, felt the electrical pulses jumping from one finger to the next. He could feel and sense all the Destroyers, he knew where they were, what they were doing, and the reasons behind becoming a Destroyer.

"And you need not worry about the one with Charon. Charon is mine to command." Isten narrowed his eyes. "Come forward

Varick Ta Farg and swear your allegiance to me. In so doing, I will aide you in controlling your powers and return unto your keeping Payne, son of Damon. And swear that as long as there is power in your blood, you'll do everything you can to keep balance in my universe."

Isten stood, his large hand held out. "I offer my hand to seal the pact. No untruth can be spoken between us from this moment on. You'll serve this pantheon and only this one regardless of any interests in Gyth's creations or reign. And you will take leadership of the Destroyers."

"And Payne will be handed over to me?" Varick narrowed his eyes. "Unharmed?"

"Yes."

Varick grabbed his hand, pain streaking up his arm and straight to his heart. The pain intensifying and blood gushing from his eyes and nose, he screamed as cold metal surrounded his beating heart and interlaced with his blood veins.

• • •

Deep laughter filled the chamber as Payne appeared to Varick's right on bended knee. Through the blood and tears, Varick and Payne stared at each other. A silent thank you hung between them as lightning danced on the marble floor and Isten's voice boomed around them. Varick roared in outrage as the lightning struck him, streaked through his body, and jumped to Payne striking him full force in the chest.

"This was not part of the deal!" Payne roared as he watched Varick's body arch as the same cold metal interlaced with his heart.

Isten's voice thundered in Payne's mind. "Our deal is simple Payne, son of Damon. You'll do as I command and swear your allegiance to me and in return, I'll deliver you unto your father."

"What must I do?" Payne gritted his teeth as the god came forward and placed his hand on Payne's cranium.

"You will find who has unwritten Chanta Timber's destiny."

"How am I supposed to do that? I'm just a Destroyer. I gave up my god powers when Gyth turned me into a Destroyer."

"You have never been just a Destroyer. You console yourself with thinking you're strong, but you're weak. Letting your emotions rule your every move has led you to every failure in your life."

With Isten's hand on his skull, Payne was immobile, his limbs as useless as a butterfly net trying to catch a dragon.

"I suggest you figure out how to get your god powers back." Isten released Payne's head. "First and foremost, do as Gyth has commanded, take Chanta through the Burning. She must survive."

"Gyth won't relinquish them. It gave him too much pleasure to take them from me." Payne tried to stand, his legs shaking. "Why is she so important to you and to Gyth?"

"Different reasons, but we both desire the same outcome. Her destiny was cut short, the events in her life have not gone as planned. As it is, now you're the only one that can save her from the Burning."

"And if I do this, you'll give me the chance to face my father? I have your spoken word?"

"Yes, you have my spoken word." Isten laughed, his voice thundering through the lightning. "Welcome Varick, son of Gyth, and Payne, son of Damon, to my pantheon."

Chapter 8

Payne gritted his teeth as Chanta wiped her hands on the towel hanging from her black apron. She was quite the beauty, except for the gothic red and black garb she was dressed in. She had changed since he had first met her. Her cotton blonde, almost white, hair was no longer long, but cropped to her shoulders in a mass of curls. Her once innocent face was now tight, hard. Even her eyes had changed, deepened and appeared darker gray than he remembered.

The extreme difference between her and Bastilla was shocking to say the least.

He sneered as her nametag flashed in the dim light. His sneer grew deeper as he carefully examined her clothes. Baggy black carpenter pants with red-laced pockets hung from her hips and did nothing to reveal what should be shapely legs. Her lacy black shirt was unbuttoned and underneath it she wore a red tank top. He could simply not fathom why a woman of her beauty would dress like that.

He had no doubt that her skin was as soft as velvet and her touch would be as hot as the breath of a dragon. The kiss he had given her lingered in his thoughts. Never had he hungered for the touch of a woman until that night.

Against his will, he stared at the face that had haunted him for the last eight years. A low growl rumbled in his chest as he envisioned his thumb running across her full lips, down her jaw, and along her shoulder. He knew he could easily have his way with her by overpowering her small frame, but there was something about her that made that thought seem dirty and barbaric. Who was he trying to kid? He was nothing if not barbaric and sinister.

Women were tools to be used to ease a man's desires, they were the blades that were used to bring down kingdoms, and they were the poison that brought about despair, nothing more! This one was no different than any other and he had no use for a woman.

Mine.

Grinding his teeth, he pushed his lust down to the pit of his stomach and centered his attention to the clothes she wore. Anger filled his mouth and the taste was bitter. Damon, the father he wished he had never had, would surely be pleased to have this one in his ranks. A firm cruel frown tightened across his lips.

His sneer turned into disgust as he eyed the pendent hanging around her neck on a leather string. The five star pendent burned into his mind: witch. Enemy! Whore of Damon! Gyth and Isten had no doubt lost their ever-loving minds. Why in hell's name did they want to make sure this female made it through the Burning?

Wondering if she remembered him, he watched her work around the tables, filling coffee cups and taking orders.

As she came closer to him, he stared at her as she nervously looked down at his tattoo that peeked out of his long shirtsleeve. Something stirred in his gut, slid down his spine, and made a beeline straight to his balls. Instant hard on.

Mine.

She eyed him cautiously, but wasn't afraid. She edged her way to his table and took out her order pad. Her fingers trembled slightly as she held a pencil over her notepad, but a determined look creased her brow and she asked, "What can I get you?"

Payne opened his mouth, closed it, and opened it again.

Mine.

"How about something to drink?" Her voice was steady, an equal blend of sassy and sweet, and licked at his ears like a soft wind that promised an even sweeter release.

He found it was difficult to speak as a lump rose up in his throat. "No." And thank the gods for the table that shielded his attraction.

"He'll have a cherry ice and a cheeseburger."

Payne's lip twitched and his eyes narrowed as Varick appeared behind her. Payne was shocked, but hid it well as he watched Varick smile at the woman and kiss her forehead. There was little doubt that Varick and the woman were well acquainted.

Payne held his breath for a second and wondered if she was Varick's lover. He didn't believe it; Varick was mated. But what did he care? She was nothing to him and deserved nothing from him including his attention. Still, he didn't like the thought of this particular woman lying in Varick's arms.

Mine.

And it didn't have anything to do with an unwarranted kiss from eight years ago. Nor did it have anything to do with her face haunting his dreams.

"I have missed you, Chanta. I must remember to visit you more often."

"Oh, you just sit down and I'll get your usual." She smiled and her silver eyes sparkled.

"You look well, Chanta. I find myself thinking of you lately. Tell me, how have you been?"

Payne bit his tongue as she slid her hands into Varick's. He watched in complete silence as the god-vampire-Destroyer brought her hands up to his lips and kissed her knuckles. A strange unknown feeling crept up his spine as Chanta reached up and kissed Varick on the cheek. He clenched his fists as the thought of nailing Varick to a post skipped through his mind.

"I've been doing really well." She looked around the diner. "And this place has finally started to pay for itself, especially since we changed themes."

"Good … good. Now, how about that burger?"

She turned and walked away as Varick settled into a chair. Payne grunted when he noticed the disgusted look she had cast his way before walking away.

Varick returned Payne's stare, grinned as he laughed, and spoke. "She's special and apparently Gyth and Isten are both insisting you do this." There was a pause. "I would also ask this of you."

Payne's jaw flinched and his steel colored eyes hardened. He had a bargain with Isten. One he would see through to the bitter end. Payne gritted his teeth at the thought.

"I want you to help her. It means a great deal to me that she comes out of this alive. Gyth chose you because she is strong and needs a Destroyer of equal strength. She may seem like an average woman, but she is so much more than you could possibly imagine."

Payne turned his head and studied her movements; controlled and collected. No, she was not average. Without the gothic apparel he knew she had a body built for sin and those eyes were spectacular. He remembered those eyes. They were the color of steel and ice.

As he stared at her from the distance, a funny odd taste of honey filled his mouth. Honey? He recalled the taste rather easily. Mine.

"Try using your empathic abilities on her."

Payne willed her to look at him, but she didn't so much as glance his way. He tried harder and stared at her back until his head started to ache. What the hell was wrong with him?

"She's special. You cannot will her to do anything. She possesses a barrier to telepathy as well as empathy." Varick paused. "I know you would rather not, but if you do this for me, I'll give you one wish, but only after it's done."

Payne grinned and turned to Varick. "One wish? Anything I desire?"

"Yes, anything that I can give … anything that does not affect the free will of anyone else." Varick shrugged, attempted a laugh. "And if I can get these damned powers to work right."

"Damn vampire." Payne shook his head. "Are you sure about this? You know what I'll want."

Varick smiled slightly. "Your wish will be granted at the end of her Burning." He paused as he turned to look at Chanta. "But there is one catch."

"Figures."

"If you hurt her, I will send your soul to the empty abyss for eternity." Varick laughed uneasily. "And I can now that I am a god and all."

"You're beginning to sound like Gyth."

"I will make sure you survive every second of eternity." Varick's grin disappeared. "I don't want her harmed, and if there is anything you can do to make her pain tolerable, do it."

Payne's anger flared. "What makes her so special? Why the hell would you be so interested in her?" He paused as he watched the woman bend over to retie her shoe. Flames of heat blasted his guts as he spoke without looking away from her rather nice backside. "I am pain! You gave me this damn name and you know damn well it's all I know how to do! Her pain is no problem of mine, and I could care less how much of it she goes through."

Varick's gold eyes flashed dangerously. "You have been loyal to my father and have served him well, but make no mistake Payne, I'll cut you down if you cross me. You'll choose your words carefully and pray that I won't be disappointed."

"You didn't answer my question, Varick."

"Look at her," Varick's eyes were on Chanta. "She's an angel, pure. And yet, she has a fire in her soul. She deserves a chance in this life and you're just the right Destroyer to help her through it. And besides, we both have orders from Isten."

"Look at you. Being a god suits you, doesn't it?" Payne had never seen Varick like this, and he swallowed his anger. "Is this all you want from me? To help her through the Burning and I can be on my way."

Varick leaned back, crossed his legs and appeared at ease all of a sudden. "For now, yes, it is. But Isten may have other plans for us after this is said and done."

"What the hell is that supposed to mean?" Payne spit out through clenched teeth. "He and I have a bargain and that's the end of my dealings with him."

"We pledged our allegiance to him." Varick made a hissing sound. "We are his to command now or did you forget that part?"

No, Payne hadn't forgot, but there was a part of the whole, 'I pledge allegiance to the almighty father of this universe' that Varick didn't know, didn't need to know. Payne had no intention of ever coming back from the Underworld. His ticket was a one way straight to hell and no return. No need to take baggage; the dead didn't need clothes.

Chanta carefully placed the plates on the table and turned away as they continued their discussion. He frowned at her as she hurriedly left the table.

"Last time I'm going to ask. You sure you want to promise me anything? You know what I'll want."

Varick grinned as he picked up the hamburger. "Make sure that you tell her everything she wants to know."

"Yeah."

Varick's soft laughter echoed around the room as Chanta returned with the drinks. She smiled as Varick took a bite of his rather raw hamburger and pointed to the chair at his side. She grinned and sat down as he chewed slowly. The rings on his long sculpted fingers flashed as he sat the hamburger down on the plate.

Payne couldn't help but notice that she scooted her chair closer to Varick than to him.

"This rather overbearing man is called Payne and he is a brute, so please excuse his ill manners. I can assure you that beneath all that brawn there is a heart somewhere."

"Are you sure about that?" Her irritation was a tidal wave slapping at the back of Payne's head, but he couldn't pinpoint what she was thinking or feeling. All he could manage to pinpoint was the one word that kept bouncing around inside his skull.

Mine.

• • •

Varick chuckled as Payne nervously pulled at the chain collar he wore. As her brother, he would have a hard time staying out of the Burning. He knew he had a job to do. Protect them both while the transition was taking place.

He watched her and smiled as she studied Payne's hands. Good, at least she wasn't completely captivated by Payne's remarkably handsome face. And he would give credit where credit was due.

He finished his hamburger and licked his fingers. Human food was most tantalizing, although it sometimes did not agree with his diet of blood, something that hadn't changed since he had been given his godpowers back. Payne stood and stepped from the table. Varick frowned and followed suit thinking that he may have to summon some lightning to hammer down on the Destroyer's thick head. Gods above knew, Payne needed some sense knocked into him.

• • •

Payne briskly went out the diner's door and took a deep breath. He was so cold on the inside his blood ran in rivers of ice. And Chanta was hot, like lava scorching his icy resolve. He didn't like it and damn sure didn't need it. But her eyes, her battleship steel-colored eyes were mesmerizing. Addictive.

Even more than he remembered them to be. They were pools that he wanted to drown in.

Gyth appeared at his side. If he didn't know better, Gyth had attached a homing beacon to his ass so he could follow him around. And Payne seriously hated that.

"I know you hate it, that's why I plague you so often." Gyth slapped Payne on the back. "In two days the Burning will begin and I expect all to go well."

Payne swallowed his anger, his pride and ego screaming at him for retribution. "Why did you pick me?"

"She's strong-minded and the beast she carries is even stronger. She needs a strong hand to guide her and you my friend have the strongest hand of any of my Destroyers."

"That's bullshit." Of course, Payne knew there were other reasons as well, but Gyth was not so inclined to speak of them. The god always had other reasons for everything he did or said. "I'll do as you want this time. But don't ever think it's because I gave in to your little pets of pain and misery."

"The why doesn't matter as long as she survives."

"You know that you are a complete jerk-off and I'll repay you for the visit with the Algea." Payne grinned. "And I hate you with an undying passion."

Gyth chuckled as he vanished leaving these words to trail behind him in the mist, "That my friend is why I like you as much as I do. It takes a hell of a ... Destroyer to admit to a god that he hates him."

"No, Gyth. The reason you like me is because I am Damon's son."

•••

Now that his next week and two days had been decided for him, how the hell was he going to approach this? He had never witnessed nor had he discussed the finer issues of the Burning with anyone. Varick could have told him the particulars on the subject, but no, it always had to be the hard way. And there was the simple fact that Payne really didn't like women. They were good for two things, sex and betrayal.

And he could do without any more betrayals and was so not up to par with the sex part.

He grunted his disapproval as her smell filled his senses. He knew she was behind him and he turned as he crushed a bug on the pavement under his boot. She frowned as he held out his hand. Her heart shaped face was soft, kind, and gentle, and it was more than enough to make Payne lose some of his hard-ass exterior. Except he didn't.

"We didn't get off to a very good start eight years ago. I am Payne." Fuck, he really didn't like to be touched. He held his hand out.

She took his hand cautiously and her nostrils flared. "I am Chanta Timbers. And no, we didn't. You're the one Gyth chose for me. I'm sure he knows what he's doing."

Her hand was small, delicate. He looked into her eyes and had to force himself to look at her hand.

"Don't think I would go so far as to say that." He slowly ran his thumb across the top of her hand feeling the wonderful silkiness of her skin. "He's a self-righteous bastard."

She tugged at her hand, but he didn't release it. "There's something I want to make perfectly clear."

He held her hand for a long minute before releasing it. "And what might that be?"

Chanta frowned. Her bottom lip quivered before she spoke. "I don't like you and the only reason we're standing here is because I don't want to die."

"No, the reason we're standing here is because after this is done, Varick will owe me." Payne narrowed his eyes, no sense in lying to her. "We're standing here because Gyth commanded me to do this, not because I want to do it."

Chanta stepped back, crossed her arms over her chest. "Glad we understand each other."

"How close is your Burning?"

"I don't honestly know. Yesterday was my thirtieth birthday, so I'm sure just any day now." She looked down at her watch. "Perhaps we can get together some other time and discuss this."

Payne growled. "When?"

Her eyes darkened, a flicker of apprehension in their steely depths. Stepping back, he took her in. She was standing on the edge of flight or fight. She hated him, but she was attracted to him, he didn't have to be a psychic to figure that out. And as much as he would like to deny the attraction he had for her, he couldn't. It was there, like a bright shining ball of flame in the darkness.

The urge to kiss her swamped his body with raw heat. Instincts took over as he stepped to his right and caught her waist bringing her back against the wall of the diner. He could see the undetermined questioning in her eyes as he bent his head to capture her lips. But he couldn't stop, like a gigantic oak tree collapsing, all he could do was lay claim to what was under him.

Mine.

His desire swirled blindly out of control as the sensation of her lips contacting his stiffened his erection to the point of explosion.

Honey! Sweet intoxicating glorious honey filled his mouth and burned its way into his senses. His desire turned to desperation as she unwittingly and instinctively wrapped her arms around his shoulders and pressed his body closer to hers.

He pushed harder and deeper into her mouth as he reached for her leg and brought it up to his hip. He ground into her core needing to let her know how much he urgently needed to be deep inside of her. Needing more, he pulled back and ran his tongue across her lips.

She pulled back, her mouth opening as if she wanted to protest. He dipped in again, covering her protest with his mouth and seeking that glorious honey taste.

He captured her tongue between his teeth, scraping his fangs against her lips. She caught her breath as goose bumps ran up her arms. He expected her to come up fighting. But he was in too deep to let her simply walk away … or run for that matter. It sure as hell wasn't like she had a choice in the near future anyway. And neither did he.

Sliding his hands down her shoulders and along her arms, her skin felt as if it had been literally singed by flames. Payne groaned his appreciation of her body as she pressed her hands against his chest and pushed, hard.

He stepped back, let her catch her breath. Her eyes were gray daggers as she pointed at his chest. "Don't ever do that again. Don't touch me unless I tell you to. We do this only, and I mean only when I have no other choice. Do you understand?" She stepped around him.

Payne shrugged his shoulders trying to hide his reluctance to step away. "Fine, tomorrow then. I'll meet you here."

Payne watched her as she walked away. Her entire body was shaking. Was it from fear? He somehow doubted that now. Desire? He couldn't say for certain which emotion was running through her. Clenching his fists and resisting the urge to follow her through the gates of hell if necessary, he turned on his heel and cursed. He didn't want to let her go, he wanted to grab her and pull her back into his arms and claim her lips as well as the rest of her body. Yeah, he just needed to get his release and then she would just be a memory.

Damn! He knew that this woman, Chanta, would never be just a memory. He had never forgotten the near kiss eight years ago, probably would never forget it.

Then Bastilla's image slammed into his mind, and his gut twisted, leaving an empty, aching spot in his chest. Her betrayal and deception had created a black void in his heart and soul. A void that was filling with thoughts of Chanta Timbers. He couldn't allow that to happen, he had to hang onto the pain. And besides, the only reason he was doing this was to finally get his revenge against his father.

Chapter 9

Precisely at five after ten, Chanta looked down at her wristwatch and tapped her foot on the pavement outside the diner. She would wait ten minutes then go home and try to forget ever meeting Payne, who had haunted her dreams last night and had haunted her nightmares for years.

She wasn't lying to herself about the nightmares. Really, she wasn't.

After wrestling with her covers and fighting her pillows, she had slept very little and it had been a long day. Chances were he wouldn't show up anyway. And after the nightmares, dreams, and fantasies she had, she wasn't so sure she would be comfortable around him. She assessed her appearance; it wasn't like she was trying to impress anyone, especially not Payne.

Not that she cared. She didn't. She learned a long time ago that men were disgusting pigs and there was simply no need to try to impress any of them. But, Payne wasn't a man. He was a Destroyer with a demon lurking centimeters under his skin.

A demon that had reminded her of Damon and at that time in her life, she hadn't needed the reminder or the immediate attraction she had felt. What she had needed was understanding and a simple friend.

Gyth, her father as it were, had been the only man she had ever had a descent conversation with and she could tell that he was always holding back something. Everyone had secrets and it was her unfortunate luck that she always knew when someone was lying about or hiding something. It was her unnatural ability. But with Gyth as well as Varick and even Payne, her ability didn't work and that was fine with her. The fewer emotions she had to deal with, the better.

What was the word that Gyth had used? Empathic. It really didn't matter what it was called, she just knew that it sucked out loud most of the time.

She grinned knowing that there were times when it came in handy. She remembered her first date and laughed out loud. He was hot as hell, but there had been only one thing on his mind, sex with a capital S.

No wonder she had lost interest in men a long time ago; reading their thoughts was a little disgusting at times and left a girl wondering if a man's brain was not indeed in his cock. Every other man she passed on the street was thinking about sex in one form or other. And often times the thoughts were perverted and purely self-centered.

She frowned all too aware that most women were the same. The only ones not thinking about sex were mostly children and elderly people, but even they were not always so inclined to turn from the matter.

She had often visited the nearby church, St. Augustine's Chapel, and had hoped to find some refuge there, but she quickly came to the conclusion that saints were hard to come by and more often than not the saints were exceptional liars and self-righteous scum.

She had found few people in this world she could stand to be in close proximity to and Gyth was one of them. Gyth was good at keeping his true feelings and thoughts buried inside so that they did not disturb her. So was Varick.

That was the only reason Payne intrigued her; it wasn't about how her body had reacted to him, it wasn't that kiss. It was because she had not been overcome with his emotions or thoughts. As a matter of fact, she couldn't read him at all. She had wished most of her life that she would find just one person on earth that she couldn't, but she was wary of Payne.

She remembered what was behind his eyes, remembered how black they had turned. And that warped evil sounding voice that she had committed to memory left her skin crawling. Only, her skin hadn't crawled last night. And like the near first kiss they had shared, the one last night left her as emotionally wrecked as a derailed train.

Payne was terrifying. He was a six-foot five-inch stack of muscles and dark desires. She couldn't help but be afraid of him, but every female instinct in her body demanded she want him. It wasn't a good combo, being afraid of what you wanted. Every time he got close to her, her body would shake, and she didn't know if it was the fear or the desire causing it. Or both.

He hadn't changed ... much. Muscles were still as large and glorious as they had been eight years ago. He was still scary as hell with that apparently permanent sneer plastered on his well-formed lips. She sighed as she replayed the scene at the diner. Never in her life had she met a man equal to Payne, he was male, all the way to the bone.

Even Damon, in his magnificently handsome form, was not as blatantly sexually attractive as Payne. She suddenly wanted to scream. For the life of her, Chanta wanted to hate Damon, wanted to hear him beg for her forgiveness, but she knew in her heart that what he had done was simply his way of crossing Gyth. She had been nothing more than bait.

And now, she meant nothing more to Payne than an order from Gyth.

Chanta leaned against the wall of the diner and took a deep breath. She closed her eyes and listened as the muffled sounds of a dozen people filled her mind. Concentrating on the male voice that boomed in the distance, she tried to push Payne out of her thoughts. It was Dave, the man she had hired to manage her diner. He was looking at the picture of his wife, Heather. Oh, how beautiful she is!

He loved his wife more than anything in the world and would die a thousand deaths for her. Chanta loved listening to his thoughts. He had a good heart although at times his thoughts did run astray. She grinned as he envisioned himself leaning across Heather in their bed the night before. She giggled and released his thoughts, those thoughts were much too private and she was sure her cheeks were getting rosy.

As she opened her eyes, she caught her breath. Barely inches in front of her Payne stood staring at her. His eyes were mute and she was sure he was not judging her, but still he was staring.

She forced a soft smile on her lips as her body instantly warmed and stepped beside him. He towered over her small frame and she had a sudden attack of unease. She still couldn't get any reading from him.

And if that wasn't bad enough, his black hair was down, not pulled back at the nape of his neck. His face was hard, the straight planes pulling tight against the muscles in his jaws. In that moment, she realized just how gorgeous he really was. A dark lethal beauty that only added to her body's hunger.

"You're late."

"Not really, you specifically said somewhere around ten." He paused and looked up at the nearly full moon. "And it's only ten after."

Chanta strained to see his expression. "Maybe this wasn't a good idea."

"Doesn't matter whether it was or not, we are both here already." His voice was deep and gritty.

"The Burning hasn't begun. Perhaps we should reschedule." And on that note, never seemed like a good plan.

"I won't be in this town for very long and time is of the essence." He looked down at the top of her head. "Your blood is heating. I can smell it."

"What? I don't stink." Her face paled.

"No. It smells like honeysuckle and fresh rain. And it's getting stronger." He paused, his head tilting to the side, his nostrils flaring slightly. "There's a storm brewing under your skin."

Chanta turned to the diner feeling her cheeks burn. "Let's just go inside and grab a table."

"I would prefer to stay outside." He looked over his shoulder, his black trench coat swirling around his legs. "These people your diner caters to are disgusting."

Chanta couldn't resist teasing him. "Oh really. The big scary man afraid of the gothic folk?"

Payne growled his disgust and grabbed the door handle. "After you, princess."

Chanta grinned and his eyes sparkled, or did they? It was a fleeting expression and perhaps she read it wrong. She took a step through the door when she caught his smell. It was a stunning odor—clean, fresh, almost like the smell on a snowy day. And there was something else, a faint musk. She took a few more steps and wondered if it was Stetson cologne. It was a good smell and she liked it a lot, more than she was presently willing to admit.

Payne followed and pointed to the corner table. It was a safe distance from the other people in the diner and the shadows would hide his expressions if he were to let one slide to his face. And she really needed to see his expressions since she couldn't read his emotions.

"You hungry?"

His answer was curt. "No."

"Well, I am. I'll be back in a sec."

• • •

Payne sat with his back to the wall as she went to the counter. He watched carefully how her expressions changed as she passed the tables. He knew she was trying to block the thoughts that were no doubt filling her mind. It took a lot of practice and by her expressions, she was not as good at it as she wanted to be. He chuckled as her mouth flew open when she passed the skinny man with black painted lips. He directed the man's thoughts and a wry smile curled upon his lips.

The man was watching Chanta's rear and was wondering if she liked it doggie style. He had fantasized about her for months and would pull out his fingernails if she would let him lick her nipples. He would lay her over a chair arm and bang her until she went weak-kneed. She had a nice ass and he was sure she would taste like almonds.

Chanta's eyes were hard as steel as she ordered the cup of coffee, black. She followed the order with a large home fries and a grilled cheese. She grinned as she turned from the counter and retraced her steps past the skinny man. Payne almost burst out into laughter as she faked a fall and her coffee cup landed in the man's lap.

Payne choked his laughter down as she made sweet apologies and swiped at his chest with a napkin from the table. In her little charade, she purposely hit his plate and its contents spewed across his jacket. He cursed under his breath as Chanta slipped away and came to the table.

"I am so clumsy sometimes. Poor guy, I hope it didn't hurt much."

Payne nodded. "I'm sure he may have done something today that warranted a rude awakening."

Chanta's lips pressed together hard. "Yes, I'm sure of it as well."

Payne fidgeted in his chair. He was not used to being around a woman, especially one he was taking a liking to. She was different from most humans. It was probably her empathic ability that made her seem different. He had no use for a woman in his life and he would have to block her out. He couldn't afford to let her get close.

"So. Where do you want to begin?"

He looked at her quizzically. "Do you want to eat first?"

"No, let's get started. I'm anxious to know some things and Varick said you would answer any questions that I have."

He grunted. "So be it woman."

Chanta frowned at Payne. "My name is not woman. It's Chanta."

Payne grunted again and ran his hand through his hair as she spoke again. "If you don't mind me asking, why do you dress like that? Do you really like leather or do you like looking like a biker?"

"I have always worn leather." Before she could answer, he added, "When I wear clothing at all."

"Okay, okay. I didn't mean to pry."

"Yes, you did. I like leather and it suits me. What about you, like looking like a gothic freak from hell?"

Chanta crossed her arms over her chest and stuck her tongue out at him. "I don't dress much different than you. Guess that makes us both freaks, now don't it?"

The waitress brought Chanta's plate and gave Payne a seductive look. "Can I get you anything?"

Payne grinned and ran his fingers across the top of her hand. "Scotch would taste good right now."

The woman leaned forward and whispered. "We don't serve alcohol here, but I live just a few blocks away if you want to come by."

Payne turned to Chanta who was rolling her eyes. "Now, just why would I want to go to your place?"

The woman leaned closer and whispered again. "I have scotch and I could give you anything you want."

Chanta choked down a fry and made a gurgling cough sound. "Go the hell away, Brenda! You can have him when I'm through with him."

Brenda turned on her heel and huffed as she wove through the other tables. One word came clearly across the room to slam into Chanta and Payne's minds. Bitch!

Chanta grinned as she looked up at Payne and decided to make a very long night talking to the man that every woman in the diner was now fantasizing about "What are they thinking right now?" Payne asked as her expression became determined.

"The truth?" She asked and he nodded his head. "That I'm going to make this a very long night sitting here talking to you since every female in this diner is fantasizing about you. And even if it kills me, which I figure it might, I'm going to leave here with you on my arm."

He grinned and looked at Brenda. "You want to make her jealous?"

"No, just going to prove a point." She looked into his dark smoldering eyes, almost sighed, but caught it before it slipped out her mouth. "And don't let that go to your head, I still don't like you."

"Mind letting me know what that point is exactly?"

"That she can't have you until I'm done with you."

"Honesty is not always the best policy." His reply was low and she studied his face as he continued. "After all, we both know I am a big scary man and we know exactly what my intentions are with you."

"Then by all means, let's hope the Burning starts soon." Chanta paled. "So we can get it over with."

"Are you ready to have sex with me, Chanta?" He smirked as she leaned back in her chair and stared at him. "Eight years ago you ran from me as if I was the devil himself."

"I'm ready to do what I have to." She didn't sound sure of herself. "And we both know what lurks under your skin."

"That demon under my skin has saved countless lives, countless innocents. Best way to fight fire is with fire." Payne leaned back in his chair and took a slow, deep breath. There was no reason to explain or justify what was within him, not to her or to anyone else. "You said you had questions."

"Fire with fire? I totally disagree. You fight fire with water." Chanta took a bite from the grilled cheese and nodded. "Who is Isten?"

"Isten?" Payne cursed under his breath. He had a bargain to keep with Isten, even if it killed him. "He created this universe."

"I know that." She finished off the sandwich, wiped her mouth. "So, is he still around somewhere?"

"I'm sure he is."

She shook her head. "Can you imagine being that old?" She looked up, met his gaze. "How long have you been a Destroyer?"

"Far too long."

Popping a french fry in her mouth, she chewed, and swallowed. "That's not really an answer. You're evading the question. Do you enjoy being a Destroyer?"

Nodding, Payne watched her eat another fry.

"Tell me about the Angels."

"They reside on the lowest level of the Heavens. They watch over mankind much like the Destroyers watch over the One Race."

"And the one called Elena? Who is she?"

Gritting his teeth, he shook his head. "Why do you want to know? The Angels don't have anything to do with the One Race."

"Just curious." She looked up, her jaw was flexing. And that was sexy. "You know, if I had a choice, I wouldn't have picked you for this."

He barked a laugh. "Don't feel lonely. If I had a choice, I wouldn't take you through the Burning. It's not a job anyone takes on lightly."

Her rejection hit something in his chest with a ping, felt like acid running in streaks along his skin. He tried to convince himself he didn't want her.

Her eyes misted. "I could die."

Payne only nodded. No reassurance from him. No emotion either.

Laying her hands on the table, she looked at her plate. "I don't want to die. But I guess no one really ever does. Not even the humans."

"Very few women make it through alive." He sat in silence, staring at the floor. "Eat your damn food."

Chapter 10

Chanta didn't know what she expected from Payne, but he was no Prince Charming. She looked at her watch. Definitely time to go.

Payne gave her a menacing look. "Do you need to be somewhere?"

She shrugged noticing that her hands had begun to shake. "The diner's going to be closing soon."

"Why do wear that star around your neck?" He looked down and snarled. "It's Damon's symbol."

"Yes, it's Damon's symbol." Chanta took a deep breath. It wasn't something she wanted to talk about. "It's a reminder. And it's just a star." She lifted it and looked at it feeling an ache erupt in her chest.

"He is Gyth's enemy as well as Varick's."

Payne continued, but she honestly didn't know what he was saying. Something about Damon being the devil and blah blah blah. She strained her eyes, tried to focus on the star in her hand, but everything got real blurry, Payne's voice bouncing around her head and banging on her emotions.

"He's a damn menace and needs to be destroyed." Payne's voice slid across her nerves and slammed into her gut. "He and Gyth are so much alike that they should have been twins."

Chanta got defensive for reasons she didn't understand. "I know the story of the war between Damon and Gyth. And Gyth knows my story. I don't have to answer to you."

"Damon is the witches' god. He's a brutal monster." She didn't have to be an empath to sense the anger rising up his throat. "He dresses in the garb you are wearing and his eyes, lips, and fingernails are as black as night. His black hair hangs to the ground like a shroud of death and his breath is as toxic as acid. His skin is the color of the moon and snakes cling to his bosom."

...

Payne watched as her eyes flickered, a small swirling gold fire radiating around her pupils threatening to eat up all that wonderful gray color.

When she spoke, her voice held a distinctive razor's edge. He knew he had hit a nerve. "Everyone, even the gods have reasons behind their actions. Have you ever considered what made Damon the way he is?"

Payne's snarl was on his lips before he could stop it. "He is the enemy, never forget that he would kill you in a split second if given half the chance just because you are One Race. And that little pendant is a perfect homing beacon just for him to get his clutches into you."

"This ... " She took the pendant off. "This is what a man I fell in love with was wearing the day he tore my world apart. This is what reminds me to never trust anyone."

"Love?" He sneered. "Love is a foolish game that leads a path to hell."

Chanta stood and cleared her throat as she turned on her heel. "We're done here. I'll make a call to Gyth and ask for a replacement."

Payne stood. "I have not finished and you will sit back down and listen!"

Chanta answered, but did not turn back around to face Payne. "For all I know you are living in some kind of nut-imagined world and think you're some kind of god instead of the Destroyer that Gyth commands."

She laughed almost hysterically. Payne watched her grab the back of a chair, stagger, and laugh again. Her scent intensified.

"Yeah ... you have a god complex!" She pouted, huffed, and crossed her arms over her chest turning to face him. "You know what I think? I think you're nothing, but a god-want-to-be with an I-am-higher-than-thou attitude! Apparently, you've been a Destroyer way too long."

"Would you be willing to test that particular theory?" he asked dryly.

Chanta took two steps forward. "The only theory I'm willing to test is whether or not you need to find professional help. I'd be glad to get the One Race phone book out and give you a list of numbers to the local shrinks."

"Your eyes are swirling." He leaned closer. "Your scent is strong. Soon, the pain will come."

She swallowed hard, her body getting stiff. "I've heard the stories about the Destroyers. How cruel and dangerous they are. I don't know why Gyth picked you of all the Destroyers, but I'm telling you right now, I've faced worse than you could imagine, so get off that dark horse you rode in on and go screw yourself."

He knew she was a fighter and he so wanted to roll around with her. He cared less that the entire diner was doing a double take of the man who was towering over the girl as if he was about to attack his prey. Taking one step, Payne stood inches from her and her scent slammed into his brain as she flushed from neck to forehead.

Chanta stopped mid-step and gulped. A heat wave blasted out of her body and slapped him in the face. "I ... "

Payne felt her temperature skyrocket and sweat popped out across her forehead. She grabbed the closest chair and tried to steady herself. Her legs trembled as she slowly slid into the chair. She groaned as she laid her head on the tabletop.

Payne pulled her to her feet and threw a ten-dollar bill onto the table where they had sat. He ushered her to the door and grinned as he tucked his arm through hers. He felt Brenda get angry and jealous and it pleased him greatly.

As Chanta took a ragged breath she uttered, "Hospital ... need to go."

Payne held her to his chest and whispered, "No hospital can help you. You are entering the first stages of the Burning."

•••

Terror Sky was leaning on a boulder in the middle of a Kentucky horse farm when Varick appeared at his side. Lines of dogwood trees were in full bloom. The sun had just disappeared and the farm was at its quietest.

"Is there something you wished to speak to me about?"

"It has begun. Chanta has entered the Burning." Terror Sky crossed his arms, the red braid dangling down to his chest. "As you were before her, she too is at a crossroads, but it isn't her actions that bear the greatest consequences."

"Riddles? I thought we were past speaking in those." Varick watched the clouds as they slid over the moon. "Just tell me, straight up, what I'm supposed to do."

"Don't allow Payne to cross over. If you give him his powers back, chances are he will kill his father and become Lord of the Underworld. He will watch Chanta die and his hatred for this world will erupt." Running his fingers down the braid, Terror Sky sighed. "There are a thousand possible outcomes, but the one that remains the strongest is Chanta's death."

"How do I prevent that?"

"I don't know. Without Jaiden's books, Isten is unable to stop what is happening. At this point, events must be controlled to the point of breaking free will." Terror Sky barked out a curse. "Her original destiny was to be Damon's mate, to bear him a son. That child was to be the Angel's savior. Now, not only is that child and Damon's destiny untethered, but so are Chanta's and Payne's."

"Fate and destiny? It's all nonsense. What's the point of free will if we are not allowed to choose our own destinies?" Varick slammed his fists onto the boulder cracking it. "And why can't

Isten control what's happening to the world around us? Why does he need those damn books?"

"Those books control all the gods' destinies, every single last one of them including all of the descendants. The only fates that they don't control are Isten and Jaiden." Terror Sky took a deep breath. "And mine."

Varick turned to face Terror Sky. "So what in the nine hells are you telling me?"

Terror Sky laughed, a cold harsh laugh that sent a chill down Varick's spine. "With my help, Isten manipulated Jaiden into creating those books. By creating them, Jaiden gave them part of his power making Isten the most powerful being in this universe." Varick didn't say anything, gods were meddlesome and this wasn't surprising.

"Someone has been changing Jaiden's words since you were born and somehow they brought Chanta into this world much sooner than she was meant to be. Whoever it is, has created so much chaos in the universe, I can feel the very seams snapping and breaking." Terror Sky growled, the sound a rumble of thunder. "There's only one problem with who is behind it."

"What's the damn problem?"

"Jaiden is the only god that could change those words." A purr of anger ripped out of his throat. "He is the only one that could possibly even allow another to do so. They are a part of him as he is a part of them."

"He's dead." Varick paced back and forth. "My grandfather had him slaughtered."

Thunder rumbled overhead as black smoke filtered up from the ground and Ania stepped out of the blackness. Varick's fangs elongated instantly.

She held up her delicate hand, her eyebrow shooting up in an arch. "Your grandfather was acting on Isten's orders."

"It doesn't matter who had him killed. He's dead and according to Terror Sky, no one can change the words in his books except him." Varick turned to Terror Sky and repeated, "Jaiden is dead."

Terror Sky's eyebrow shot up and he shared an exasperated look with Ania. "Jaiden was the most powerful god in all the universes when he fell into Isten's hands and he was just a babe. Do you really think he's dead?"

Ania pointed to the braids hanging from Terror Sky and Varick's temple. "Those are of Jaiden's will. Before he was slaughtered, he would pick a handful of gods and goddesses that he trusted and relied on. Seems, he has chosen both of you."

Varick laughed. "So, this meeting is basically initiating me into treason against Isten and Gyth."

Terror Sky nodded. "But it is much more than that. Payne and Chanta's destinies were unwritten and I have a feeling that Jaiden is the one rewriting their scripts."

Ania spoke, her voice dropping an octave, "Jaiden can destroy us all. He is the end all, be all. He is destruction, he is creation. If he knows that Isten and Terror Sky used him to create this world and those books, he will seek revenge."

Varick closed his eyes. "And Isten will try to destroy Jaiden before that happens. That's why Isten wants Jaiden's books."

Chapter 11

The Tree of Life swayed as the River Styx, an invisible river that divided the Heavens, the earth, and the Underworld, rushed around the island hidden in its depths. Charon looked up into the branches, his face switching from human to skeletal bones. The tree swayed again, its branches reaching down to touch Charon's robed shoulder.

In the silence, with his eyes closed, Charon tried to remember his life before becoming the caretaker of the tree. He tried to remember his son. The only images coming to his mind were the books, the tree, and the faces of all those he would have to cross paths with to achieve what he sought.

No, not what he sought. He opened his eyes, realization dawning on him. He was doing what the *Book of Creation* was ordering him to do. He was a tool, nothing more.

He looked down at the silver trunk of the tree and sighed. The *Book of Creation*'s cover glowed, a distinct hum of power radiating from within its pages. The other two he had collected began glowing as well, each one desperate to be in their master's hands. But their master, Jaiden, had been slaughtered in the Heavens, his books scattered across the universe.

Twelve books of knowledge, the *Book of Creation*, and the *Book of Destruction* were essential in maintaining the balance of the universe. Jaiden had been the hand that kept the balance according to the words written in those books. But now, so many years after Jaiden had been killed, the books were at unease and the universe was swirling blindly out of control.

Charon had been enlisted by the *Book of Creation* as its new protector. And he had protected it for many years. Until one day, the book had awakened, called Charon forth and longed for the future the book had been forged to protect.

The ground rumbled as fourteen wooden pedestals erupted from the ground. As they slowly rose, Charon laughed. With great care, he laid the *Book of Creation* on the first pedestal, the *Book of Resurrection* on the second, and the *Book of Darkness* on the third. The *Book of Light* would need to be placed next. The next nine books would need to be placed after and the final book, The *Book of Destruction*, would be placed last.

Closing his eyes, he reached out, called to the missing books. The seven that were in the Heavens answered, but remained hidden. The *Book of Destruction*'s soft lull was barely audible in his mind. His burning red eyes cast a glow as he continued reaching out to the other two books. They were on earth, but they refused to answer, refused to awaken.

But the *Book of Light* had awoken, the pages ringing out demanding to be answered. His robe fluttered in the soft wind as his hood covered his face. Charon would see to it personally that the book was returned to the Tree of Life.

Not by choice. By command.

• • •

Chanta awoke and sat straight up on her bed. Vivid images of Payne's hands on her body, plundering in secret places, raced through her foggy mind. Erotic thoughts of chains and biting came to surface as she took a deep ragged breath. She definitely had been dreaming!

She bolted out of the bed and looked around. The light was on in the hallway and she edged to the door. Slowly and with great anticipation, she peeked out into the hallway. She took a deep breath, crept out, and tipped toed down the hall to the front room.

Chanta turned the corner and caught her breath. In the center of her couch sat Payne with all four of her cats curled up on his lap. The big psycho scary guy had a soft spot for cats; now imagine that.

Oh hell, she could imagine more than just that. For instance, she could clearly see his strong powerful hands sliding up her legs and caressing her hips. She groaned softly as she wondered if his lips would still feel like silk against her skin. And if not only to add to her misery, she wondered if he was a gentle or rough lover. Rough, yeah, he would definitely be a lover who knew how to control her passions.

Chanta stopped, looked down at her trembling hands and shaking knees. What passions? She looked at Payne, instantly heat claimed her core. She knew it had to be the Burning that was causing her body such turmoil yet she couldn't deny how.

She stared at him, felt like she was staring at a wild animal that had been caged and refused to be tamed. And she was the one that had to let that animal out or die if she didn't.

His head was leaned back against the wall and his eyes were closed. He looked peaceful and asleep, almost content. The hard planes of his face were soft, almost gentle. She edged closer and slid into the black velvet chair that sat across from the couch. She had to admit he was rather good looking with all that black hair and those bulging muscles. Okay, he was flipping right out gorgeous. Groaning again, she tried to imagine him naked on her couch holding out his hands and begging her to come for him.

Shuddering from the erotic havoc dancing in her mind, her body warmed from the tip of her toes to the top of her head. She had no doubt that she could get off just by looking at him. And that was downright nuts.

She wondered how often he had to work out to maintain that gorgeous physique. Rolling her eyes, she couldn't remember the last time she had looked at a man without being disgusted. And to her astonishment, a soft smile slid across her lips as she roamed Payne's body. She especially liked his hands, clean and neatly maintained and powerful. Her skin glowed and the warmth in her body turned to a devastating heat that spread throughout her limbs making her ache deep inside.

Chanta! You're doing it again! You're only torturing yourself. What the hell would someone like him want with someone like you? Devour you? Scare the crap out of you again?

She eyed Payne; he couldn't be all that bad if her cats had taken a fancy to him.

Chanta licked her lips bringing her fingers to her mouth. He had tasted so good, clean, and powerful. She shivered as she recalled how good it had felt to be in his arms. No, good was not the right adjective; she had felt things she had never felt before. Passion, desire, need, want, and damn if the list wasn't getting longer by the second.

Which made absolutely no sense whatsoever. Eight years ago, she had literally run from him. But that kiss . . .

"Why are you staring at me like that?" Payne drawled out his words as he blatantly roamed her face for an answer.

His voice was so deep and gritty that Chanta jumped. It was a slow rumble in his chest, like a lion giving off a small warning to any would-be trespassers. It was sexy—too damn hot to be anything but supernatural. "I was just admiring your ... your ring."

The lie fell from her lips and her cheeks went red with embarrassment. Well, she couldn't very well admit that she had been checking him out. She looked at the floor and hoped he believed her.

"You're lying to me. Don't worry, most people find me frightening." He paused. "Do you find me frightening?"

Chanta twisted in the chair and looked up to meet his obsidian eyes. "I don't find you frightening, just weird as hell." And sexy as hell.

"You should be very afraid of me." He grinned, one corner of his mouth lifting. "You were very frightened of me eight years ago."

"If you were going to harm me, Gyth would not have sent you, so why should I be afraid of you?"

"Because I am the devil's son."

That must have been the cue for her cats to start stretching and purring. Chanta grinned. "How am I supposed to find you scary when my cats have all curled up in your lap?"

"Cats are territorial and find comfort in the dark, much the same as I do."

Chanta lowered her gaze. She had to ask. "Are you territorial also?"

"Yes."

Chanta watched as he shifted and ran his hand along Jazz's back. "How did you know where I lived?"

"Your address is on your key ring."

"Oh." Her throaty reply rang in her own ears. What was she expecting? He was a Destroyer, a killing machine designed and created for one specific purpose—to protect the One Race and she guessed that included taking members, like her, through the Burning.

Turning her head, she hid the tear that was threatening to slide down her cheek. With a quick swipe, it was gone and she took a deep rattled breath. She wondered just how many women Payne had taken through the Burning. How many women had lain in his gorgeous arms and transformed from human to demi-goddess?

And just why the hell was it bothering her to think of other women in his arms?

Chapter 12

Payne ran his hand through his hair and stared at Chanta's bare foot and the birthmark that hovered above her ankle, a purple circle with a crescent moon attached to each side. He had seen the same symbol somewhere else. His memory failed him and he grunted as his eyes slid farther up her leg. The length of it was torture and the scent that was reaching his nose was flaring up desires he didn't want to face.

He gritted his teeth and frowned as she stood. She was looking better and better each time he saw her. She stretched and he sucked in the air around him as her breasts peeked and her nipples hardened. He would like to see her naked, and he knew that soon he would and a soft grin came to his lips.

Watching her move was a pleasure all its own and he knew beyond a shadow of doubt that he was going to enjoy this. Yeah, he would indeed, even if it killed him in the end.

She turned and headed back down the hall. "I'm going to take a shower and get this makeup off. Would you be a dear and fix some hot chocolate? The cocoa is in the cabinet above the stove."

Cocoa? Chocolate? What was she trying to insinuate? Chocolate was an aphrodisiac.

Payne growled, but stood carefully depositing the cats on the couch; he didn't have the faintest clue how to fix hot chocolate nor had he ever been asked to do such a thing. The fat black cat that had been on his left leg stretched as he purred. Jazz jumped down to the floor and meowed up at Payne as he waltzed by. He walked across the room and went into the small kitchen turning around and meowing to Payne once more.

Payne rolled his eyes and followed the cat's path to the kitchen. Jazz pawed at the refrigerator and Payne opened the door. The cat rubbed against Payne's leg and meowed again. Scanning the contents of the refrigerator, he found a gallon of milk.

Okay, so he had the milk, now what?

He twisted the cap off and poured some into the bowl that was sitting in the floor in front of the stove. The cat happily lapped at the cold liquid as Payne reached into the cabinet and pulled out the can of cocoa. He carefully read the instructions on the side of the can.

It seemed easy enough. He looked around the tiny room trying to find a microwave. The directions called for a microwave, but none was to be found in this kitchen. He eyeballed the pan that sat in the dish drain beside of the sink.

"I am not a fucking maid, she can do it herself if she wants it. Who the hell does she think she is ordering me around? And why the fuck does she smell so good?"

He carefully sat the can down on the counter and looked down at the black cat. "You fix the shit for her!"

Jazz purred and rubbed up against his leg as the other three cats came running into the kitchen at the sound of his voice. He grinned as they jumped up onto the counter and pawed at the pan. They were loyal to her and he did appreciate that.

Loyalty he understood, cooking he did not.

Payne grabbed the pan and slammed it down on the burner, wincing slightly at the harshness of the sound. He poured it about half full of milk and turned the knob until flames shot out from underneath the pan. He stepped back and grinned; he could have used his fingers to achieve that. He took the lid off the can and tipped it over the pan. The tabby squalled out as a few drops of the powder poured into the milk. He jerked the can away and frowned as the powder landed on the stovetop.

"What the hell do you expect from me? I haven't ever done this shit before."

The tabby growled and hissed as she went to the dish drain and pawed a spoon. Payne grunted as he took the spoon and slammed it into the can. He dumped two tablespoons into the milk and glared at the cat. He stood over the stove and stared at the milk until it started to boil.

As his stare hardened, he listened to the water running in the bathroom. He could hear her humming and smell the soap she was using to wash her hair. He wondered what she looked like without all that makeup and Gothic clothing. Growling, he could picture her in a black negligee with her hair damp and clinging to her. He wondered what kind of lover she would be as he pictured her sitting in the middle of his bed. The image was sexy. He groaned as he imagined her naked in his arms and begging him to take her.

Mine.

The tabby squalled again and Payne watched as the chocolate milk boiled over the pan's side. "Son of a bitch!"

He grabbed the pan's handle and cursed again. The tabby jumped off the counter and hissed at Payne. He sat the pan on the counter and mentally shook himself. He grabbed the mug that was turned upside down and slammed it on the counter. He gritted his teeth as it split up the side. Picking up the pieces, he looked for a trashcan. His nostrils flared as he threw the broken shards into the ten-gallon can. Jazz purred and pawed at his black combat boot as he ran his hand through his hair.

"What the fuck am I doing?" He looked at the cat and suddenly felt like a fool.

In all his life, he had never been like this, jittery and acting foolish.

He reached to the cabinet above the sink and pulled out another mug. He poured the mug full and carried it to the front room. Grunting his discord, he placed it on the table beside the black velvet chair. He reached into his pocket and took out a pen and notepad. He scribbled on it and tucked it under the mug's edge. Taking a deep agonizing breath, he turned on his heel and stomped to the front door growling as he quickly left and locked the door behind him. This night had definitely not gone the way he had intended.

His body was hard wired for Chanta Timbers, ready to embrace her Burning. His mind was another matter. The witchy woman had done something to his body and to his head.

Mine. The word spun loops in his brain, zigzagging across his nerves like the teeth of a saw blade. She could never be his. His future didn't have any place for her, it didn't have a place for anyone.

He was famished and needed to feed. And there was no denying that he needed to put some space between himself and the bewitching woman in the shower. Cursing under his breath, he left the building and shimmered out of sight. Right now, he needed control and patience and those were two things that he seriously lacked.

. . .

Chanta dried off and slid the purple gown over her head. She caught her reflection in the mirror and smiled. She was back to her normal self and her face felt a lot better without the make-up on. Wearing all that stuff made her skin itch, but it hid the dark circles under her eyes. Her light blonde hair dripped as she ran her fingers through it. She wondered if Payne liked her natural whitish blonde tresses. It was an odd color, almost white.

But then why would she care? Why did she care? It wasn't like he was going to stick around.

She wiped the fog from the rest of the mirror and frowned. She hoped he thought she was pretty. Hell, she was praying he thought she was sexy because she sure as hell was thinking that about him. She closed her eyes and imagined him standing in the bathroom naked. All those beautiful muscles and that silky long black hair and his hands, oh lord, those hands. Her face flushed as she wondered what he felt like under those clothes of his.

Chanta grinned and turned to the door. She took a slow long deep breath and opened the door. As she stepped out of the bathroom she heard the front door close. She frowned and went to the front room. It was empty. She slid into her chair and noticed the mug steaming on the end table.

Without thought, she took the cup and raised it to her lips. Sipping the hot chocolate, she realized something was stuck to the bottom of the mug. She pulled it and looked at the fancy writing. It was old English and as neat as it could be and her jaw dropped as she read it.

It read: *Sorry about the mess in the kitchen. I will be back tomorrow night at ten sharp to finish our conversation; make sure you are home. If you feel the burning before I return tomorrow, call me immediately. Payne.*

Underneath the words nine numbers were scrolled, it was a cell phone number. Payne, crazy as he may be, had left her his phone number. Knowing it was silly, she smiled as if he had left her a bouquet of flowers. An odd feeling crept up her skin. She felt as if she had cracked the surface, had somehow took an inch off of the mile where he was concerned.

Payne was a Destroyer, a lethal weapon against the demons that Damon commanded. And even though she knew he had a demon of his own under his skin, she couldn't help the way she was feeling.

With a sigh, she shivered. Payne was just more male than anyone she had ever been around. He was the total package except for his ill moods; those she could live without. The same ill-mooded, almost frightening, thick-headed Destroyer with no manners who she knew would rock her world. Reading the note again, she laughed. She was already feeling a burning, but she was sure it was not what he meant.

Chapter 13

Payne collectively retreated inside of himself as he left Chanta's apartment. He needed to find that black void where he felt so comfortable. His back went straight and rigid as his hands curled into balls at his sides. The smell of this town was almost clean, almost.

His eyes flashed and turned yellow as he caught the distinct smell of witch. The grimace on his face deepened as his eyes glowed orange and then red. It was hunting time and his blood boiled with the excitement of the kill. His fangs extended over his lower lip as he grinned.

He reached around to his back and pulled the Egyptian scimitars from the sheaths that hung from his shoulders. They were his favorite weapons, forged by his own hand with the power that ran through his blood veins. The smile on his face widened as the smell grew closer. He knew the witch was strong and old and he hoped for a good fight. The stronger the witch, the more fulfilling her blood would be.

His image shimmered and disappeared as he stepped into the shadows. He reappeared inside of an old barn that lay on the outskirts of the small town. The low chant of the coven filled his ears. His eyes narrowed as his mind was thrown back to the past, a past that burned into his soul every second of every day.

. . .

Egypt. During the reign of Thutmose III
Payne was known as Damian, the son of Damon. He was not coveted or treated as one would expect a prince of the Underworld to be. Instead, he was starved and scared, and stayed huddled in

the corner of the dark cave. His fear and loneliness isolated him as much as being Damon's son did.

He watched as his mother painted a five-pointed star in blood on the cave's wall with her long finger. She was as beautiful as sin, long black hair and eyes the color of the deepest ocean. Her beauty was devastating, but her heart was as black and cruel as they came. She was a witch, a worshipper of the feared Damon.

The star she had painted was from the blood of an innocent child, her child. Damian's blood slid down her fingers as she turned to him. He was crying and holding his wrist. She smiled and walked to his side slowly sucking the blood from her fingertip. She knelt beside of him and grabbed his wrist. He bit his tongue as she raised it to her lips and licked the wound. His skin crawled as the tears ran down his dirty cheeks.

"Do not cry. You're serving a great purpose. Your blood is innocent and Damon loves you." Her ancient Egyptian language spilled from her mouth as she ran her finger down his nose. "You're his son and he needs you. Love and obey your father and he'll give you immortality in the end. Hate your father and he'll torment your soul for all time."

She pulled him to his feet and ran her fingers through his thick mud packed hair. He leaned against his mother and took her other hand in his. He walked by her side out into the cave's opening. Over thirty witches stood waiting for them. His mother, Re-Mona, held her hand up and silenced the coven. Their chant subsided and she pushed the boy to the center of the crowd.

"He must be beaten with your wands. Take care to lance his skin and lick the blood from the wound. His blood is pure and tonight Damon commands that we all partake of him and taste what he implanted inside of me."

The little boy fell to his knees, but his tears dried as the witches formed a line. The first witch stepped forward and held out her wand over his back. The little boy stared at the ground and waited.

The wand came down and bit into his flesh. His mother smiled as the witch fell to her knees and licked the wound. She stood and went to Re-Mona's side with his blood on her lips.

The next witch stepped forward. Damian looked up as a little black haired girl, Bastilla, came running at him. She threw herself across his back and screamed in utter defiance to his mother.

"No, please stop. I love him. Why do you cause him so much pain?"

Re-Mona frowned and went to the young witchling. She grabbed her hair and pulled her to her feet. Bastilla kicked her shins and fought as Re-Mona dragged her into the cave. She commanded the ceremony to continue as they disappeared into the opening of the cave.

Even though the witches continued the beating, Damian turned and watched his mother, listening to every word being said.

She threw the girl into the corner and took out her wand. "He is the property of Damon! His blood is still human and is unfit for your love. You disgrace your god by loving him. It's your duty to love Damon!"

Bastilla pleaded, "But coven mistress, please. He is your son!"

Re-Mona stopped, her face going pale. "He is Damon's son. I may have carried that demon inside of me, but he isn't a child of mine! My pain was greatly rewarded."

Bastilla's eyes widened as she stared out of the cave at Damian. "You sold your body and your son to Damon."

Laughter echoed through the winding cave. "His pain is a blessing from your god!"

"A blessing?"

"Yes." Re-Mona grinned, her eyes glittering like diamonds. "You should not worry about the boy, you should be more worried about yourself. I have given you to Damon. He has chosen you as his next bride-to-be and wants you to understand that you will mother his next child!"

"No!"

Bastilla scrambled to her feet and tried to run past her. Re-Mona caught her by the hair and slammed her to her knees. She lashed out and slapped the girl several times and spit in her face.

"You ungrateful little urchin! It's time you met your god."

Damian heard Bastilla's scream. Scrambling to his feet, he raced to the cave, fear clutching his heart. He knew that his mother would beat her for trying to protect him, but that wasn't what worried him. His father would do unimaginable things to Bastilla.

Pushing through the two of the witches at the entrance, he fell scraping his knees. Slipping through one of the witch's legs, he ran as hard as he could to Bastilla. He slid to a stop in front of her unconscious body and fell to his knees. As he reached for her hand, he was kicked in the side. Unwilling to feel the pain, he crawled to her hand. His fingers grazed her skin as he was pulled to his feet in front of his mother.

Re-Mona's eyes were cold and hard as she slapped him across the cheek. She threw him face forward to land in front of a pair of black boots. He looked up and bit back the scream in his throat. The man who stood before him was death, disease, famine, murder, hatred, and pure evil. His straight hair hung down to the cave's floor and fanned out around his black boots. His face was cold and as white as the linen worn by virgins. His eyes were red and set in dark sockets. The black horns that protruded out of his skull were twisted and jagged.

Damian tried to look away but couldn't. The man's body was lithe and skinny and snakes curled around both of his arms and slithered around his chest like clothing. They hissed and bit at Damian as he scrambled backward.

Damon laughed and the sound of his laugh froze the cave's air and the cold mist settled around Damian's body as the cave disappeared. The boy scrambled to his feet and tried to see a way to escape. He reached out into the mist and screamed as his hand was bitten by snakes that appeared out of thin air. He fell to his knees as the snake god stepped forward and grabbed his hair.

As he lifted Damian from the ground by his hair, he said, "Is that any way to treat your father? It has plagued my soul to have to be away from you."

The boy twisted and cried out as his hair began to pull from his scalp. Damon released Damian's hair and let him fall to the ground. A throne of twisted naked female bodies appeared and Damon sat down. He peered at the boy and pointed at him. He crooked his finger and Damian slid across the cold floor to his booted foot.

"I want to share something with you, my son."

Damian closed his eyes as the mist cleared and two woman dressed in white appeared. They were chained to the floor by their ankles. Damon grinned and opened the boy's eyes with a flick of his wrist. Damian watched in horror as another man dressed in red satin robes stepped forward holding an axe.

The women in white were virgins. Damian knew because he had witnessed these executions all of his life. He also knew that they were members of the One Race and had not yet gone through the Burning. He didn't know how he knew, he just did.

He swallowed hard as his mother appeared in front of the two women. She was naked, painted with blood from head to toe. Damian tried to look away as his mother took the axe in both of her hands, but his head refused to turn.

"Lesson one, my son. Fear will win you more servitude than any other emotion." He leaned forward, grabbed Damian's chin. "And when that fear turns into devotion ... " He pointed to the women in chains. "They'll want to die for you just so it will bring you pleasure."

Damian jerked away, fell backwards as Damon laughed. "I don't want anyone to die."

"Watch Damien, watch how your mother serves me." Damon grinned, his black hair falling over one of his eyes. "Soon, you'll serve me as well. The rivers of blood that you'll create will give me insurmountable pleasure."

Chapter 14

Payne watched in the shadows shaking off the memory as two witches carried a black candle from the front of the barn to the back. The smell of hay and horses filled his nostrils, the scent distracting his thoughts. It reminded him of the kiss he had never forgotten, of the woman he had tried to forget, but hadn't.

And he had just left that woman in her apartment, naked and wet. Chanta was becoming a major distraction and it was presenting a problem for him. For the life of him, he didn't know what he was going to do or to how to handle the situation.

The doors of the barn opened and a red haired witch stepped in followed by ten more witches. All of them were naked and all painted red. The red head was strong and no doubt the high priestess of her coven. She wore the mark of Damon on her forehead as if it was an honor to have endured his touch. Payne's lips curled into a cruel grin as he saw the scars that ran across her nose and down her jaw.

Damon was an enigma. He lived on the pain and misery of others and even convinced his followers that through the pain he inflicted, his love was in the purest form. How crazy was that? Damon really was a snake, in every possible way.

The scimitars hummed in his hands, anxious to taste blood. Damon had taught him well in the time he had been his prisoner, he taught him how to kill without mercy, without fear, without emotion. And Varick had honed those skills to perfection. He was born to be a killer, born from the semen of a god, born from the womb of a witch. Reborn with revenge and bloodlust in his heart. He was Payne!

He stepped out from the shadows and his war cry scolded the ears of the coven. They fled in ten different directions as he crossed the small space to the head witch. His blades were raised as she shielded her face. Her screech of anger flooded his mind and he grinned.

He swung the scimitar and sliced through the flesh of her arm. Black blood gushed from the wound as she whirled around with her wand. The edge of the wand contacted his left forearm and he laughed. The witch stepped back with a wild unbelieving expression on her face as blue flames rose from her attacker's fingertips and flowed up his arms.

"Who are you?" she screamed as he leapt forward.

"I am your Destroyer. Prepare to meet your fate."

No sooner than the words left his twisted mouth, she fell to his thrust. The blades penetrated her body as if it were made of soft butter. Her blood poured down his hands as he heard the scream of another witch.

Payne's double fangs lengthened as he whirled around and caught the screaming witch midair. He flung her against the barn wall and sliced her in half, blood splattered the wall as she exhaled her last breath.

He turned and smiled as eight witches, five males and three females, surrounded him. They each extended their hands and weapons appeared. His body, fueled by the intensity of his rage, took on a persona of its own. His maddening dance of destruction lashed out at the witches, and his laughter filled the barn as they fell one and two at a time.

Blood splattered and spurted across his face and chest. It ran down both of his arms as he roared curses and insults. The black horns of his inner demon appeared on his forehead as the smile stretched across his hate-filled face.

The eighth witch fell into a severed heap at his feet. He looked down with contempt written on his face. Bitch of Damon! He growled as a solid wallop to the back of his head made him step forward. He turned and smiled as the witch dropped the iron bar in her hand and cowered from him. Payne sheathed his scimitars and lunged for her.

He caught her by the hair and slammed her face into the center post of the barn. It cracked under the force and groaned as Payne slammed her face into it again. The witch fell and her screams turned to gurgles. The bones in her face were caved in and one could no longer even guess what she had looked like. She threw her hands to her face as Payne carelessly twisted her neck. She fell forward against the post with her eyes bulging from the torn sockets.

Payne knew there were three more hiding in the shadows and his eyes flashed turning yellow once more. The strongest was waiting against the back door, carelessly picking at her long, black fingernails. The smug expression on her face seared through his anger as he reached into the shadows to his left and drug a male from his hiding place. His fingers squeezed around his jugular and crushed his windpipe. The witch fell backwards as Payne turned to the witch who stepped out from behind a large pile of hay.

She laughed as Payne stepped forward. "So you are one of Gyth's piglets?" Her black fingernails extended as she continued. "I won't let you kill my mistress. I will feast on your flesh this night."

Payne's arms blazed again and his eyes turned as red as blood. "Then come on whore of Damon. Stop your useless chatter and come get some of me."

The witch snarled and leapt forward with her claws slashing at the air. He raised his left arm and blue flames flew from his fingertips and slammed her backwards into the back wall. She slid down the wall screaming in pain. The flames covered her body and melted her eyes. The stench of charred flesh filled his nostrils as he watched her flesh turn to blackened mush and slowly slide from her bones.

Payne grinned as the flames entered her ashy sockets and devoured her insides. Damon's gift was ironic to say the least. It was the one power that he had kept after his transformation into a Destroyer. The blue flame of the Underworld's fire was torture to any soul and could melt any metal with his slightest touch. It was time to harvest the witch's souls and seal them inside of the pendants of Damon. It was all rather ironic, but self-satisfying all the same.

The last witch strolled up to the haystack and smiled. "I know who you are Destroyer. Your name has crossed my mistress's lips more than she cares to admit. You are Payne, son of Damon, son of Re-Mona, bringer of death. Your reputation precedes you. Cold, calculated, brutal, and so full of hate."

Payne gritted his teeth as the witch walked closer and touched his forearm. "Your father has sent me here to find you, but I knew you would find me instead. I've waited for you as you have played caretaker to Gyth's offspring."

Payne narrowed his eyes, but held his tongue as she ran her fingers across his chest. Her eyes rolled into the back of her head, her neck cracking and popping. Payne stepped back, the witch's eyes bled black tears as fangs emerged and her skin stretched tight and split open as if tiny knives were lancing her skin. Small streams of black blood flowing from the cracks.

The witch's mouth opened, moving slowly as saliva dripped from the corner of her lips. Damon's voice, warped and twisted, poured from the witch's mouth. "Yes my son, she is Gyth's daughter. He wants you to use those hands of yours to help her through her Burning. Gyth is a selfish god. He knows that it could very well kill you to use your power on a transforming soul."

"No. You lie." She couldn't be Gyth's daughter. That would make her Varick's sister. "Show yourself."

Damon's laughter echoed around the barn, the witch's face contorting as her body twisted, her bones breaking. Payne recalled the birthmark on Chanta's ankle and his nostrils flared as Damon spoke again. "Don't you see what Gyth is planning for you? Are you really going to let that bastard use you? Are you going to let his daughter use you?"

Payne laughed. "I'm used to it."

"He uses you because you are my son! Don't you see the pleasure he gets from knowing he can bend and twist you to his will? He thinks you are weak, nothing more than a trophy for him. And she will think the same. Once she transforms, you will be nothing to her."

Payne's howl of anger erupted from his chest, the horns of his demon protruding from his head. His chest tightened, the past scratching its way to the surface. "And what was I for you? A trophy as well? Just another victim of your terror and perverse pleasure?"

"You are my son. My flesh covers your bones, my blood runs through your veins, and as much as you don't want to admit, you are just like me."

"I will never be like you!"

Payne struck hard and fast and roared in anger as Damon released his hold of the witch.

Shock filled the witch's face as she grabbed at the sudden pain in her stomach. Terror filled her eyes as Payne's teeth came down on her neck. She cried out as the blood flowed from her veins into his mouth. Whispering, she pleaded with her mistress and no answer came.

She whispered to Damon and tears flooded her face as Damon's face appeared above Payne's head. The evil sarcastic grin was glued to his lips as his words filled her mind.

"He is such a brutal killer and so much like his father."

She twisted in sheer agony as her heart slowed to its last beat. Her eyes hazed as Payne pulled away and threw her lifeless body to the ground. Without emotion or any trace of regret, he gathered all thirteen of the pendants and slid them into his pocket. Her power flowed through his veins and he braced himself for the coming impact.

His body jerked and fell forward to his knees as her blood made contact with the flame of the Underworld. The pleasure he felt was indescribable as it coursed through his limbs, strength, power, knowledge, and an undying feeling of superiority filled his soul. He would kill them all, every last one of the bitches. They would all pay for the crimes against him and others that had suffered by their hands, they would all be consumed and their souls eaten. His revenge would be fulfilled!

He threw his arms up and screamed as flames leapt from his fingers and licked at the inside of the barn. "I'm coming for you, Father!"

Chapter 15

Damon watched Payne from his throne and grinned as his son's heart filled with hatred and vengeance. He had outdone himself with this one. He was proving to be Damon's greatest accomplishment.

His evil laugh filled the throne room; and to think that dear Gyth had taken Payne into his care just as Damon had planned so very long ago. He stood and looked at the witch who walked into the throne room. Yet another accomplishment: Bastilla.

Her stilettos clicked on the floor, their echo a reminder of another set of feet that once had crossed a marble floor to him. Looking into the cauldron before him, he marveled at Payne's anger and hatred. It was a thing of beauty.

Damon waved the image of Payne away as she came closer. Bastilla, who had been no challenge to dominant, had once captured Payne's heart. He recalled the perfect pain and misery Payne had felt, had relished in it. Now she was Damon's wife, lover, and his worst enemy all wrapped up into one very pretty little package. She frowned as Payne's image disappeared.

"Why do you watch him? Have you not had your fill of fun with him?"

"The fun is only just beginning." Damon reached out and captured a stray strand of her black hair and jerked it. Hard. "What have you been up too lately ... wife?"

Bastilla stepped back and narrowed her eyes. "Protecting my position."

"Your position?" Damon threw her hair into the flame that arose from the pit around his thrown. Bastilla grimaced as pain shot through her temple. "Exactly what position are you protecting?"

"Bastard!" She picked at her long black fingernails. "I am your wife."

"Yet, you continually cross me. Did you think that I would not know what you were up to with the slut you have been catering to?"

"Which one do you speak of husband? The one I am sleeping with or the one I have had spying on your dear son?"

Damon waved his hand and Bastilla was thrown against a rock wall that appeared out of the ground. She twisted and gritted her teeth as snakes curled around her body and pinned her to the slab. He held out his hand and a small dagger appeared in his palm. He licked the blade and laughed as Bastilla's eyes widened.

"What should your punishment be? Should I kill the slut you have been sleeping with? But wait … " Damon turned and his image melted and in his place stood a very beautiful blonde woman. "I am the woman you have been sleeping with."

Bastilla jerked and tugged as the snakes tightened their hold. "You bastard! Can I not have any fun without you poking your ass into it?"

Damon's female form laughed. "How long has it been wife since I wed you? How long has it been since I took you in my true form?"

Bastilla caught her breath and closed her eyes as Damon's image transformed once again. She couldn't bear to look upon him as he truly was, as he had been the night he took her through her Burning. His face and body disgusted her and her stomach lurched as she felt his hand slide up her thigh.

"Open your eyes and answer the question."

"Not since I went through the Burning." Bastilla's eyes opened and tears ran down her cheeks. "Please, not like this."

Damon threw his head back and the snakes that framed his white face hissed as he laughed triumphantly. "It turns me on when you beg." His eyes narrowed into slits. "But you already knew that."

Bastilla bit her tongue as the snakes from his crotch slivered up her legs and bit into the flesh of her thighs. Damon spread his arms and opened his mouth as hundreds of the bastard snakes poured from his fingers and mouth. Bastilla bit back her scream of pleasure as they swarmed her body entwining themselves around her limbs.

The body of Damon that remained was little more than a skeleton draped with black hair. His eyes were as yellow as the sun and emotionless as he leapt onto the slab of rock and thrust his tongue into Bastilla's mouth. She accepted him greedily and tried not to groan. His eyes showed the pleasure he was feeling as he slowly slid his tongue out of her mouth.

Bastilla cocked an eyebrow. Damon bared his long jagged teeth and nibbled her chin as she rolled her eyes and grinned.

"Is that the best you can do?"

Damon's smile spread across his demon skull-like face as he pressed against her crotch. She arched as the snakes released their hold. She laughed as they slid back inside of Damon's body. He growled with intense pleasure as she spread her legs and threw them around his waist. Her arousal was intense as he pushed inside of her. He took her hands and placed them above her head as he slammed inside of her. She cried out in pleasure as he slid his hand up her thigh.

"So eager for me." Damon's groan of pleasure bounced around the throne room.

Bastilla grinned as he licked his lips. "I want him."

"My son is and always has been off limits." Damon's whisper beat at her skull. "Have you forgotten why I sent you to him in the first place?"

Damon thrust harder as she begged for more. "Please give him to me. Please, let me have him."

"Beg more."

"Please, I beg of you. I'll give you anything you want, I'll do anything you want. I want him!"

"The one thing I wanted from you, you could not give me." Damon threw his head back and his cold laughter slammed into Bastilla like a brick wall. "You will continue wanting Payne for all eternity."

Bastilla closed her eyes and moaned as he caressed her skin and flung his head back in pleasure. As Damon released his seed inside of her, she trembled. Damon stepped back and let her fall to the floor as his red robe appeared around his shoulders. His laughter filled her ears as she tried to stand.

"Make no mistake, wife of mine, the next time you interfere with my son I'll cut out your heart and eat it." Damon turned, his smile hovering on his black lips. "I fear your position as my wife has been severed. Consider yourself … what do the humans call it … divorced."

"No." Her brown eyes swirled with rage. "You cannot do this to me."

Walking towards his throne, Damon said nothing, waited for Bastilla to soak up what he had said.

"What makes him so special?" She screamed, "What does he have to offer you that I cannot?"

"Isn't it obvious? Your position has been to give me a child. That's all I ever wanted from you." Damon stopped and stared down at his hands. "He's my favorite creation. He is my son."

Bastilla fell forward as she cried. "But he hates you and kills your followers. He has sworn to kill you!"

He raised an eyebrow. "You hate me as well and yet, I have kept you around for centuries. But alas, I have grown tired of these pointless games with you. And your one and only purpose has not been full-filled."

Her fists slammed against the floor. "He will be your downfall."

Damon chuckled lightly as he strolled back to his throne taunting her. "He has the heart of a killer, the soul of a snake, and the hands of the Underworld. What do you have?"

• • •

Bastilla's anger flooded her cheeks as she scrambled to her feet. "I hate you!"

Damon hissed as she turned and stomped out of the throne room. She held her head high as she rounded the corner. Looking over her shoulder, she made sure that she wasn't being followed as she quickly stepped through the roots that hid a doorway. Her bitter laugh echoed as she stood before a mirror, its depths shimmering with a green glow.

She would have Payne one way or another, even if it meant Damon's death. Her body jerked as her mind conjured up images of Damon's lifeless body … cut up into small pieces and being fed to Cerberus along with all the witches he had slept with. Every last one of them.

He had taken every single one of them through the Burning himself, delighting in their pain and misery, making sure that Bastilla was tied to a chair and watching him.

Pounding in her chest, her heart threatened to explode. And now, after everything she had endured for the bastard, he wanted a divorce? For the gods, a divorce was humiliating. No other god would dare enter into a relationship with someone spurned by another god. She wasn't going to go down without a fight.

Seething rage festered in her heart. Oh, he would pay with blood and bone.

She would have to play her cards right and she knew just which card to lay down first. Varick Ta Farg, son of Gyth! If she could get him to believe that she was here by force and get her clutches into his heart, things just might start turning her way.

And even if she couldn't get to Varick, he would lead her straight to Payne. And that's exactly where she wanted to be. One thing, she had learned from Damon, always have a back-up plan. And if the back-up plan didn't work, always have an escape route.

Thanks to Charon, her newfound friend, she could travel to the earth's surface on demand. The surface of the mirror rippled as she stepped through and was swept into the currents of the River Styx.

Charon hadn't asked much of her in return, just the unborn fetus that she had hidden from Damon. With a little help from a goddess, she had successfully placed the fetus in stasis. After all, she wasn't about to give Damon the one thing he desired most, another son.

The smile slid onto her lips as she vanished and reappeared on the earth's surface in Fether, California. Damon could not track her footsteps in this realm unless she wore his pendent next to her heart and oops she had accidentally left it lying on the floor of his throne room.

She forced her wounds to stay fresh as she scribed for Varick. He was nearby and the smile widened across her lips. Soon, she would be in Payne's arms and according to Charon, she would become queen of the Underworld if she could make Payne fall back in love with her and have Payne kill his father. Unlike Damon, who refused to give her the power she needed to be queen, Payne could be manipulated as she had when she had met him. All she had to do was make certain Payne knew Damon's weaknesses.

Damon was not as smart as he thought he was.

Chapter 16

Payne stood still as the vampire crouched over the hidden entrance to the cave where he and others had been hiding. His grin spread, there were more than twenty of the bastards huddled inside. Slowly they came out, looking from left to right as they slinked across the grass. Payne's fingers twitched, he was ready for a good fight, and he needed to let out some major frustration tonight before seeing Chanta.

He reached back and grabbed the hilts of his swords. They felt good in his hands, like old friends. Sharp as razors and two feet of unbreakable steel; he loved these weapons and they had served him well. His eyes narrowed as he counted, twenty-three, twenty-four, twenty five.

Prepare you motherfuckers, death is coming!

Payne held the swords pointed down and crouched as he steadied the power of his beast. He didn't like using him unless it was necessary and tonight he wanted the physical exercise of the kill. He looked down at his pants pocket as it vibrated against his leg.

Who the fuck would be calling now? Everyone knew what he would be doing this hour of the night.

He chose to ignore the cell phone for the time being and redirected his attention to the fight at hand. With a loud cry, he leapt through the air and soundly landed in the midst of the vampires. They crouched and hissed as their tongues tasted the air that whipped around them. Destroyer! The bravest few stepped forward and laughed as he raised his swords.

"Destroyer. What do you think you are doing? We are many, you are one. Your soul beckons to me. Strong you are, but stupid to come here."

The vampire licked his lips and hissed as ten more stepped forward and circled him. The grin on his lips and the glint in his eyes should have worried the vampires, but they were lusting after his soul and cared not that he may be a powerful enemy. After all, they weren't entirely very smart.

"Perhaps, we all will feast on that savory soul of yours."

Payne closed his eyes and forced the demon to be still as he rushed for the male who was talking. The vampire sputtered as Payne's sword sliced through his neck. The bright red blood flowed down the vampire's chest and bubbled as the vampire started to melt. Payne opened his eyes as the vampire's body exploded into ashes. He turned and swung his left sword as a female vampire grabbed his ankle. She burst into flames as the sword sliced her skull in half.

Three came from the right and fell back as Payne's swords danced through their chests. Ashes flew around Payne's head as he sidestepped and dodged two female's attacks. One at a time they fell at his feet in flames. He sliced and diced as the rushed to their deaths. To the right, a swarm of twelve gathered as he fought off four males who were latching onto his back. One by one, the four were flung threw the air and hacked at. Arms and legs flamed as they landed on the ground at Payne's feet.

Payne growled as a female leapt over his head and landed on his back. Her black claws dug into his shoulder and pain shot down his arm. The sword in his right hand fell to the ground as another female grabbed his left leg and bit into his thigh. His rage escalated as he saw twelve more coming out of the corner of his eye. He fought to keep the beast contained as he grabbed the vampire from his shoulder and held her up by her throat.

He snarled and flung her to the ground in front of him. The female latched onto his leg and screamed as his sword plunged into her back. Flames licked his leg as he slammed the toe of his boot onto the ground. A long metal spike surged from the boot hill and in seconds landed down on the other female's skull.

He tried to keep count as he turned to face the oncoming swarm; thirteen were down, twelve more to go.

Payne rolled, catching his sword in his right hand and forcing the beast to stay put. The first of the twelve leapt onto him as he swung upwards. Two fell in flames as the other three jumped back. He was aware that five had jumped up into the tree to his left as he was covered in ashes from three more who misjudged his next move and felt the sting of his boot heels. The three that were wary clung back to the safety of their cave as he fell to one knee and groaned.

His Destroyer, the demon under his skin, was screaming to be released and it clawed at his skin as the five leapt from the tree onto his back. Payne's anger soared as he felt two sets of incisors sink into his flesh. His eyes rolled back into his head as the demon took over. Two of the vampires screamed as a long black-scaled snake ripped out of his side.

Payne roared as his snake shot through their chests like a deadly arrow. Another one leapt back as it swung forward and slammed her down into the ground. The one at his shoulder looked down in shock as a horn ripped from Payne's shoulder and pushed through his stomach.

The vampire on the ground flamed as his snake swooshed down and struck hard, ripping the vampire's heart out. The one remaining on his back was sucking hard as Payne reached over his head and grabbed him by the hair. The vampire screamed as he was pulled from his meal and slashed out at the hands that held him. The shock on his face was replaced by pain as the pressure of Payne's hands crushed his windpipe. The vampire exploded as Payne's fingernails lengthened and pushed into his chest.

Payne stood and screamed, raged, and cursed as he held out his arms and his shoulders ripped open. He fell forward onto his knees as the demon claimed his body. The other three vampires huddled inside of the cave in fear as the entrance was filled with dozens of snakes.

Isten's shadowy image appeared and shook his head. "Really? You can't even control those snakes? And you think you're a Destroyer?"

"She is Gyth's daughter!" The claws between his knuckles slid out, four inches of lethal weapon. Balling his fist, he pointed the tips at Isten's ghostly visage. "Why should I help my father's worst enemy? Why should I bother with her at all?"

Isten's silver eyes swirled. "Because I command you!" Gritting his teeth, his jaw flexing, Isten swallowed hard. "It is necessary for her to survive. This isn't about Gyth, it's about the fate of the universe."

"Like I care about the fate of this universe."

"You're not your father, Payne."

"Aren't I? His blood runs through my veins."

"You will be and are what you make yourself."

Payne in his truest form, turned, a crown of blood forming above his brow as Isten continued. "If you plan on keeping your end of our little bargain, learn to embrace who and what you are. You better get your ass together and figure this out. Chanta must survive. Was I wrong when I chose you, son of Damon?" Isten laughed and teased as Payne swiped at the snakes hissing in his ears. "You're over two thousand years old. It's about time you put your past behind you."

• • •

Gyth stood in the foyer of Isten's castle with Varick, Chanta, and Payne on his mind. The black marble floor shining in desolation, a gentle reminder of the chaos that was yet to come. The soft chime of a clock inundated his senses, pushed him further and deeper into his own thoughts and emotions.

How he wished he had raised his son, how he wished that Payne had not been part of the game at hand, and how he wished that Chanta could be spared this torturous journey.

When Ania appeared beside of him, he caught his breath, her black eyes bored into his seeking his miseries. He stepped aside, growled low in his throat.

"Are you angry?" She pouted. "Angry at me?"

He shook his head. "Never. You did as you were told."

"But I pledged my allegiance back to Isten." She circled him, her graceful legs carrying her with a confidence only the goddess of misery could have. "And your plan is succeeding?"

Gyth could only nod as she stepped back and glanced at Isten who was seated on his throne, his body a silver statue.

Her eyes flickered and turned back to him. "Where is he?"

"With Payne. Teaching him how to center and control his powers, preparing him to be the hand that defends Isten's pantheon."

Ania frowned. "Using him for his own purposes is a more accurate way of putting it. But then, Isten uses us all in one form or another."

Gyth couldn't stop the lift of his eyebrow as he stared at her. "Is there something that you know and you haven't told me?"

"I have been around a long time, my dear old friend." Ania laughed, her voice a melody of pain and sorrow. "I have forgotten more things than you will ever know."

He couldn't suppress his irritation although he really did try. He liked Ania, she was one of the few that he trusted. He barked a laugh. To be honest, she was the only one he trusted.

"Then tell me, what am I missing here?" Gyth paced back and forth waiting for her to answer. He knew not to push her. "I did exactly what needed to be done in order to save my son and my daughter. And yet, everything is going in the opposite direction, the game pieces are not taking the steps I need them to take."

She shrugged. "What you perceive to be needed is not what destiny perceives. You meddled with your daughter's fate, meddled with Damon's, and tried to prevent Varick's. And yet, you never gave thought to Jaiden's books."

Gyth frowned. "Why should I? Jaiden was destroyed when my father reigned the Heavens, his books became meaningless."

"Did they?" She glided past him, her hair a soft whisper of silk as she turned and faced him. "How can something become meaningless when they are a part of someone?"

Gyth rolled his eyes and shook his head. "You and your riddles, Ania, can you just please say what you're getting at?"

She smiled. "When Isten used Jaiden's powers to create this universe … " She paused, her eyes sparking to life as if a fire had been thrown into two pits of oil. "When Isten used a babe's powers, took from a child born from time itself, he crossed into divine territory. Good must be balanced with evil, rights and wrongs must stand on equal ground. Free will must prevail."

Gyth felt his jaw flex. "More riddles?"

Her smile widened, her eyes returning to their black state once again. "It is all I am allowed to give you."

Running his fingers through his hair, he snorted. "One of these days, hopefully before my own demise, I will think back to these moments and remember them with sweet reverence."

She pursed her lips, narrowed her black eyes, and snorted. "That's not going to happen."

"Yeah, you're probably right."

She laughed. "Trust in this. Jaiden's books are not meaningless. Even though Chanta, Damon, and Payne's destinies have been erased, that doesn't mean the books won't rewrite them."

"What else must I do?"

Her black eyes pinned him, stared straight into his soul. "There isn't anything you can do to stop this. Gyth, please, if you want your daughter to survive, stop tampering with her destiny."

Gyth jerked around as Ania vanished. Her words echoed around his skull, the sound of her voice sending pain along his nerves. As he pushed her voice from his mind, he gritted his teeth so hard his jaws ached. He had a feeling that his only true ally had just become a wildcard.

Chapter 17

Varick watched the door, his senses going into overdrive. Standing at the bar at Tortured Souls, he glanced around the dance floor. Strobe lights flickered and pulsed as bodies danced to the hammering music. Mostly they were One Race members, a few Destroyers, and the occasional human.

Something wasn't right, he could feel the low hum of chaos in his backbone. The door creaked open, the wind swirling in and stirring the black napkins on the tables. He narrowed his eyes, the feeling in his spine hammering into his brain.

As the door swung wide, a woman with long black hair appeared in the doorway. Her make-up minimal, just dark liner around her eyes. Dressed in a long white dress, Egyptian sandals on her feet, and beads hanging in her hair, she looked like she had just stepped out of time. She made her way through the teaming crowd and went to a table in the back. He noted that as soon as she sat down, her eyes went directly to his.

Varick stared at the woman as he turned the bottle up. Yeah, there was something amiss with her. He couldn't tell if she was a witch, a werewolf, or a vampire, but she was not human and she wasn't anything he had ever encountered before. So much for his gods be damned powers. He cursed and went to her table.

She looked up, her eyes misting with tears. "I am Bastilla."

Varick grunted once, ran his hand over his chest. "What do you want?"

She lowered her eyes and pushed her sleeves up so that he could see the bite marks that riddled her skin. "I need help and I didn't know where else to go."

Varick swallowed and sat down across from her at the table. "Who did this to you?"

"I don't know his name. He comes to me while I sleep. The others tell me that it's a great honor, but ... "

Varick took her hand and pulled it across the table. He carefully inspected the wounds and frowned. They were snakebites, large, probably constrictors, and no poison. He released her hand and looked at her chin. She had teeth marks, jagged and sharp, but teeth marks all the same. He watched as she pulled her sleeves down and nervously shifted in her chair.

"What are you?" The question was simple and he expected an answer.

She looked up and met his stare. "I'm not sure what I am. I know that I am different. My clan ... .they are ... different too, but I am not like them either."

"What are they?"

"Vam ... " She lowered her gaze. "They are vampires."

Varick finished his beer and held up his hand. The waitress that Alexander, a fellow Destroyer, liked brought him another one and asked if the woman wanted one as well. She shook her head and politely said no. The waitress bounced away as someone called her name.

"What are you?" he asked yet again.

The woman shrugged her shoulders. "I'm not sure."

"And exactly what do you want us to do for you?"

"Help me escape them and the man who plagues my nights," she whispered nervously looking around the dance floor.

"Are you asking for asylum?"

Bastilla frowned. "No, I want this world rid of them all. They are evil beyond compare and I don't think I would be safe until they are all dead."

"Where are they?" He knew she was lying.

He felt excitement race through her veins, but she bit it down as she answered. "On the outskirts of town. There is an old abandoned warehouse with an underground storage compartment. That is where they sleep. I watch over them ... if I don't, they will hunt me down and kill ... kill me."

"Have they fed from you?"

"No."

"Why did you come here?"

"I need your help."

"My help?" He paused, let the silence between them grow until she started fidgeting. "How did you know where to find me?"

"I have a friend. He told me where to come and to look for a white haired man."

"And what is this friend's name?"

He watched her eyes dart back and forth. "Charon."

"Charon?" Charon's name struck a chord in his gut. Varick searched her face as an odd feeling snaked up his spine. "What do you offer in return for their deaths?"

"I don't have anything except for my body."

Varick looked her over as if she were a piece of meat. Her black hair was lovely, her eyes were an odd bright brown and satin gray color and her complexion had an olive tint to it. Her shoulders were strong and her fingers were soft. She was a very beautiful woman, but he felt the evil that clung to her. She had no doubt been subject to many horrors, but she was no saint.

Bastilla met his eyes. "If you will do this for me, I'll give my body freely."

Varick narrowed his eyes. "You would offer yourself?"

"I have heard the rumors that Destroyers are powerful lovers … and I feel that it is I that would be rewarded."

Varick was not born yesterday and he could sense a trap when one was being laid out so politely in front of him. He didn't need god powers to see it. Did this female expect him to fall so easily? Or was that part of the trap as well?

He gritted his teeth and commanded. "You will tell the truth of this visit. Perhaps you will find solace in another man's arms," he whispered, "But you won't find it in mine."

Bastilla gritted her teeth as she clutched his crotch. "I will do anything you want me to. Please, I beg of you, help me."

Varick growled as his zipper came down and her hand reached inside. Her fingers were warm and soft, but her grip told another story. He groaned as the beast clawed at his eyes. It was getting harder to control as she reached around him and cupped his butt. Instantly, he slammed her into the wall and picked her up from the floor baring his elongated fangs.

"You know not what you seek. When I finish with you there will be nothing left except for your crushed dead body!" Varick shook his head. "What brings you into this sanctuary?"

Bastilla grinned. "I am stronger than I look. And I need your help."

"It has nothing to do with strength and you will keep your distance from me or die." His voice deepened as his eyes cast a soft white glow over her face.

In his present state, he caught a strangely familiar odor, Payne. But he was in Kentucky. He released his hold of the woman and turned on his heel.

He knew of Bastilla, Payne's one and only desire. Could this be her? He would have to speak to him in regard to this matter. Speaking with Payne about his emotions was like pulling your fingernails out one at a time, complete torture. He growled as he turned back to the woman. Time to play the game at hand.

"You can have asylum until this issue is resolved. Go to the office in the back and ask for Alera. She will show you to a room and see that you are protected throughout the night. Do not leave this building or speak to any demons that may be here. Do you understand?"

Bastilla stared at the only man that had ever refused her, complete confusion on her brow, "And what about the man who comes while I sleep?"

"No demon can come into these walls and cause harm to another."

"And what am I going to owe you?"

"We shall see."

"All I can offer is what stands before you."

Varick laughed hatefully. "Not interested."

Bastilla's rage flared as he turned and walked back to the bar. He would regret this refusal soon enough. No one refused her will, no one! But for now, she would play the part of the damsel in distress. She turned to the door as a gorgeous woman walked into the club from the back.

Bastilla watched her as she looked at Varick. Her blood boiled as she saw Varick turn to the woman and smile. She caught her breath as Varick' power surged at the sight of this woman. Disgust and hatred welled up her throat as his eyes feasted on the female.

The woman was the reason he had refused her. No matter, she would have what she wanted as soon as she found Payne and had him falling for her all over again. Time for plan B.

• • •

The clock on the wall above the picture of a lion chimed. Chanta nervously picked at the hem of her black dress. She had taken great care in preparing herself for Payne's visit. Her light tresses framed her face in an upswept fashion, her fingernails were painted red to match her toes that peeked out from the high heels that she was wearing, and the sleeveless dress she wore was perfectly fit to her soft curves.

She sat straight up in the black velvet chair and took a deep breath. What would she do if he came on to her? But that was the point of the whole situation, right? Would he? Was he mated or did he have a love interest? He couldn't be either, or Gyth would never have chosen him, right? Was he crazy? She stood and covered her mouth as her thoughts ran wide open.

Hell, he was probably gay. She grinned, his penis was probably little too. Did that even matter?

She had had sex several times. The first time was quick and hurt a little, but she hadn't enjoyed it at all. She had known what her boyfriend was thinking and her arousal soon died as his thoughts turned to the secret he was trying to hide.

She gritted her teeth; men were pigs. It was a hell of a secret and she had burst out in intense laughter and later her laughter had turned into disgust. He was gay, refused to acknowledge it, and had to think about a man to keep his erection. She had been such a fool!

Her thoughts ran back in time to her twenty-first birthday and her skin crawled. She shut her eyes and tried to refuse to relive that night of horror. It had been the best and the worst night of her entire life.

Damon, the lord of the Underworld, had seduced her. And she had fallen right into his cold hands. But they weren't cold until after she had slept with him. He had hidden his true identity from her, had indeed treated her with respect and had appeared to cherish her. Until after she had professed her love for him and had slept with him.

His hands had been so cold; she could still feel the scale-like tongue that had been forced into her mouth. She gritted her teeth and choked her past down her throat. She had not let that night rule her life even back then and she wasn't about to let it do so now.

She looked down at Jazz as he curled around her foot. "Well, Jazz, my furry little prince, what do you say about my new friend?"

The cat purred and meowed up at her. She grinned and reached down to pet him as a heavy knock sounded at the door. Chanta jumped and turned to the hallway. Could she go through with this? For a second she wished she had put on the baggy clothes she worked in, but the thought quickly disappeared as the knock sounded again, much louder.

She went to the door and grabbed the knob. "Who is it?"

"Payne."

She unlocked the door and removed the chain. She opened the door and caught her breath. The expression on Payne's face was dark and there was not an ounce of kindness to be found. He came in and pushed past her. He scanned the living room and looked out of the window. When he turned around Chanta was standing by the black chair and she had every intention of turning tail and running.

And to think she had been fantasizing about this Destroyer? This arrogant, hateful, and uncompassionate Destroyer?

Chapter 18

Payne looked her over and his heart pounded in his chest. Isten's words thundered in his head as he simply stood and stared at her.

Of all the times to remember, now, he recalled the symbol on the white robes that Gyth had worn to the celebration the night the son of Dark Fever had been born. The same symbol that Varick had on his wrist and had never spoke of.

He gritted his teeth as he looked at her fair hair, she was blonde, light blonde … almost white. He wondered if she knew as his eyes slid from her lips down her soft neck and settled on her breasts.

She was beautiful, but then again, she was a half-god and gods were either beautiful or scary as hell. With a snarl on his lips, he stood staring at her. She was a beauty and he was the beast. A beast with a death wish.

He ran his hand through his hair as he turned away from her. Varick swore that he would give him one wish and he had never broken an oath. He turned back to Chanta and grunted. As far as he was concerned he had told her enough, it was time to get down to business.

"This is some serious bullshit," Payne stated angrily. He turned on his heel, ran his hand down his forehead and rubbed his eyes.

• • •

Chanta eased around the chair and sat down. He was aggravated and it sure as hell didn't take an empath to figure that out. She watched him as he turned back to the window; she definitely wasn't going to try to charm him tonight. Swallowing hard, she figured the best course of action was to stay out of his way.

She rolled her eyes, how she wished she had worn jogging pants and a t-shirt. The two hours she had spent getting ready seemed like a waste of time. She curled up into the chair and leaned her head against the back of the couch.

Well, Chanta, what the hell were you expecting? A knight in shining armor? A dozen roses? This is what happens when you let your guard down! Not to mention, he was a Destroyer, aka, demon under his skin.

Chanta studied him, watched as he looked at the couch and sat down, kicking his feet out and crossing them at the ankles. Maybe he just planned on waiting until the Burning kicked in. It was time and the sooner the better. She felt the warmth of tears rim her eyes, prayed that she wouldn't cry or at least not do it in front of him.

"What the hell is wrong with you?" She jumped at the sharp edge in his voice.

Chanta didn't bother to look at him as she lied. "It has been a long night. I just got back from a date and I'm tired."

"A date with whom?"

"That's none of your business."

"Did he get what he wanted?" Chanta gritted her teeth as he waited for a response.

Chanta closed her eyes. "Let's do this some other time. It's obvious that you don't want to be here and I don't think it's a good idea for you to stay."

"What's wrong? Did I insult you? Hurt your feelings?" he questioned with a rough voice that made him seem detached.

Stretching, she slowly pulled her heels off. His smug expression angered her. What the hell did he think she was? A whore? She narrowed her eyes and flung both of her heels at him. One hit him in the chest and the other landed with a thud against the wall. He grinned as he threw her heel to the floor.

The four cats, who had all graced the room with their presence, perched themselves on the back of the couch and stretched out.

"Just leave, Payne. You don't want to be here and I don't want you here. I have your cell number, I'll call you."

"Can't do that just yet, but I will leave soon enough. Tonight you will go through the Burning." He crossed his arms over his chest. "Well, did you fuck him?"

Chanta stood and turned on her heel as her face reddened. "When I come back you had better be gone!"

She marched to her bedroom and slammed the door. She threw herself on her bed and screamed into her pillow. Where the hell was Gyth when she needed him? Why the hell would she need him? Her father who had been missing all her life. He was just another man, god or not, and they were all the same, assholes, pigs, and perverts! She beat on the pillow with her fists and tears misted her eyes. How could she have been so stupid?

Chanta lay there for an eternity before she finally stretched and sat up. She pulled the dress up over her head and flung it in the floor at the foot of the bed. She unclasped her strapless bra and threw it backwards over her head. In her underwear, she opened her door and went to the bathroom. She didn't bother to look in the living room, she knew he had left; they all did when they saw that she wasn't going to put out.

But this wasn't a date, it wasn't something she could even control. And Payne was here to service her at the command of his leader. His leader and her father no less.

Taking a deep breath, she laughed. On her second breath, she reminded herself that Payne was here to have sex with her, nothing more nothing less. It was what it was. And it wasn't going to be easy or fun or sexy. It was going to be painful.

And she needed to quit trying to romanticize it. It was biology, not chemistry.

She slid her underwear to the floor and stepped into the shower stall. A hot shower, a cup of hot chocolate, and a good book was all she needed. To hell with men, to hell with Payne, and to hell with life. She was tired of it all, tired of the perverts, tired of the lies, and tired of the nonstop rumbling in her head. She just wanted a life, a normal life. And that was something she was never going to have.

The hot water streamed down her back as sweat beaded on her forehead. She stepped back and tears rushed down her face. Why had his mood upset her so much? Was that not the real reason she was so upset? She had wanted him to be interested and it had hurt when he lashed out at her. Her insides tingled and her throat went dry. She had wanted him, hell, she was going to throw herself at him tonight. She was a fool and she wasn't going to make that mistake again, not now and not ever.

Chanta stepped out of the shower and wrapped herself in the towel hanging on the door hook. She wrapped her hair in another towel from the rack over the toilet. She opened the door and walked to the living room. Her mouth flew open as Payne walked out of her tiny kitchen holding a coffee cup.

"Why are you still here?" Heat instantly swamped her, drenched her already wet core.

He shrugged as he took two steps and was standing in front of her, holding out the cup as if offering a truce. He looked out of place in her living room. He was dark, lethal, and dangerous. He was a predator in his own right, menacing, cold, and she was sure his cruelty knew no bounds.

He put the cup in her hand. "Careful, it's hot."

She looked down and smelled the steam coming from the hot chocolate. As he went to her couch, she suddenly felt overwhelmed and tired. She groaned under her breath as her four cats jumped up on the couch with him. She tapped her bare foot on the carpet as he closed his eyes and leaned his head against the wall.

"Look, Payne, you're going to have to leave. I'm tired and I'm going to bed."

"Go ahead."

"Leave!" she screamed as she sat the cup down on the end table.

"Can't do that."

Chanta walked over in front of him and kicked his leg. "I don't know what kind of game you're playing, but I'm not interested. You leave now or I'm calling the cops!"

Payne didn't even chuckle at her worthless threat. "And what are the cops going to do?"

"Make you leave my residence." She balled her fists at her sides when she saw the glimmer of a smile touch his lips. "Just leave. Gods above, I know you don't want to be here let alone do this Burning thing. I'll just call Gyth and request another Destroyer."

"Sit down and shut up. You make too much noise."

Chanta kicked him again. "I said to leave! Get out! I can't go through with this. I know the consequences and I accept them. So you can leave now."

She reached for his hand, but he grabbed her wrist. She jerked, but he only grinned as he pulled her to his lap. The towel around her loosened and she grabbed at it as she landed on his thighs. The towel came completely undone and she sat bare-butt on his legs. Her face went scarlet-red as he grabbed her other wrist. The towel fell to her lap as he looked down.

"Let me go!"

"No, I don't think I will." His eyes narrowed and he asked again, "Did you fuck him?"

Chanta jerked and tried to pull from his grip twisting one way then another. She tried to bite his hands as she twisted and landed on her knee between his legs. He was smiling as he put both of her hands into one of his. She cursed as he pulled her into a sitting position across his lap.

She was face to face with him with her hands captured behind her back. She took a deep breath as he slid his free hand up her thigh. Her breasts heaved and her body trembled as he ran his fingers up her ribcage.

"You fucking bastard! Don't touch me!" Even as the words left her mouth, she leaned into his touch.

Payne pulled her forward and released her hands. She pulled back and slapped him across the cheek. He didn't say a word so she slapped him again. He watched her eyes flame as she continued slapping him.

Chanta crossed her arms over her breasts and glared at Payne. "Is this what you like?"

Payne knitted his eyebrows together. "What I like?"

"Yeah, you fucking asshole, do you like raping women?"

Payne snarled at her. "If I was going to rape you, I would have done it already."

"Then what the hell do you want from me?" she screamed.

"I want nothing from anybody. I came here to help you."

Chanta stilled, her body becoming heavy, her voice a hoarse whisper "Oh, that's right. The Burning. And let's not forget, Varick's going to pay you for … " Her voice trailed off, the words lodging themselves in her throat.

Payne wrestled around until he had the towel in his hand, offering it to her. "Cover yourself."

Slowly, Chanta took the towel and climbed off of his lap and scooted to the other end of the couch. She couldn't find any words to spit out so she sat silently staring at the floor. She felt like a fool. Payne was basically a prostitute, getting paid to do the wild thing with someone he obviously didn't stwant.

"I'm sorry I slapped you. But like I said, I don't think I'm going to do this. I don't think I want immortality."

"Don't be sorry. And you don't have a choice in the matter. You'll go through the Burning and you'll survive because I say you will." Payne stretched out once more. "Trust me, there are much worse things than immortality."

She shook her head. "I'm just an assignment to you, aren't I?"

In a fluid motion, he was on his feet, her cup of chocolate in his hand. "Drink this as I tell you a story."

She took the cup, sipping as he sat back down. Her tears slipped down her cheeks and she quickly wiped them away.

"As most know, after the Titans, the Olympians emerged and ruled over the universe for a long time. What most do not know is that Isten fathered a son. His name was Charioton and he fathered Charon. Charon in turn fathered Tanterious."

He stalked around the room. "Tanterious overthrew the Olympians, the Sumerians, the Egyptians, the Norse, and all other pantheons. He then fathered a son with Athena. And in his state of greed for more power, he destroyed Jaiden and most of the other old gods. Somehow he managed to imprison the godkillers and he changed the laws that they had once protected, took powers from the gods that had ruled before him or defied him, and used those powers to create other gods."

"Go on," Chanta insisted even though she knew this tale.

"He used those powers to create some of the gods that rule now. Damon, Zekel, Daertha, Zena, Adale, Amay, and Grace all have powers that formerly belonged to someone else."

Chanta shook her head, curling her feet under her. "You don't have to tell this story, I know it by heart."

He said nothing for a few seconds. "The ruling god is Gyth, Tanterious' flesh and blood born son. He is a direct descent of Isten, this universe's creator."

She nodded.

"He ruled for many years and one day, he stood before his pantheon and handed Gyth the throne to the Heavens. He gave Damon the rule of the Underworld. He then divided the remaining six gods between the two realms."

She laughed suddenly, couldn't stop herself. "Well, now that explains everything!"

He was still pacing in front of the couch, his brows knitted together. "Not exactly. What most don't know is that Tanterious didn't do it because he wanted to, he was forced by Terror Sky to give Gyth the throne."

Chanta didn't even bat an eyelash. "I've never heard of Terror Sky and I'm a teacher. I know the creation myth word for word and that name has never been mentioned."

"He is an Elemental god and he serves Isten faithfully."

"Well, guess even teachers learn something new every day." She snorted. "And honestly, that was well over two thousand years ago and I don't see how that pertains to me."

"Gyth is Varick's father. He's your father."

Chanta burst out in hysterical laughter. "Father? He may indeed have been the sperm donor, but that doesn't mean I have to like it or deal with it. One day, Gyth and I will have a little father-daughter talk about all those little details, but until then, don't refer to him as my father."

The look on his face killed the laughter in her throat, caused her to temporarily forget how to breathe. She stood shaking her head not wanting to ever have to deal with Gyth being her dad. A part of her was screaming it was all a big farce, a concocted scheme of lies. Another part was standing in the corner of her mind taking deep breaths and trying to put all the pieces together.

As she stood there and stared into Payne's eyes, it all came crashing down on her. She was Gyth's daughter. Not just any of the gods, but the one who sat on the throne apparently at Isten's command. Sinking down to her knees, she sat there numb to her core.

And for the first time in her life, she sent a silent prayer to the mother she had never known.

Chapter 19

Chanta narrowed her eyes as she looked up at Payne. He looked simply delectable standing there trying to hide the smile that threatened to break free. The man was intoxicating, the total package. Her insides trembled, sweat beading her forehead.

He smiled as he stepped closer, the tips of his fangs peeking out. "I can smell you. Like a storm brewing, growing and swirling with desire."

"Do you find something amusing?" She whispered, afraid her voice would fail her.

He knelt in front of her, his nostril flaring as he took a deep breath. His fangs peeked out again and she shivered.

Lifting one hand, he ran his fingers down her jaw, the barest touch sending rivers of goose bumps along her skin. "Your body is responding to mine, like a bee to a flower."

She swallowed hard, found her voice. "That's not how I would put it."

"Then tell me, how would you put it?"

She swayed toward him, her entire body feeling like Jell-O. "I feel like a herd of nymphomaniacs just lodged themselves into my body and overthrew my brain."

He stood and towered over her small frame and slowly shook his head as he held his hands out to her, a small chuckle escaping his mouth. "I applaud you for handling the situation so well."

"You're laughing at me? Do you think this is all some kind of big joke?" She looked around her tiny apartment, looked anywhere but at him. "I don't even like you and yet my body wants you, needs you. Do you know how infuriating that is?"

His smile was blinding, bringing a soft flicker to his eyes. "I'm laughing with you, not at you."

"Do you see me laughing?" She reached up and he pulled her to her feet. The contact was electrifying.

Jerking her hands away, she closed her eyes trying to ignore the heat that was threatening her sanity. "Why must the One Race go through the Burning?"

"The race is descended from the gods, but they aren't pureblood." He shrugged. "For whatever godly reason, the law was decreed that to prove themselves worthy of godly powers, they must endure the Burning."

"Meaning?"

"Everything comes with a price. You want to live with godpowers, you must earn it."

"And if I don't want it?" She opened her eyes, stared into his, and watched his eyes harden, darken, and swirl with an odd blue light.

His voice twisted, a slight deep resonating sound that thundered in her ears. "Then you will die, like so many others before you and Damon will have one less member to try to kill off or to turn into a witch."

She nodded. "Damon ... " A tear rimmed her eye, but she refused to remember times best forgotten. "Why does he want to kill the members of the One Race?"

"Witches, vampires, werewolves, and other beings of that sort take pleasure from One Race deaths." His eyes traveled down the towel she was wearing making her shiver. "Gyth and Damon have been at each other's throats since Tanterious gave Gyth the throne and condemned Damon to the Underworld."

Damon. Her heart stopped. Damon, the Lord of the Underworld. The years came crashing around her, the memories alive and as vivid as the days she had lived them.

Chanta sat down, slumped back in the chair, and just stared at Payne. Yes, she had always known she was different from most people, even different from most members of the One Race. Yes, she had come to terms that her brother was a god. Not completely on board with Gyth being her dear old dad, but she didn't have any reason not to believe Payne.

She should have figured as much about her father, but she had known Gyth forever it seemed. And now that she thought about it, it did make sense. But the rest of it? Damon included. Had he honestly been out to kill her? She just couldn't handle it, not that part of it.

Information and emotional overload.

"There is more that you will need to know."

"No, it's time for you to shut it up." She made a gesture as if to zip her lips. "No more talking from you."

"But?"

"No!" She stood, the fierce look on her face evidence enough that she was done, or it should have been at least.

"I am not finished. We have barely skimmed the surface of the things you must know," Payne insisted. "The gods are all mettlesome creatures and at some point in your life I'm sure you will end up dealing with some of them."

"Do you know what *no* means?" She swallowed hard, clenched her teeth, and rubbed her temples. Payne had no idea of the things she had already dealt with. "I have heard enough."

"The Destroyers are protectors, fighters." He grunted as she closed her eyes. "We kill the minions that would do harm to the One Race."

"I know that Payne. I get it. I'm just not sure I want to live basically forever." Putting her fingers in her ears, she shook her head, and replied, "Shut up Payne! I cannot bear to hear any more. For the love of the gods, let me digest what you have already told me before you carry on."

Her gasp was lost in his growl as he hauled her up from the chair by her wrists. "You will listen! I don't want to be here wasting my time with you when I could be out there killing something."

Slowly, she collected herself and jerked her hands away from him for the second time. Retaliation burned in her guts as he stomped to the window.

"You are the daughter of a god. Like it or not, you will go through the Burning. I will be your only salvation, but trust me it was by no choice of my own." He turned back to her with his eyes glowing blue. "It will serve you well to sit down and listen to everything I have to say or I will tie you to that damn chair and show you exactly what I am."

He had some nerve! "What you are? I know what you are."

His eyes flashed as he spoke, his fangs elongating. "I am the devil's son or have you forgotten when we first met?"

"Don't you dare stand there all high and mighty! You can take your tall, dark, and I am your worst nightmare bullshit and stick it where the sun don't shine! And by god, if you don't want to be here, don't let the door hit you in the ass as you walk out of it!" Her finger pointed to the door. "Go be someone else's salvation because I damn sure as hell don't need you to be mine!"

• • •

Payne was speechless. He was utterly speechless and completely enthralled by this small wisp of a female that had the backbone of a Destroyer. He watched as her jaw flexed, knew she was gritting her teeth, and had a sudden appreciation for her sprout in his loins.

He could only listen as she continued her rant. "And if you think you are going to stand around acting like Mr. Badass and command me to do this or that, you are sadly mistaken! Trust me, I have dealt with men far scarier than you are and for the life of me, I have no idea why I agreed to listen to anything you had to say!"

He stalked to her, standing a mere inch away, his breath cascading down onto her upturned face. "If I were a man right now, I would kiss you until you had nothing left to say."

Her eyes latched onto his slightly parted lips. "If you were a man, you wouldn't be standing in my apartment right now."

Heat flooded him, her face glowing a soft red as he raised his hand and ran his fingertips down her cheek. Instantly, sweat beaded across her forehead. His tongue ran across his bottom lip and she groaned, his body jerking with the sound.

He had never experienced a more erotic moment than this one.

Payne staggered back, his body's reaction sending spasms of alarms going off in his brain. He had never been this attracted to a female before, never wanted to take one down to the floor and have her screaming his name.

"Payne?" Her hoarse whisper lodged in his ears, made him crazy with need.

He took two steps back, tried to get the visions of taking her on the floor out of his mind. His erection hurt, pounded and threatened to erupt at the slightest touch. With no alternative at hand, he dematerialized.

• • •

Chanta followed Payne and reached for his arm to steady herself because her legs felt wobbly. She grasped air as he vanished right before her eyes. Sinking down into the carpet, she closed her eyes and tried to breathe through whatever it was causing her to turn into a sex crazed lunatic.

Man, she really couldn't be falling for the brute. She didn't even know him, didn't trust him, and wasn't even sure if she liked him. Her body jerked as if to disagree.

"Yeah, okay," She begrudgingly admitted to the empty apartment, "I'm kind of, sort of, maybe attracted to him."

Chapter 20

Varick waited rather impatiently as Isten explained again how to control the power inside of him. It wasn't for lack of trying that he was still having such a hard time.

Tapping a finger to his temple, Isten said, "The power is here, tangible from the mind's eye. Every volt of power must come together within your mind, be centered, travel to your heart, and flow through your veins. You must know it, sense it, need it, and never fight against it as you have been doing. It is as much a part of you as your blood, organs, and limbs."

Taking a deep breath, Varick relaxed, closed his eyes, and let his powers fuse together, let them blend, and pulled them together.

"That's it Varick. Let it travel through your body, become a part of them as they are a part of you."

A glowing ball of energy appeared hovering over Varick's hand. It grew brighter as he opened his now white glowing eyes.

"Now focus on what you desire to see. Let the power guide you to her."

The ball of light dimmed as Chanta's face appeared. She looked up to the full moon and her steps faltered as she stared. Somewhere in the distance, the distinct howl of a wolf brought her out of her reprieve. She hurried along the dirt path glancing over her shoulder occasionally.

"Her name is Chanta Timbers, mine sister," whispered Varick in an eerie voice that caught him off guard. "She is the first of her kind, part god and part angel."

Isten nodded. "You must protect her at all costs."

The light disappeared as Varick turned to Isten. "Is she the reason you wanted me to be a part of your pantheon? Does she have something to do with your future? With Gyth's?"

Isten shrugged. "Perhaps."

"Not much of an answer," Varick returned. "Now about Payne. What role do you want him to play?"

Isten frowned. "For now, he has his own destiny to deal with. He must make a choice soon enough and if things fall as they should, he will come out on top, so to speak. And he and I have an agreement of sorts that is best left unspoken."

Varick rolled his eyes. "What is it with you gods? Do you ever just give straight out answers?"

"Of course not," laughed Isten. "It's part of the mystic. Now, what do you know of Tanterious?"

"Not much. He overthrew the other pantheons and took most of the powers of the gods he defeated."

"How?"

"I don't know." Varick grinned mischievously knowing that Isten was fishing. "Perhaps you should ask Gyth."

"Perhaps." Isten waved his hand and an image of Charon appeared. "Tell me about this pact you have with Charon."

"He is after Jaiden's books and has several of them already. He wants me to help locate all of them. And don't ask me what for either because I don't know." Varick shook his head. "He has made some kind of deal with Bastilla, the woman who has plagued Payne all these years. She came to Tortured Souls."

Isten's nose flared. "Was she not in the Underworld serving Damon?"

"As far as we knew, she had pledged herself to Damon, one of the reasons that her memory plagues Payne."

"And Charon has allowed her passage to the earth's surface."

"Seems he has." Varick took a deep breath. "Charon is becoming a pain in my ass."

Thunderous laughter fell from Isten's mouth. "I am becoming aware of that sentiment." He waved his hand again and an image of Gyth appeared before them.

Varick growled as he watched his father move a game piece on a large chess board. The piece was an image of Chanta. "What in the nine hells is he doing?"

"Laying out the board and preparing for the game at hand." Isten pointed to a piece that oddly resembled Varick, but should have been a rook. "Looks like you are part of the game."

• • •

Damon waited, the game of being the Underworld ruling power stretching his nerves tight. He sat on his throne, almost impatiently as black horned demons led Charon into his throne room. Another bargain he was sure would follow Charon's appearance.

Menacing shadows crept along the ceiling and down the walls of the room as thirty more demons followed behind Damon's old acquaintance. As the throne room doors closed, Charon abruptly vanished in a wisp of smoke and reappeared in front of Damon's throne, an eerie smile lingering on his lips.

Damon's instinctive defenses fired, warned him.

The god had changed, his entire demeanor now dangerous, lethal. A surge of cold air whipped about the room as a large green portal appeared in the center of the throne room. Charon laughed, the portal swirling and cracking with power. Damon could feel the power radiating from not only the portal but from the god in tidal waves, menacing dark waves of energy.

Damon kept his thoughts and emotions hidden, deep within and brought his I-am-ruler-here attitude to the surface. Charon's smile disappeared, his eyes glowing red.

He watched in silence as Charon bowed slightly. "The debt I owe you has been paid. Bastilla is on earth searching for your son as we speak."

Damon held out his hand. A soft glowing ball of light lifted from his palm. "Her soul as promised. Of course, you know that to fully own her soul, you must be the one to end her life."

Charon pulled out a jar from his robes, opened the lid, and waited patiently as the ball of light floated to him. With a delicate motion, he guided the light into the jar and sealed the lid.

"And the fetus she carried? Where is it?" Damon asked slowly, his eyes narrowing as a female, dressed in white and with long white-feathered wings stepped out of the portal. "Explain this female's presence!"

Charon turned slightly, glancing at the beautiful Angel. "This is Elena, Chanta Timbers' mother."

"Why would you dare bring an angel to this domain?" Damon stared at the angel. Her skin was almost translucent, an iridescent glow hovering around her. "It's forbidden for her to come here."

Elena stepped forward, standing beside of Charon. "I forbid your son to be with my daughter. I have erased his destiny." A book appeared in her right hand and a pen made of bone in her left. "With Jaiden's bones, I have crafted a set of pens to rewrite his destiny. The decisions you make this night will result in what lies ahead for him."

"You, an angel, dare to threaten my son!" Damon roared, the walls trembling from the power of his anger. "Your kind are nothing but the keepers of mankind, not of the One Race!"

"And you are nothing but a collage of dead gods reborn from their ashes!" Elena spat at his feet. "Do you even have a soul of your own? Do you even have a destiny?"

A pain surfaced in Damon's heart. It was a dull ache that had gnawed at him for centuries. An ache he wanted to ignore yet he couldn't, but he wouldn't speak of it to anyone, let alone an angel.

Damon laughed, a soft caged animal sound. "No angel in her right mind would come to this domain of her own free will and insult the Lord of the Underworld. With the simplest thought I could send you to your death and snatch that bright shining soul away from you and torment it for the remainder of eternity."

Elena's body shifted, her wings spreading wide as silver armor appeared encasing her body in its protective grasp. In her hand, a flaming sword of fire appeared. Her soft yellow hair became completely covered by the helmet of the Commander of the Angel Legion.

"I am no second rate angel." She pointed the sword at Damon's chest. "If your son defiles my daughter with your unrighteous blood, I will kill you both!"

"Empty threats … " Damon wanted to laugh at her, but kept his calm. "I am not Gyth and I won't make bargains with an angel that defiled herself with his blood!"

Elena barked an unladylike laugh. "Dare you question the strength of his blood? He is directly descended from Isten himself."

Damon grinned. "Your daughter is a shining star among dead suns. She tastes of rainbows and honey on a warm spring day."

Damon pointed to the book in her hand. "What does Jaiden's book foretell of your daughter's destiny?"

Elena stepped back, her eyes showing her fear. "It has been unwritten! So it matters not."

Charon spoke, the sound of dead leaves crunching around him. "We are at an impasse. Elena wants her daughter untouched by your son. You Damon, you want her daughter and the fetus Bastilla has hidden from you that I now have in my possession. And I want … " he looked at the book in Elena's hand. "I want what belongs to Jaiden."

Damon paced in front of the throne, his thoughts gathering. "I have had a wonderful taste of Chanta. You both want bargains from me and so I shall begin with what I want. I want that fetus Bastilla has hidden from me and I want Chanta."

"Never." Elena handed Charon the book and the pen and held out a slender silver chain that appeared dangling from her fingers.

"In return for this book and the remainder of Jaiden's bones, I want to ensure that Damon never has my daughter."

Damon narrowed his eyes. If he couldn't have Chanta, there was something else he wanted. But timing was everything. He had not become Lord of the Underworld without a heavy dose of patience and cunning. And always a back-up plan … or two.

"If you want the fetus, you must give me something in return." Charon's nostrils flared. "I want your sworn oath that you will leave Chanta alone."

Damon replied, "You will need to be more specific than that."

"Very well. What Elena wants is for you not to fall in love with Chanta nor for her to fall in love with you. Under no circumstance are you to physically touch her." He turned to Elena. "To change destiny is an almost futile quest; however, it can be done. Destinies have a way of rewriting themselves even after a destiny has been erased. I can change their fates, for a price, of course. And I will require more than just Jaiden's bones and his book."

She nodded. "What do you want?"

"Are you prepared to pay the price?"

"Yes." She cast a glare at Damon. "I will pay the price to keep Damon away from her."

"Very well. I want an angel's soul."

She took a harsh breath and slowly nodded. "Done."

Damon controlled his anger and interrupted the conversation. "In that case, if you want my sworn oath not only do I want the fetus, I want Chanta Timbers to carry the fetus to full term. I want her to raise the child as her own."

Elena grabbed Charon's arm. "No," she whispered. "You must not do this. That fetus could ruin her, its blood will be tainted."

Charon's eyes swirled with liquid fire. "The bargain is not yours. As with all bargains, there are two sides to every deal. If she agrees to carry the fetus, it will be done."

Damon smirked. "And we all know that Charon has never been refused a bargain."

She turned to Damon. "If that abomination harms my daughter in any way, I won't stop until I have your head on a stake and your son's heart burned!"

"Still threatening my son? Really? He could break your neck before you even knew he was near you."

With a flare of defiance, Elena went back to the portal. "Mark my words Damon, if anything happens to my daughter, you will pay the price for it."

As Elena entered the portal, Charon spoke, his shoulders once again becoming at ease. "You gave up your son to Gyth's command so he could become a Destroyer." Charon's eyes flashed. "However, the agreement between us about your use of the portals has been broken. Payne is no longer under Gyth's command."

"What?" Damon's voice rattled the walls of the throne room. "How can that be? Gyth would never give up his command of my son!"

"Isten has been awoken and your son has pledged his allegiance to him."

"Isten?" Damon stalked back and forth in front of his throne. "Why would Payne do that?"

"Because he hates Gyth almost as much as he hates you. If he can't get his revenge by one means, he will use another."

Damon grinned. "So much like his father."

Chapter 21

Payne's body ached and he was harder than he had ever been in his entire life. Chanta was the hottest thing he had ever touched. The situation in her living room had rapidly spiraled almost out of control. She was the daughter of a god, Varick's sister, and she deserved better than his purebred lust.

Nothing would have ever prepared him for the desire that was coursing through his entire being. He couldn't let it continue controlling him, he had to put a damper on it. Only, he didn't really want to. He enjoyed her touch, wanted to touch her more and in all of her secret places. And gods above and below, the way she responded to him was shocking. Even the irritation in her eyes had turned into a molten blend of desire and lust.

And that turned him on even more. He didn't know why he felt guilty of anything. Sex was why he was here, sex with her. Shaking his head, he swallowed trying to rid himself of the thirst crawling up his throat.

Crouching on the rooftop of Chanta's apartment, he peered into the streets below. He did many things exceptionally well. Fight. Kill. Protect innocents. He wasn't so sure he was going to be good at the sex thing. In his youth as Damian and even later as a Destroyer, he had never lain with a woman, not once. Not ever. He was a virgin.

...

Varick stood in front of his fireplace and closed his eyes. The low hum rumbled deep within his chest as the room grew dark. When he spoke, his voice twisted, warped, deepened.

"Payne. Payne. I'm coming. We need to talk."

"Not now!" Payne's voice boomed inside Varick's mind.

"Now! Bastilla … I think she's here. She's asking for asylum from a clan of vampires and a man who haunts her nights."

"She's in the Underworld with Damon!"

"I'm positive it's her." He strained to keep the connection with Payne.

"There's no way that it could be her. She must be an imposter. Kill her."

"She asks for help." Varick waited impatiently as Payne remained silent.

"Bastilla always did know when to make an entrance." Varick felt Payne dematerialize from the rooftop and appear in a dark alley. "Well, Come on. I don't have all night to wait around for you."

Varick appeared to Payne's right. Payne spoke without turning to face him. "You sure it's her?"

"She stays on the eighth floor. I have a few of the Destroyers watching her. They say that she sneaks out in the early hours of night and returns right before dawn. While she is out, they have had difficulty following her. It's like she disappears into thin air … like a … "

"Witch."

Varick nodded. "She's here for a reason. Something's going on in the Underworld. She made a pact with Charon to get here to find you."

Payne's jaw flexed, his hands fisting at his sides. "No doubt, Damon sent her."

"Payne? She's still the Bastilla that you loved." Varick eased into the subject knowing Payne would get defensive. "She may be in need of our assistance."

"She's Damon's puppet. The only assistance she'll need is called gravedigger."

"Can you take care of her if need be? Or do you want me to do it the need arises?" Varick leaned against the wall. "I know the attachment you felt with her, the pain of losing her."

"Yeah … my mother was also my mother and it sure as hell didn't bother me to cut her fucking head off and it won't bother me to do the same to Bastilla."

"When?"

"Tonight, if you can manage it."

"I can manage."

"You're weak from … whatever it is you're going through."

Varick gritted out, "Fuck you Payne! I can manage! Just tell me when you're ready."

"No time like the present."

"Give me your hands." Varick paused. "Just give her the benefit of the doubt, she may need your help."

"You just love this shit, don't you?" Payne took Varick's hands.

Varick grinned. "What? You mean you don't like holding my hand? I'm hurt! And here all this time I thought you loved me. And you'd make such a pretty girlfriend."

• • •

Payne roared, but his words were lost as time swept them back through the eons. The purple light beat into Payne's skull and he gritted his teeth as he went numb from head to toe. His heart pounded in his chest as the pressure of the leap forced tears from his eyes. The entire trip he watched Varick's face. Varick held his expression perfectly as his fingers entwined in Payne's. Payne heard his thoughts as he sagged forward.

"I'm right here my friend. I've got you and I won't let go. Relax and come with me. Let me hold you. Relax Payne. I've got you."

Tears filled his eyes as Varick cradled Payne's weight against his chest. Time travel played with the emotions and Payne's were deep and tortured. Varick gently held him as the warp slowed and swirled around them. The purple light sparked and grew brighter as the neon lights of tortured Souls appeared in the distance.

"We're here."

Payne stood and grabbed his head. That hurt! He settled and his mind went to the night on the Nile River that had changed the course of his life. They were swimming across the water and he knew that it was Bastilla and himself. In less than a half an hour, he would reveal his secret to her and she would break his heart with her traitorous act.

Payne watched the memory play out in silence as he remembered how they had flung themselves to the ground laughing. It was the best and worst of his memories with her. He watched in horror as her face welled with fear and terror as he showed her the demon under his skin. The muscle in his chest tightened as she stood and ran back to the river.

"Payne?" whispered Varick.

"Varick, she betrayed me … "

"Payne … just let it go."

Payne turned to face Varick as his eyes filled with tears. "She betrayed me, Varick. As all women did. My mother, her … "

"But I never will and it was her betrayal that led me to you." Varick's eyes darkened, swirled with emotion. He and Payne were tight, closer than brothers and he felt his pain. "I am Varick, I am your friend, and I will never betray you."

"My friend? You're Gyth's son. Chanta's brother! Why didn't you tell me?" Payne's head sagged and his eyes darkened. "Why didn't you trust me with that information? Or are you so much like Gyth that you planned on using me as well?"

Varick closed his eyes as the purple light flashed around them. "I am not my father." He uttered a truth, a whisper. "You are my only friend . . ."

Varick gripped Payne's shoulder hard. "And you … you are my brother if not by blood … by tears my friend. Your pain is mine."

"And yours is mine."

They waited patiently until Bastilla stealthily slid around the corner of the building. They recomposed themselves and followed her footsteps. She led them to the outskirts of town and shimmered. Payne closed his eyes and searched the night for her.

"She's close. In a field with two barns and a cave and there's another building. She's going down a tight steep flight of stairs. There's a sign. Fether Hills Vineyard."

"That's just east of here."

Payne grinned and opened his eyes. "Ready for a good fight?"

Varick laughed as he pulled his blades out. "I'll let you show me what you've learned pupil."

Payne laughed as they shimmered and reappeared at the end of the first barn. Varick started counting as vampires followed Bastilla into the vinery. Thirteen, fourteen vampires and twelve, thirteen, fourteen witches filtered into the building. He looked at Payne and shook his head.

"Might not be a good time to mention it, but I may or may not now be able to control my powers."

"Yeah, I know old man … you rest and just watch how a pro does it."

Varick rolled his eyes. "This old man will have to come to your rescue."

Payne grinned as he slipped out and made his way to the building unseen. Varick grinned as Payne went into full Destroyer mode. Scimitars clutched in both hands and eyes glowing, Payne was a lethal weapon.

"You know you are kind of sexy when you look like that."

"Shut the fuck up Varick! Son of a bit … there's twenty four more down here … come on old man!"

"Thought I was going to rest and you were going to show me how a pro does it."

"I'm beginning to think you're afraid old man."

Payne laughed heartily as Varick appeared by his side with his blades flaming. Two mighty war cries sent chills up the spines of the fifty-two demons. Vampires and witches sprang into action as the terrifying scene played out before them.

And Bastilla turned to watch them. She grinned as Payne sliced three witches down and leapt to his left slamming his hilt into a vampire's face. Black blood splintered through the air as the Destroyer skillfully brought his blades across the vampire's chest.

Beautiful!

One mighty stroke after another, one war cry after another, and one terrific slice after another, the two Destroyers battled on the ground before her and she was in awe of it all. The fierce beauty of it was overwhelming.

Varick turned as two vampires came from behind and grabbed his arm. His flames leapt up to his shoulder and the vampires lurched back as the fire spread up their arms and engulfed them in black flames. Their screams and hisses faded as ashes flew into the air.

A witch appeared to his right as he sliced up and back at another vampire and the witch latched onto his shoulder with her claws digging deep into his skin. His eyes blazed as the white robe ripped. The witch screamed in pain as a blast of fire came from his mouth and slammed her to the ground. In a swift fluid motion, her head rolled as his sword danced through the muscles of her neck.

Payne charged three witches and blasted them back into a crowd of five more with his purple flame. Body parts went flying in several different directions as he blasted through the swarm of Satan spawn.

Pure energy. Gods, he lived for this shit.

One fell to the right, one to the left, and two more as he turned on his heel and swung his swords in perfect balance.

"How many?" Payne screamed as Varick slammed a vampire to the ground and coughed as the ashes filled his nostrils.

"Thirty-eight."

"How the fuck do you do that?" he asked as he swung to the left and blasted another to the right.

"Lots of practice!" Varick answered as two more vampires fell at his feet. "Forty-two!"

Varick trembled and fell to one knee. Payne stepped in front of him and growled as four witches and six vampires stepped forward. Payne let his flame pour from his fingers in full force as Varick slowly stood.

"No. Payne, let me have them all … " his voice turned dark and eerie, "You must … go … Bastilla!"

"I won't leave you like this!"

Varick chuckled as his back cracked open and he fell forward with steam flowing from his nostrils. "Damn you, go now! When my dragon form comes, I'm not able to control him!"

Payne turned and caught his breath as Varick's black-scaled wings ripped out of his back. Without hesitation, he ran for the stairs going into the basement with a grin on his face. Varick was going full blown beast and pity to the idiots that tried to run.

Bastilla turned to face Payne as he sailed down the steps after her. "Damian … "

Payne replaced his swords and cracked his knuckles as cold bitter hate filled his eyes. Bastilla stepped forward and her tears sparkled in her eyes. Payne grinned as his incisors extended past his bottom lip and his flames licked at his ears. This moment had been a long time in the planning and he was sure as hell going to enjoy her groveling at his feet.

"Damian, I have missed you!" she confessed as she stepped forward to embrace him, but stopped short on his words.

"Whore of Damon! You betrayed me!"

"Damian, I was afraid! Your mother would have killed us both! Please Damian, listen to me. It was I that took you to the dessert to save you." Bastilla's face softened as she edged closer. "I am not his whore! He forces himself on me and if I fight back he hurts other people to make me … "

"Lies!"

"Please listen to me. He takes what he wants and gets what he wants. I don't have the power to stop him … but you do! I need your help … help me escape him … help me kill him!"

Payne narrowed his eyes. "Why would I help you? You waste your breath!"

"Please Damian, I beg of you … please!"

Payne's cruel laughter filled the room and sent a blast of cold air up Bastilla's spine. "I am not your Damian anymore! I am Payne! Prepare to meet your fate witch!"

Falling to her knees, she let the tears flow as she looked up at Payne. "I beg of you Damian, please kill me so that I will never have to return to Damon. I have suffered so many of his beatings, his rapes, and his bloodlust that I would rather die than go back to him."

Payne hesitated as he stared at her face, the face he had once loved so very much. "How did you escape the Underworld?"

"A god named Charon came to me one night, offered to help me find you and the Destroyers." She gently reached out and ran her fingers down his leg. "I know I betrayed you Damian, but that was so long ago. I was afraid."

"You willingly gave yourself to Damon!" Payne roared as his heart broke again. "I would have protected you! I would have loved you!"

Slowly, Bastilla came to her feet. "You couldn't even protect yourself from your mother or from Damon back then. How were you going to protect me?"

Payne's scimitars hit the ground. Memories filled his mind, burned into his heart. "We could have left the coven." The sound of his own voice rattled his bones. "We could have stayed together."

"They would have hunted us down, destroyed us." She ran her hand up his arm, over his shoulder, and caressed his cheek. "I have always loved you, Damian. I gave myself to Damon to save you."

Closing his eyes, he placed his hand over hers and whispered. "I'm no longer Damian, I am Payne. That boy that loved you without question, without pause died in that dessert."

"If you have any love for me left, you will help me kill Damon." She kissed his chin. "You will end my torments and the tortures he puts me through."

"I could have loved you for a lifetime." Payne captured her hands. "I would have loved you!"

She stepped back, her eyes narrowing. "Loved? Past tense?" Payne watched the tears fall from her dark eyes. "Please, tell me you still love me. Tell me you only want me to know how much I hurt you."

"You know nothing and will never know of the pain I went through. You betrayed me, watched the coven and my mother beat me with a smile on your face." Payne pulled her roughly to his chest. "And as I lay in the mud and my own blood, you gave yourself to my father."

As he towered over her, she leaned her forehead against his chest. Her hot tears soaked through his tattered shirt. His heart hardened. Searching his feelings, he found he only held her in contempt. Nothing more.

"I made a bargain with your father that day. My soul for your life." She lifted her head. "I agreed to let him have my body so that you could have a half way normal life with the Egyptian man that found you."

He let her hands go, wondered why he had ever loved her, and thought of Chanta. "You should have let them kill me. Instead you gave yourself to the devil knowing that I would take that memory with me to the grave. And worse than that, you stand here trying to convince me that you loved me? You have no idea what the word means."

She pulled back. "Never doubt that I love you. I have always loved you, only you."

Before Payne could answer, she shimmered and disappeared. He roared, the anger in his heart manifesting into the air he breathed. Bastilla had used him to get to Damon. She had known the entire time that in order to gain his father's attention, she would have to pledge her soul to him. And as he lay face first in a puddle of his own blood, beaten and humiliated in front of the coven, Bastilla had willingly gone into Damon's arms.

Chapter 22

Chanta opened her eyes, blinking and trying to clear her vision. The last thing she remembered was that she had curled onto her couch after Payne had disappeared. Sitting up, her head swam like her brain was surrounded by dense fog hell-bent on keeping her thought process suspended.

"This will pass," a female voice whispered as Chanta was eased into a sitting position. "Breathe slow and deep."

Regaining her vision, she swallowed hard at the sight before her. Across from her, sitting on a cloud was an angel in a sparkling sapphire robe. She glanced down and inhaled sharply. She was sitting on a cloud too. Funny, she would have never guessed they felt like silk.

Staring into his sea-foam green eyes, she asked, "Who are you?"

He smiled, a slow seductive smile that would have made her heart melt. "I am Lysander. Your mother's consort."

"My what?" She stuttered as she watched large white wings unfurl from his back. "What are you?"

"Some call us demons, some call us spirits." He laughed at the confused look on her face. "We call ourselves Angels."

Rubbing her temples, she closed her eyes and asked, "If I click my heels three times will I wake up at home?"

"No," a female voice spoke. "You will open your eyes and you will still be here."

Chanta opened one eye and stared at the female angel who now stood beside Lysander. "Where am I?"

The female's wings stretched. "You are in the Heavens, the lowest region of them as a matter of fact. And you belong here. This is our home. We watch over mankind in much the same way that the Destroyers watch over the One Race."

Chanta pinched herself and gulped as her skin burned. "Am I dreaming?"

"No," the female stated. "I had Lysander deliver you to me in your time of need. Soon, you will become who you were meant to be."

"Who the hell are you?"

Chanta stood on shaking legs, fearful the cloud would split open and she would plummet to the ground far, far below.

"I am Elena, your mother."

Chanta's heart stopped, lodging itself somewhere in her throat.

"When you were but a babe, I placed you on earth at your father's demand. Not a moment has passed that I have not thought of you."

Lysander stood, his arm pulling Elena closer as her tears flowed. "Your mother has suffered so much with your absence."

Resentment bubbled up in Chanta's throat. Too much was just too much. Both of her immortal parents left her, she had a brother who was a god, Payne was a Destroyer, reborn none the less, and now, all of them suddenly wanted to make an appearance in her life.

"Why didn't you raise me? Why didn't you stick around, you know, watch over me or something? Protect me?" Her voice cracked. "And why make an appearance in my miserable life now?"

"Your father is king of the Heavens. He commanded me to deliver you unto the earth's surface as was his right." Elena took a deep breath. "I had no choice in the matter, I had pledged my allegiance to him."

"And now? Now you want to make amends for leaving me?" Chanta tried to control her temper. "Is that what you want? For me to forgive you for not being my mother?"

Elena looked at Lysander and Chanta shook her head. "It isn't, is it?"

"Try to understand. I had no choice leaving you down there." Elena stepped forward, her bare feet floating above the clouds as she came closer to Chanta. "I have pledged my allegiance to another god, so I am free of Gyth's demands."

Chanta turned and jumped, her feet barely landing on another cloud. She scrambled to her feet and looked for another cloud. She had to get away from Elena. She didn't want to hear anything more from anyone. She wanted to go home and wake up from the nightmare she had been living.

"Please Chanta." Elena followed her every move. "You must listen to me. Payne is not what he appears to be. Do not trust him."

Before Chanta could jump to another cloud, Lysander grabbed her and turned her around to face her mother. Tears fell from her eyes as she stared at the angel.

"When he told you he was the devil's son, he wasn't lying. He is Damon's son. He's in love with Damon's wife, a female named Bastilla." Elena's sorrow was etched on her perfect features. "If you let him, he will take you through the Burning, but he will use you any way he can to get what he wants. And he wants nothing but revenge against his father for taking Bastilla from him."

"Damon's son?" Chanta fell to her knees not wanting to believe Elena's words. "Payne is his son?"

Elena nodded. "I know what happened between you and Damon. I know how your heart broke, how fear took over your life. I was tormented that I could not help you. I begged your father to protect you from him."

"What do you want from me?" Chanta screamed as she struggled in Lysander's hold.

"I want you to come home. Be a part of the Legions."

As she calmed down, Lysander loosened his hold. "The Angel Legions have sworn their allegiance to Isten. We are in his command now as it should have always been. Your mother, your ancestor Isten, and I would be honored if you would return to us and take your place at your mother's side."

"What do you mean? My place?"

Elena smiled tenderly. "I am the Commander of the Angel Legions. Lysander is my right hand and my consort. You, my darling daughter would be my left hand. You won't want for anything and you would be a judge of mankind, deciding their fate as they come before the altar of judgment."

Chanta jerked out of Lysander's grip. "I don't even know you. Why would I want to judge anyone?" She held out her hands, looked out across the fluffy white clouds. "I am no angel."

"Not yet." Elena snapped her fingers. A white robe appeared on Chanta's body, her feet bare. "To become the angel you were meant to be you must not allow Payne or any other to take you through the Burning."

Chanta snorted. "In other words, I have to die to become like you. I have to endure the Burning whether I die or live. So, basically the whole base line of this sad predicament is to have sex or not to have sex even though either way, I'm going to be in a world of pain."

"Yes." Elena stepped closer, her hand landing on Chanta's shoulder. "Please, my daughter, don't let Payne destroy the only chance you have of becoming an angel. Don't let anyone destroy the only chance we will have at finally being a family."

As Chanta's body began to shimmer, she whispered, "How can I trust a mother who left me when I was just a baby?"

"How can you trust the father that let Damon hurt you so much?" Her mother's words echoed in her mind as she reappeared sitting on her couch in the white robe. "How can you trust Payne? Or your half-brother who is also half vampire?"

Insanity was creeping up on her. Chanta wanted to scream, to deny everything that was happening around her. Gods and angels, demons and witches, and more myths and legends coming to life than she could handle.

Jazz jumped up into her lap. "How can I trust anyone?"

"You can't." The sound of Payne's voice brought her to her feet.

His black eyebrows were knitted together, the frown on his face and the piercing glint in his eyes all, but screamed he was in an ill mood, but it seemed he always was. Chanta couldn't help but notice he looked tired and there was a sadness etched into the lines of his handsome face.

When he turned to the kitchen, something about the way he moved struck her hard, like a hot lance guiding itself straight to her core. It made her want to reach out and touch the very beast that she knew had a demon lurking under his skin. Even after her mother warned her that he was Damon's son, she still wanted to touch him, smell him.

She couldn't help but wonder if he was like his father. Gritting her teeth, she shoved her memories aside and stared at Payne's broad shoulders.

Without any warning, he stopped in his tracks and turned his head in her direction. "Is there something you wish to say?"

Chanta clicked her fingernails, but stared straight at him. "Are you Damon's son?"

He turned around, his eyes swirling with blue fire. "I told you I was the devil's son. Can you deal with that? Can you let the demon inside of me get inside of you?"

She tried to swallow, her mouth going dry. He closed the distance between them before she could blink her eyes. His face turned to stone, those magical eyes of his going electric blue with that intense flame. He was terrifying in a drop dead gorgeous kind of way.

"I don't know if I truly want to go through with this." The sound of her quivering voice made her insides shudder, but she continued. "I don't know who to and who not to trust. Or who to believe any more. The Burning is upon me and I have two options. To have sex with you and become a demi-goddess or to die and … "

His face twisted with anger as he cut off her words. "There is no choice to be made. You'll go through with this because you're Gyth's daughter and you don't want to die."

She stepped back. "My mother is an angel." The confession was out of her mouth before she even realized what she was saying.

"Yeah, and mine was a cold blooded witch. What difference does it make?"

Was Damon's wife the reason behind Payne's actions? Was she the reason he was willing to have sex with her? Chanta didn't even know if what the angel had told her was true or not. But she was going to ask him anyway.

"How can you go through with this when you're in love with someone else? How can you justify taking me through the Burning?"

Payne just stood there, the tips of his fangs slowly creeping past his top lip. When she figured he didn't have anything else to say, she started to turn away from him.

He grabbed her arm. "I don't love anyone. When this is done, I'll get the one thing in this life that I have always wanted."

Chanta jerked away. "Oh that's right. My dear brother promised you that you'd get a wish after you have sex with me. It's her, isn't it? You want Damon's wife."

Chapter 23

Payne stared at Chanta suspiciously. "Who told you about her?"

"My mother." She ran her hands down the sides of the robe she was wearing. "I had a visit with her tonight after you left."

"And?" Payne watched sweat bead her forehead as her hands began to tremble.

"She said not to let you take me through the Burning. If I don't go through with this, I'll ascend to the Heavens and become an angel."

He snorted. That wasn't likely. "She lied. Half-breeds aren't allowed in the Heavens. End of story."

She scoffed. "Maybe you're the one lying. It's not like you're not getting paid to do me."

Forcing himself not to laugh at her choice of words, he let his fangs elongate in a show of dominance. "I have no reason to lie to you. And to be honest, I don't care if you believe me or not. The fact remains, you will go through with this, like it or not because I will get what I want. So get used to the idea of me getting all up inside of you princess. It's going to be one hell of a ride."

Her face darkened, her cheeks staining with the loveliest red hue. Catching him off-guard, her eyes began to swirl; he did a double take. Her eyes were whirlpools of silver and black and they stared at him hard, and oddly enough her cotton blonde hair streaked with blood red highlights.

So much for her not being like her father.

"How dare you?" Her voice was a symphony of velvety sounds, twisting and turning inside his head creating a blinding pain right behind his eyes. "I'm not a piece of meat to be bargained for! You want Damon's bitch, find another way to get her!"

Payne grabbed his head, her voice booming louder, her words ringing in his ears. Varick had said she was an empath, but this was much more than just that. He felt a sharp crisp pain in his heart that made him gasp. He staggered back as he locked eyes with her again.

A cold look fell upon her face as she raised her hand and pointed at his chest. "I can feel your agony. I can feel what your mind refuses to acknowledge."

"Get out of my head." His order went unnoticed and he decided to take a different approach to the matter.

He lunged forward, wrapping his arms around her waist and lifting her from the floor. With a step to the side, he threw her on the couch and held her hands over her head.

"Listen princess, you need to calm down before you get hurt." Payne planted his knee between her thighs. "If you want bullshit laced answers and sweet words of innocence about what's happening to you, talk to someone else. Simple and to the point, this is the way it is. You have to have sex or you're going to be dead. And like it or not, if you die, your soul will not go to the Heavens with the angels, that's for humans not for the One Race."

Her eyes calmed, returned to their steel color. Her rigid body went slack under him as tears pooled in her eyes. Releasing her hands, he ran his fingers down her face wiping away the tears that ran from the corners of her eyes.

She spoke softly, her voice a mere whisper of sound. "I saw inside of you. I touched some dark part of your heart."

"I know I'm cold. I'm not the gentleman you deserve, but I can take you through the Burning safely." He breathed in her scent. "I got a boatload of bad shit in my head and more agony inside of me than even the Algea can handle, but I won't lie to you about anything."

He could handle the pain, the betrayals, and all the bad shit he had been through. It fueled his hate for his father and the demons he commanded. It kept him sequestered, cold, and untouchable.

Unlovable. But he wouldn't wish it on anyone else, especially not on Chanta.

"The pain inside of you is so intense, so agonizing. I am so sorry for intruding." She took a deep rattling breath. "I don't know what came over me. I have never been that overcome with anger."

"It's part of the Burning." He tried to smile. "And besides, that is the one emotion I seem to elicit from just about everyone that crosses my path."

She raised her hand and touched his face. Her touch was soft, warm, and something inside his heart snapped. No one had ever touched him to soothe him. No one had ever looked at him as she was doing. The compassion in her eyes made him feel weak, made his heart skip a beat.

"Why would my mother want me to die if I won't ascend to the Heavens?" He wiped away more tears as she continued. "Why would she lie to me?"

"I don't know." Payne ran his finger across her lips. "I wish I did know so that I could ease your mind with the answers you seek."

The words were out before he even knew what he was thinking. He clamped his lips tight, felt the edges of his fangs tearing into his flesh.

He wanted to kiss her, to taste her again. She was infectious, addictive. And the way she was looking at his lips, her skin flushing made him want it even more.

When she laid her hand against his cheek, his entire body jerked. As he took possession of her lips, she wrapped her arms around his neck, pulled him closer until there was no space left between their bodies.

Chanta tasted of honey and she was so warm and soft. Her scent drilled its way home, pushing his erection to full mast. He deepened the kiss and she arched under him, a soft moan slipping from her lips.

In an instant, he brought her up to her feet and turned to sit on the couch pulling her into his lap. Tugging at the robe, he slipped it over her head and threw it on the couch beside of him. He watched her emotions dance across her face.

Chanta reached for the robe, apprehension written on her face. Shivers of pleasure rippled down his spine as she paused and ran her hands down his arms. Her hands were hot and his body was hard, hard everywhere.

She quickly grabbed and pulled the robe to her chest as her nipples hardened. He smiled as he traced little circles on her knees and she groaned.

Payne watched as her face reddened at his touch. He made a path from her knees to her waist and liked her response. She grabbed his hands, the robe falling and revealing her breasts. He slid up along her thigh, her hands urging him on. He was shocked and relieved that she was enjoying his touch and it pleased him. His eyes moved to her lips as she leaned forward.

When she stopped, he almost didn't look into her eyes, afraid that she had realized what she was doing with the devil's son. What he saw there stopped his heart.

The gentleness and understanding that stared back at him made him tremble. Him, of all the Destroyers, trembled under a woman's soft touch and compassion-filled eyes.

She cupped his face in her hands and leaned her forehead against his. "I barely touched what is inside of you and yet I know you aren't evil. After all you have suffered and been through, your heart is still pure. You would give your life to protect someone innocent, to ensure they don't suffer as you have."

Payne swallowed at her soft tone, her heartfelt words wrapping around that cold muscle in his chest. He didn't know how to handle what he was feeling, didn't know what to say or do, and he didn't understand how she could stand the sight of him let alone be touching him simply because she wanted to. The only woman ever to stand the sight or feel of him had been Bastilla.

He ground his teeth as he dropped his head. If he allowed Chanta to continue, would she betray him as well? Would she chisel her way into his heart and then destroy it as Bastilla had done?

And then there was the sex part. All his life, he had witnessed nothing but the roughest, most grotesque sexual acts known to man and even more than an ordinary man could ever dream of in a thousand lifetimes.

"Payne?" Chanta was in his ear, her naked body tempting him beyond reason or sanity. "I can feel your hurt, your heartache."

He shoved her back, fearful of what she was doing to him. "You need to stop. I'm not some game you need to figure out or feel sorry for. All you need from me is sex and that's all you're going to get."

Her breath fell in and out, smooth and calm. "It's not all you're going to get from me. And no, you're not a game. But you know what, if that's all you're able to give me, then I'll take it because I know that's all that wall around your heart is going to let you do."

Chapter 24

Chanta ran her hand up Payne's chest to his neck and leaned forward. She had to kiss those amazing lips before she chickened out. Her lips brushed his and she pressed harder as his hands went to her back. Almost timidly he kissed her back as if he was unsure what to do. But she knew he could kiss. It wasn't like she hadn't been reliving the kiss he had given her every single minute of every single day. His mouth opened as if he were going to speak and she slid her tongue into his mouth.

The pleasure that rocked her body was unreal and intense as she licked his tongue with hers. He groaned as she deepened the kiss and crushed her body closer to his. She had never experienced a thing like this. He growled as her crotch rubbed against his and he caught his breath as she pulled away from his mouth and nipped at his bottom lip.

Chanta slowly opened her eyes and looked at Payne's face. His expression was a look of utter fascination. She couldn't tell if he was shocked, happy, mad, turned on, turned off, or upset. Suddenly embarrassed with her actions, she hid her face in his neck.

They sat still in the silence and it stretched on for what felt like hours. In the moments when she had been out of control, her anger so intensified that her emotional blocks slipped away, she saw Payne for what he was. His soul was teetering on the edge between good and evil. One small push could make him go either way.

She whispered, "I'm sorry. I shouldn't have done that. Just let go of me and I will get off of you."

"Do it again." He whispered back as he pulled her head from his neck to face him again. "Do it again."

Chanta tried to read him as she leaned forward and ran her tongue across his lips. He tasted good, salt and sugar all mixed together. She slid her tongue into his mouth as his hands went to her butt. As she wrapped her arms around his neck, she felt his erection through his pants. He groaned and held her hips as he arched up. She moaned as she pressed down and pulled from his mouth. He caught her lips as she tried to pull away and greedily kissed her.

Chanta's insides went wild as his hands moved up her back and came around to her breasts. He slowly cupped them and released her lips. She arched forward and pulled his head to her chest. He grinned as he took one of her nipples into his mouth and sucked hard. Her response thickened his arousal and he bit down. She grabbed his face and he slid his tongue around her nipple.

His other hand traveled down her ribs, down her stomach, and down the inside of her thigh. She opened her eyes and met his as his hand went between her legs. She moaned and tried to lean forward, but he held her still.

"Look at me," he whispered.

She watched his face as he slid his fingers across her womanhood. She was wet with excitement and he smiled as he slid one finger inside of her heat. She kissed his lips as he went deeper inside of her. The sensation that was driving inside of her body was unlike anything she had ever felt; she was hot—hell, she was on fire. His fingers were delicious, long, thick, and were hitting all the right spots.

His eyes held hers as he made love to her with his hand and the look on his beautiful face was satisfaction enough, but damn it, she wanted more. His grin widened and she felt his temperature rise. Was she going through the Burning or was he? She was unable to differentiate between her heat and his. His breath hit her in the face like a wave of hell's heat. He had some serious fire in him and it was coming out one way or the other. Her eyes burned, but she refused to shut them as she licked his lips again.

Chanta was lost in a whirlpool of colors, sweet chaos, and a rising heat. Her skin blazed and felt like it was melting, but there was no pain, just overwhelming pleasure. Her eyes closed as she let the feeling carry her body and her hands found his. His—oh it was Payne's hands, Payne's body, Payne's eyes. She wanted him, she needed him, and she had to have him. She arched back as her birthmark bit into her flesh. She wanted to cry out but the pleasure was more intense than the pain.

She heard Payne's voice. His tender tone catching at her heart. "It's going to be okay. Just go with it. Don't fight it." As if she wanted to fight her body's desire to have his? "I'm right here."

As she leaned back and let the pain from her ankle run up her body, her heartbeat sounded in her ears and her spine twisted underneath her skin. She wondered why she wasn't afraid; she wondered what was happening but his hands were so warm, gentle, and creating a fierce need inside of her.

Her shoulders ached and she fell forward as something hot gushed down her back. She screamed out as she felt the skin on her shoulder blades rip open. Her fingernails dug into Payne's hands as the pain intensified. She felt as if her spine was forcing itself out of her skin.

•••

Payne honestly didn't know what was coming next; he had never taken a woman through her Burning, but so far he was enjoying it. She arched against his chest and grabbed his hair. He watched in amazement as her eyes turned red and her hair flew back from her face and went completely white except for the red highlights that appeared. Payne's eyes narrowed as her fingernails dug into his hands.

Her skin glowed with a pale white light as delicately etched black and red flames raced up her legs like tattoos appearing without the needle. He squeezed her thighs as the flames ran up her stomach and under his hands.

Her skin was on fire—hot, beautiful, and worthy. Payne growled in pleasure as the flames circled her arms and ran up her neck to lick at her cheeks. She was everything and more; she was breathtaking and intoxicating, and he would die for her in this moment.

Payne beheld her, in her true form, and what a gorgeous sight to behold. She was covered in black and red flames that seemed to have a life of their own as they licked up her body. Her eyes had turned from red back to that swirling silver and black and her lips seemed fuller, healthier. The wings on her back extended, the feathers were white and each one was tinged with red. Her white hair fell across his chest like silk and shimmered as he ran one hand through it. It could have very well contained the stars from heaven within its shine.

He reached to her face and pulled it up to look into her brilliant shining eyes. Tears ran down her cheeks and steamed as the flames licked them away. She was amazing and sexier than he had envisioned her before. True, she resembled Gyth, but this woman before him, this goddess, she was special, she was Chanta.

He smiled; she was his Enchantress. His.

"This is the Burning."

• • •

Chanta's body ached and burned as she tried to fight the pain that was cutting down her pleasure. She cried as Payne ran his knuckles gently down her face. She was hurting in places that she couldn't fathom. Every bone, every muscle, every nerve ending was on fire.

She tried to pull away and lashed out at him as he gently lifted her and stood. She twisted and screamed in outrage at the pain.

"The pain you're feeling is going to get worse. You won't be yourself as the Burning eats your blood and devours your soul. You must fight, you must want to stay alive. I'm right here to help when the time comes. When it does, you'll know what to do."

Chanta barely heard his words as he walked to her room. She screamed as he laid her on the bed, every touch, every slight brush of air felt like someone was ripping her skin from her body.

Anger flooded her heart and she kicked his stomach as he reached for her hands. He flew backwards and landed against the dresser. He grunted but kept calm as she twisted to her side and begged him to make it stop.

"Stay with me, Chanta. Focus on my voice. Hear me."

Payne pulled his black leather trench coat off and threw it on top of the black dress on the floor. He pulled his scimitars from his back and hung the sheaths over the mirror on the dresser. He watched her as she twisted and curled on the bed. She was in a great deal of pain, but he knew it was going to get worse.

He slowly unbuttoned his shirt and pulled it from his leather pants. Chanta took him in. His mark, his tattoos, ran up both arms and across his broad shoulders. Skulls, bones, faces of demons and black serpents riddled his back and arms. They all were covered in red flames and seemed to be screaming. In the center of his shoulder blades was a deep scar from his childhood, a five star pendent had been painstakingly carved into his flesh with fire.

"I'm right here, Chanta. You're not alone in this. That's it, keep listening to my voice."

Chanta sat up as Payne sat down on the edge of the bed. Her canine teeth lengthened as Payne reached for her hand. She reached up to her mouth and her eyes widened in disbelief as the pain eased. Her stomach was still on fire but her body calmed.

"What … .how … why?" she shook her head. "I'm not a vampire, why do I have fangs?"

Payne caressed her wrist with his thumb as he tucked a stray strand of her hair behind her ear. "When a female goes through the Burning, she transforms into her true form. This is yours."

"I have fangs."

He nodded as he continued rubbing her wrist. "Every member of the One Race has a true form and everyone is different. You're part god and part angel. And the fangs, they have a use when the time comes. The pain has eased?"

"Yes … but my stomach … "

"Your blood has pooled into your stomach and soon it will need to be released."

"Released?" She cried as her hands flew to the pain that stirred inside of her belly.

Payne bared his teeth and they slid down over his bottom lip. "This is how I am going to help you."

"What are you going to do to me?"

He pulled her into his arms and gathered her hair from her neck. "I'm going to take your blood and rid it of the impurities. You will no longer be human, you will become immortal."

Chanta grabbed his forearms and cried harder. "Are you a vampire?"

"No. Vampires aren't the only beings that have fangs. As a matter of fact all the members of the One Race have fangs."

"What if I don't want this? What if I … "

"If you refuse to let me, you will die." His eyes softened. "I don't want you to die, Chanta, I have just met you. I seem to have taken a liking to you."

Chanta pulled away and searched his eyes. "Why?"

Payne ran his hand down her cheek. "I expected you to be like your father. Imagined later that you would be like your brother, but you're not, you're so much more."

"I was adopted," she whispered as she took Payne's hand in hers. "I didn't know I had a brother and I didn't know Gyth was my father until Varick told me. I never met my mother until today."

Payne's nostrils flared. Gyth couldn't even raise his own child but then he did have enemies that would have loved to slit her throat in front of him. Gyth had never held her when she had nightmares, had never told her he loved her, had never tucked her in bed at night. At least his father had taken an interest in him, even though it had tormented him and would for all eternity.

"Your father is a god. He had to protect you by not being with you."

Chanta threw her arms around Payne's neck. "Then he's a fucking bastard for making me go through this!"

Payne grinned. "He is a real piece of work, that's true. That is one thing I am sure of, but Varick and your father sent me here to help you. The Burning isn't something Gyth or anyone else can control."

Chanta jerked away. "They sent you? The only reason you're here is because Gyth commanded and because Varick made you that promise. You don't really want this, do you? But you'll do it because you want that woman you're in love with."

Payne gritted his teeth as he watched her face twist in pain but he wasn't going to lie to her. "I was promised one wish for helping you."

Chanta laughed and it sent a chill up Payne's spine. "Fuck Gyth and fuck you!"

"That's the general idea."

Chanta slid to the edge of the bed and tried to stand on her unsteady feet. "Go back to your fucking god and tell him he can kiss my cold dead ass!"

Payne grabbed her waist as she sagged into his arms. "I'm afraid I can't do that."

"I don't want this! I don't want to be the daughter of a god who … get your hands off me!" Her voice cracked and her words were more of a growl than a reply.

Payne jerked her around to face him. "You won't die. You're going to let me help you through this!"

"Fuck you! I'll tear your limbs from your body if you dare to help me." Her voice boomed in his ears and he narrowed his eyes.

"If I have to, I'll do this by force."

Chanta's cold laugh hit him in the chest. "I can feel the power of him coursing through my veins. Are you sure you want to fight me?"

Payne's lip curled up in a sarcastic smile. "I'm going to let your little sweet ass in on a secret. There is nothing you can throw at me that I cannot withstand."

Chanta jerked away from his hands and hissed at Payne as her blood thickened in her veins. "Then prepare yourself, Payne!"

"I keep hearing that lately."

Chanta balled her fists at her sides and the flames on her arms grew and burst out of her skin. She held out her hand and smiled as the flames leapt from her palm and hit Payne in the chest. His feet slid backwards as he grabbed the bedpost to steady himself.

He grinned and rushed her. She fell back onto the bed as Payne grabbed her hands and pulled them over her head. His hair fanned down over her face and she arched up as flames leapt from her feet and traveled up her legs.

His smile widened. "I'm afraid your flame has no effect on me."

Her eyes softened, her fingers running along his skin. "In case I forget, thanks for this … for trying to save me."

He softly kissed her lips. "You don't have to thank me."

His body pressed down on hers as her flame completely enveloped him. It felt good, right, and his erection pounded inside of his pants. She fought and twisted underneath him as the fire in her soul roared to life. Payne let her hands go as she screamed and her face revealed the physical and mental torture she was going through.

It was time, but he had to wait for her to acknowledge her need of him. He held her face as the tears of mental stress poured from her eyes. Dropping his empathic shields, he let her emotions and thoughts pour into him.

The anguish of a hundred million human souls filtered through her mind. She witnessed and felt them all at the same time. The One Race souls from the abyss cried out to her and tried to pull hers to their endless torment. She fought and scratched at them as she tried to flee their thoughts, their past, and their tormented futures.

Payne pulled her hair from her neck and whispered into her ear. "Tell me you want this and I will make them go away. I can save you if you'll let me."

Chanta grabbed his shoulders and screamed, "Payne!"

His name from her lips sent a thousand sparks of fire into his soul. She needed him. Someone needed him and to have her need him was a pleasure that he had never felt.

Payne gently caressed her neck and lightly sucked on her tender flesh. The flames danced out of his way as he bit down and sank his incisors into her throat. Chanta moaned and pulled him closer to her body.

His heart somersaulted. A vision claimed him, one from Chanta. She didn't see him as a demon or a monster, she saw only him. The wall around his heart shattered.

Her anguish diminished as he sucked and her blood rushed from her stomach to her veins. It flooded his mouth and slammed into his stomach where the flame of the Underworld awaited its arrival. He pulled back and sealed the wound with a kiss. She closed her eyes and unconsciousness claimed her.

Chapter 25

Flames licked Payne's insides as he pulled himself from Chanta's body. He violently fell backward and landed on his side. The flame inside of him cut through her blood and steam poured from his mouth as he tried to stand. Her blood was strong, stronger than he had expected and her pain was even stronger. He pulled himself to his knees and braced himself against the floor with his hands.

Tremors of pain ran up his back as the blood boiled inside of him. The horns of his demon burst from his forehead as the purple flames leapt from his hands and ran up his arms. He groaned as her memories flooded his mind.

Since her first awakening experience in the womb, she was beautiful. Her childhood spun around his brain as she was passed from one home to the next. The foster parents all thought she was a freak of nature. And they were afraid of her and the uncanny ability that she possessed. But most of all, they were all afraid of what lay behind her odd eyes.

Payne witnessed her teen years and pain fueled his heart as she yearned for comfort, a soft hand, and a tender touch. She had been beaten, hidden, and locked in a closet. And the torments had not ended there. One of her foster fathers had threatened to kill her because she had caught him cheating on his wife.

Her eighteenth birthday flashed in his mind. She was finally free of foster parents and had met a man. Her heartbreak swirled in his mind as two years passed and Payne tried to deny what he was seeing. Damon stood on her steps waiting for her as she locked the door. Chanta was smiling as she threw herself into Damon's arms and kissed him.

Payne wanted to scream, wanted to erase what he was seeing yet he couldn't and it continued. He saw Damon on bended knee, saw the ring that he placed on Chanta's finger. His groan of despair was unheard as he slammed his fists onto the floor cracking the wooden panels.

Her memories swirled, danced, and bled together. Then he saw her again.

Chanta was walking down the dark alley to her new apartment, one she was sharing with Damon. She was happy and carefree as she strolled along. She had gotten a job and things were finally looking up for her. She smiled as the dark clouds passed the moon and closed her eyes as her apartment came into view from the alley.

Payne growled as a man stepped out of the shadows behind her. She screamed as he grabbed her neck and dragged her into the shadows. Payne tried to block the vision and clutched his head as the memory refused to let him go. Payne slammed into the nightstand as Chanta was forced to face the cold block wall.

The attacker ripped her shirt and pulled it from her body. She cried out and tried to twist around to face her attacker, but he punched her in the side and she fell forward. The man used her ripped shirt to blindfold her and tie her hands behind her back.

Payne screamed his outrage as the man slid his hands around her breasts. Not her! Why would Gyth allow her to be defiled? Bastard! He would find him and brutally pull his entrails out as he died! Payne tried to see the man's face and his rage overwhelmed him.

Out of nowhere Damon appeared as the blindfold fell from her eyes. Damon licked his lips as the man stepped back, letting go of Chanta. Her fear escalated. She watched in complete horror as Damon's body shifted, as snakes poured from his fingertips and engulfed her attacker.

"Nooooooo! Fucking son of a bitch! Not you!" Payne screamed as he watched Damon turn to her and pull her to her feet.

Damon's fingernails sliced her hair to her shoulders as he spoke. "Fear not, Chanta. You belong to me and no other will ever have you."

She tried to jerk away, her tears blurring her vision. "What are you?"

Damon laughed. Taking her head into his heads, he let his fangs slide down, his face becoming white and his lips turning black. "I am Damon, Lord of the Underworld. And you Chanta, you belong to me."

She shook her head violently, begging for him to let her go.

"Tonight, you'll become mine in more ways than you can possibly imagine."

Damon had touched everything in his life with his disgusting hands, everything! Contempt and disgust for his father fueled his desire to kill him and now his desire soared to the Heavens as Damon pressed his lips against hers. Bile rose up in Payne's throat as Damon forced his snakelike tongue into her mouth.

Payne laughed bitterly as Chanta bit down and Damon's black blood ran down her chin. So, he did bleed! The memory started to fade as he watched Chanta fall to her knees.

He desperately tried to keep it in his mind needing to know what happened.

But the memory disappeared and was replaced with another one, a less frightening one, but no less effective on her soul.

Chanta was with another man in a bed and his thoughts were careening around her mind like metal ping pong balls. Payne wanted to puke as the bile rose up in her throat. He was no virgin to the ways of the perverted, but Chanta felt like she was dirty, unwanted, and being used. She was hurting and she ran from the bed to her car.

The man came after her begging her not to go. Chanta had screamed her disgust at him and accused him of what she had seen in his mind. His anger showed on his face as he slapped her. She grabbed her cheek and cursed him as he grabbed her hands. They fought over her keys in the driveway of his white picket fence house. She bolted down the driveway as he grabbed her hair and jerked her to a stop.

The memory blurred as the blood transformation completed itself and heat gripped Payne's insides. He had to let her have the blood back and he crawled back to the bed. Payne grimaced as his skin contacted hers; she was as cold as ice.

• • •

Damon stood from his throne of bones as he felt Payne become weakened. He gritted his teeth and went to the cauldron of flame. He waved his hand over it and Payne's image appeared as he kissed Chanta. Damon's lips tightened over his teeth and his eyes narrowed; he couldn't have him falling in love with her.

Damon's hand flew to his bare chest, to the spot where his heart should have been.

Love! Of all things Payne was finding, it fucking had to be love! It was the one emotion that Damon could not touch or twist to his needs.

The image blurred and Damon waved his hand over it again trying to keep it from fading. He raged as it shimmered and disappeared.

Flames and snakes poured from his mouth and fingers. He turned to the witches who were showering him with sacrifices and their bodies twisted in agony as he curled his fingers into a fist. Their screams were pure pleasure to his ears and the snakes hissed and swayed to the music of their cries.

Someone would pay dearly for this. With a roar, he sent his snakes out from his body and watched with a snarl on his black lips as they strangled the witches in his throne room. Their pitiful cries of pleading went to his ears, sent shivers of pleasure down his spine.

He had once intended on bringing Chanta to the Underworld and now it seemed he couldn't lay a finger on her. When he took Bastilla, he had placed Chanta's face over hers and had found the only real pleasure he had ever felt. Chanta was going to be his queen, his lover, his new wife, and his mistress! But those things had changed. Now she would carry his child. A child that would have no part of the Underworld, no part of the torments and tortures of Damon's life. Her name was a soft whisper in his mind. In his entire life, she had been the only woman that had offered him a real challenge. He could have feasted on her pain and misery for the remainder of his lifetime.

He could still taste her and had kept her hair in the satin bag that hung from his belt. He pulled it out and brought it to his nose. She smelled like honey and he ran his tongue over the light blonde curls.

But now, he had to settle for what she could give him, what she could do for his unborn child. His son, his prize, had taken what should have been his. His soul was in a rage, his temper escalating beyond reasons that he couldn't understand.

Damon's insides trembled, his guts twisting into knots. His hand grasped at his chest, his claws digging into his flesh until black blood poured over his knuckles and dripped onto the floor. Something inside of his chest broke, snapped into tiny pieces.

Falling to his knees, he watched as the snakes dragged the dead bodies of the witches into the flame of the Underworld. Their souls cried out in agony as Damon shimmered and vanished. His cold laughter echoed in the Underworld and the demons cowered under its ferocity.

Chapter 26

Chanta was twisting and jerking in her unconsciousness as Payne pulled himself onto the bed. Every muscle in his body felt like it was frozen, his teeth chattering. His strength was fading as he pulled her closer and dragged his fingernails over his heart. Blood oozed from the wound and he placed her lips over the deep gash.

Payne wanted to scream as her body seized and jerked again. He knew it was time, but she wasn't taking his blood. His hand began to shake, his heart pounding in his chest. An ache developed inside his heart, his mind. What if she didn't survive this?

His stomach jerked as her thoughts spilled into his mind. Part of her wanted to let go, wanted no part of the life that was waiting for her as an immortal. But he could sense the part of her that wanted to survive. All he had to do was find a way to reach her.

"Chanta." Her name was a pathetic plea from his lips, but he didn't care. "You must survive. For the love of the gods, take my blood."

A scream ripped from her throat. Her body jerked again, her fingernails extending. Without warning, her eyes flew open, a white glow so bright Payne winced. Her fangs elongated as she inhaled and turned her face toward his chest.

"That's it. Take it." Payne urged her harder, pulling her closer hoping that the scent of his blood would push her on over. "Don't die on me. Please, do it for me. Survive for me."

Immediately, she responded and grabbed his shoulders as she bit into the wound and sucked. Payne's eyes rolled back into his head as her lips created a powerful lust-filled sensation. He became all too aware of how much she wanted him and if he had been able, he would have taken her as she fed from him. He groaned as her hand slid down his chest and went to his erection. His pants came undone and his zipper went down as her hand slid in and found his tender flesh.

Her name rolled off his tongue as she stroked him, "Chanta … "

Her mouth released him and she licked her lips as she slid down his body. Payne's eyes flew open as her mouth covered the head of his erection and his hands flew to her face. She sucked on him and he groaned with pleasure as her hands slid his pants off.

Payne's heart thundered, his body so alive and pumped up that even the soft brush of her hair against his skin made his erection jump. He had never wanted a woman like this, had never felt this overwhelming need to have sex. Even after the horrors and depravity that he had been subjected to in his youth, he wanted this.

His thoughts melded with hers and they became one, needing and wanting. Visions of him poised over her arching body, his erection buried to the hilt inside of her brought out a growl of pleasure from his throat. Her naked flesh rubbing against his, tiny beads of his sweat dripping onto her pearled nipples, and her hot breath whispering on his skin was too much to bear, too much to resist. He cursed as her face blurred and his eyes closed.

Not now! Let me enjoy this!

• • •

Varick settled on the roof of Chanta's apartment. The clouds overhead rolled in silence as the moonlight cascaded down. He waited and watched through the shadows from his perch. His mind drifted, the night reminding him of his mate, Angelica.

The sound of crunching leaves brought him out of his thoughts. In a wisp of smoke, Charon appeared, his black robes fluttering in the light wind. Varick nodded as Charon pointed down.

"One of the books is in Chanta's apartment." Varick searched Charon's face for any sign of emotion. "She is mine sister. No harm is to come to her."

Charon bowed slightly. "Do you wish to make a bargain with me?"

"No." Purple sparks jumped from Varick's fingers. "I will protect her with my life."

"Of that, I am certain you will. Fear not Varick, I will cause her no harm on this night." Charon looked up at the moon. "But I cannot promise others will not."

Varick nodded. "Is it true?"

"Truth is deceiving, no matter the subject." Charon laughed. "I assume you are asking about Jaiden."

"Is he alive?" Varick stepped onto the ledge of the building. "Is he seeking revenge against Isten?"

"Why don't you ask him yourself?"

"I'm asking you."

Charon's face switched from human to skeleton. "I have lived countless ages. I have served the gods before me with unwavering devotion. I have given up family, home, soul, and even my free will for the sake of the hierarchy because someone had to do so. Someone had to make sure the balance remained."

"Is Jaiden gunning for Isten or not? It's a pretty damn simple question." Varick spun around and stepped off the ledge taking two steps to Charon. "And does Jaiden plan on destroying this world that Isten created?"

Charon laughed, his body slithering away into ribbons of smoke. "Only time will tell that tale."

Varick spun around as the sound of dead crunching leaves echoed in the night air. The clouds darkened hiding the moon's light. With stubborn pride, Varick launched into the air, his body shifting into dragon form. With a roar, he rose above the clouds and circled Chanta's apartment.

His job was to protect his sister and Payne, not worry about the fate of the universe. But he couldn't fight the need to know and the curiosity of Jaiden and those damn books.

Chapter 27

"Awaken Chanta!"

Chanta bolted upright in her bed as the sound of misery wailed around her. At first, she thought she was dreaming; then she thought she had died and gone to hell.

In front of her bed stood the grim reaper of nightmares, his bony fingers wrapped around a scythe of bone and blood. Her bed was completely surrounded by darkness except for the eerie red haze that radiated out of the reaper's eyes. When he spoke, she cringed, his voice sending the misery of millions of souls careening around her bed. Like ghosts, images swirled around her running their fingers along her skin.

"There is a choice to be made on this night of agony. A choice that will lead to destruction or salvation." He pointed the scythe toward the right side of her bed and Payne's frozen body appeared as if reaching for her. "Some say that pain is the harbinger of vengeance. Some say it's the one thing in this universe that will condemn all species."

She tried to scoot up in the bed, but found she was immobile, her voice lodging in her throat. The reaper laughed as her fear came crawling up her throat. He waved the scythe through the air and pointed to the bottom of her bed. Her eyes latched onto the book that appeared, her mother's book. Opening his bony hand, a glowing ball of light appeared hovering an inch above his palm. Inside, she could make out the silhouette of a fetus.

"There is a war coming. The Heavens above and the hells below are rising against one another and all that you have ever known and loved will be destroyed." Chanta tried to scream, but the reaper shook his head. "Payne will die and Damon will arise from the Underworld and lay havoc to this world. Gyth will fall and the

Heavens will descend upon the world of man. Would you change the future of this condemned world if you could? Would you save those children you are so fond of?"

Her head became mobile and she nodded slowly.

"The Apocalypse is upon this realm. And the decision is yours to make." His voice swirled, winds whipping about the dark room like razor blades. Her skin burned as sulfuric black smoke rolled from Charon's mouth and nose. "The destruction this night will be on your head."

He held out his hand, the fetus glowing brighter. The sound of crunching leaves screamed in her mind and the wail of the unborn child wrapped around every one of her nerve endings.

"This fetus is Payne's brother. If you don't accept him into your body and raise him as your own, he will never exist. But be warned, he is Damon's son." The fetus disappeared as the reaper pointed back to Payne. "In two days, Payne will die giving his life for yours, but it will all be in vain."

Chanta shook her head, her voice still lost. She didn't want anyone to die.

"You'll die as well and that death will unleash Varick Ta Farg's powers of destruction and he will kill your father in his blinding pain." Again the reaper laughed sending goose bumps along her spine. "Your mother will take the throne of the Heavens and all humanity will be condemned. But I can change those destinies for a price." He paused, the bones of his face shimmering as muscle, blood, and skin covered them. "Speak now and ask what questions are in your mind."

"Who are you?" She wasn't expecting much of an answer, was seriously expecting to wake up from the nightmare. "What do you want from me?"

"I am Charon, descended from Isten the same as you." His red eyes glared at her. "I want to make a bargain with you. You have something I want."

She had heard his legend. He was infamous ferryman of the River Styx and he had a lust for bargaining with members of the One Race and the gods. But what could she possibly have that he would want?

"What kind of bargain?" Chanta contemplated the reaper's words. "And how do you know what will and what won't happen. Destinies aren't preordained, they are made."

"As the guardian of the Tree of Life and the Book of Creation, I know all destinies and how to change them." He clicked his tongue. "Only humans have the right to make their own destinies." He reached down and picked up her book. "In exchange for Payne's life as well as your own, I want this book."

"Before I commit to a bargain with some demon I know virtually nothing about and before I can even begin to trust your words are true, I'm going to need some kind of proof or something." Chanta snorted as Charon threw his head back and laughed. "And furthermore, even if I consider your little bargain, I may have some bargaining of my own to do for that book."

Charon's now handsome face hardened. "Indeed."

She nodded although her feet were itching to run. "And before anything else is said, tell me why that book is so important."

Charon tilted his head as if he was studying her face. "It's the Book of Light, one of many books that belonged to Jaiden."

"But why do you want it?"

"I have been commanded to gather his books and place them at the roots of the Tree of Life." Charon grinned, almost mischievously. "I have been given free reign to do as needed to collect his books."

"Who commanded it of you?" She narrowed her eyes. She was sure he was barely skimming the surface of the reasons.

"I'm offering to save this world from the Apocalypse, to save Payne and you, does it really matter who commanded it?"

"Do you want the book?" She tried to move her toes, but they refused to budge.

"Yes. I must have the book."

She idly wondered why he didn't just take it. "Then here's the bargain. Payne's life and mine as well as the baby's and answer some questions truthfully in exchange for the book."

He held out his hand and a slender silver chain appeared. With his scythe, he sliced his palm next to the chain. Taking one of his hairs from his head, he wrapped it around the chain and closed his fist around the blood, the chain and the hair.

She vaguely recalled the myth of such a pact.

He spoke low, his voice a mesmerizing lull. "Body, flesh of mine. Blood, power of mine. Soul, power of the gods. I give you my word." He held out the chain. "If I break my word, my soul will belong to you."

She hesitated. "And the baby? Will he be like Damon?"

He raised an eyebrow. "A personality is one's own. I cannot guarantee he will be any different than Damon."

"Do you know what his destiny is?"

"Yes." He grinned slightly. "He has two roads before him, one evil and one good. If you wish for me to interfere with his choice, I can do so, but the price will be higher than just that book."

"What else do I have that you want?" Most likely some very important details were missing in this whole bargain of Charon's. "And just how did you get Damon's baby?"

"We have not made the bargain so I must decline to answer any more of your questions." He held his palm out, the silver chain glowing. "The choice is yours."

"Once I make the bargain, you can't lie to me about anything can you?" She racked her mind for more information on Charon.

"That is part of our bargain and so I cannot lie."

"And I can ask as many questions as I want?" She stared at him searching his face for any clues about his character. "At any time I want?"

His red eyes swirled. "There will be a limit. No more than five questions."

"Is that all? Seriously?" She felt her jaw flex as she tried to move her toes again. How was she going to get all the answers she wanted out of five questions? She needed like thirty or fifty. But five was better than one.

She looked at him apprehensively. "I need to move my hand to take the chain."

At once her hand lifted and he slowly laid the chain into her palm. "It's going to hurt."

"What?" No sooner than she said that one word, the pain started, her flesh burning, melting around the chain. Her brain was slow to register the fact and seconds passed before a scream of agony ripped from her throat. As soon as her flesh covered the chain, her hand returned to normal and the pain was gone.

"What is your first question?"

She thought for a moment. "Why did my mother tell me to die?"

He grunted. "Isn't that one obvious?" He shook his head. "Your mother wants Gyth's throne, always has, always will. If you die, your brother will destroy Gyth and she will have what she wants. And just to show my good nature, I'll let you in on another secret about your mother. She made a bargain with me to keep Damon away from you. Before your destiny was unwritten, you were to be his consort, giving him a child that would destroy her."

She sat there slack jawed. "But she is an angel."

"Angels aren't always good." Charon's eyes flashed. "Next question."

Boy, she had a million questions she wanted to ask about her mother, but her questions were limited and there were other things she needed to know. "How did you get Damon's baby?"

"I made a bargain with Bastilla. She is now on earth and she searches for Payne." He grinned. "She hid the fetus from Damon and in exchange for passage to earth, she gave the fetus to me."

She clutched at her stomach. Could she carry a child that belonged to Damon and to the woman Payne was in love with? Would she be able to raise that child knowing he was a part of Damon. She shuddered. Not from fear, but from the hurt he had put her through, but she knew she couldn't let an innocent child die even if it was Damon's. There were so very few members of the One Race that even one child could make a difference.

And how would Payne feel about the child? Did it matter? It wasn't like Payne was going to stick around after he got what he wanted.

Chanta looked at her book, the questions there were endless. She didn't even know where to start or even how to form a question where it was concerned. But she knew the legend of the books of knowledge.

"Why didn't you just take the book from me?" She wiggled her toes and caught her breath wondering if Charon's hold was weakening. "And if memory serves me correctly, how can destinies be changed or unwritten since Jaiden is dead?"

"Once the books have attached themselves to someone, they must be given or traded." An odd look crossed his face, his eyes narrowing into tiny slits of red light. "Jaiden's power manifested into his books when his physical form died."

Physical form? Did that mean he had another form?

Chanta raked her hand through her hair as Charon waited for her final question. The legend said that Jaiden died by Gyth's father's hand and that he was completely destroyed, his bones laid to rest in a vault in the Heavens and his books scattered into the four winds. He was the god of destiny and even the legends and myths surrounding him never spoke of his actual birth, just that as a babe, Isten and he had forged the books.

She heard Charon chuckle and she looked up as her book disappeared. "This bargain between you and me, it ensures that the world will not be destroyed?"

Charon nodded. "The world will not be destroyed this night."

She snorted. "This night?"

His image swirled, his red eyes the only thing remaining of him. "Just as your brother before you, you can save this universe from destruction. But destruction is always just one step away. Pray that all others whose destinies fall upon this crossroads do the same as you."

As his eyes vanished, the room spun out of control, her vision blurring and the pain of the Burning returning full force. Her back arched as she looked at Payne whose body was encased in ice. Slowly, the ice began to melt and all she could hear was Charon's cold misery filled laughter as the Burning claimed her.

• • •

Elena came to a dead stop as Lysander entered her private quarters. His eyes were downcast, his wings drooping. Since, she had given birth to Chanta, he had become more and more detached, sullen, and depressed. Lysander was for the most part, a good upstanding angel, one who didn't take his duties lightly. For centuries, he had been her most trusted ally and her lover. Her slave of sorts.

His only problem, he had fallen in love with her. She barely controlled the sneer that was threatening to appear on her face. Love? What had love ever brought her? Misery.

With the blondest hair of any of the angels, uncanny handsome blue eyes, and a body built for every sinful wish she could possibly imagine, he had served his purpose without flaw and without hesitation. And now, he stood before her with disappointment written so clearly on his face.

"What news do you bring me?"

"Chanta has decided to endure the Burning." His voice was low. "Odds are she will survive as well as Damon's unborn son."

"She must be destroyed. I don't care how, but it needs to be done quickly before she allows that monstrosity, Payne, to save her." Elena stretched her snow white wings. "Even with the bargain I made with Charon, I don't want to take the chance that destiny will rewrite itself."

She turned to Lysander, a soft smile on her lips as she gently laid her palm on his cheek. "You'll do this for me so that I can survive. I must rule the Heavens if I am to condemn mankind for all their sins." As an afterthought, she whispered, "And after it is done, you and I will consummate our relationship. You will no longer have to stand by my side as a consort. When this is over, we will rule as Lord and Mistress of the Heavens. According to Jaiden's book, all that I will require is her death and the rest will fall into place."

Oddly enough, his eyes narrowed, his voice unwavering. "Is there not another way? Does Chanta have to die?"

It wasn't the response she was expecting. "There is no other way. It must be done, tonight. With each passing hour, the window of opportunity is getting tighter and tighter."

He nodded. "Varick is protecting her and Payne as well. What do you want done with Varick?"

"I want him dead as well. Gyth will fall all that much easier if the only two things in his entire existence he cares about are dead." She watched the flicker of regret cross his face. "If you are not capable of doing this, I'm sure I can enlist someone else's aid."

He scowled. "I have always been at your side no matter how wrong you are in things. Not once have I ever went against your wishes. Not even when you conceived that child with Gyth."

Elena slapped him, her hand stinging. "You'll do well to remember your place, consort."

"I don't have to remember it, you remind me every single day." His jaw flexed. "I'm bound by oath to do as you command."

From the folds of her robe, she withdrew a small glass jar. Inside the jar, a soft white light glowed, flickered, and swirled around. Lysander's eyes latched onto the jar as he took a step forward, his hand instinctively reaching out.

Elena shook the jar, chuckling softly as Lysander went to his knees. "When you pledged yourself to me and agreed to be my consort, you gave me power over your soul. You will kill her or we shall see what happens to an angel's soul when it is flung into the deepest region of Hell with nothing to occupy its time, but the endless torment of the condemned."

Facing him, she tightened her grip on the jar. As she gracefully stretched her wings and stood before him, she laughed knowing he would do as she said.

"There will be many who stand in the way." His jaw clenched. "Many who have no part of this conflict with Gyth. To get to her, I will have to go through them."

"Then do it. Kill them all." He flinched as she ran her fingers over her hand print. "Take a few of the guards and make sure that Chanta dies tonight."

"And if I fail?" His eyes narrowed as she smiled at him.

"Don't fail me in this, Lysander. If you do, it will be your downfall." Taking a deep breath, she stepped back. "Now go."

As he turned and stalked away, she laughed softly. Lysander was the sexiest of all the angels, the tallest, and the most skilled. There was nothing she enjoyed more than controlling his every move except making Gyth suffer.

The god's name made her skin crawl. Her lust for him had created a destiny she would defy to the bitter end. She would have accepted that destiny save one little detail. Gyth had ordered her to send Chanta to earth and had ended their little love affair. In her tears and heartache, the bastard had apologized, tried to convince her it was for the best and that they could never be together. If she couldn't have Gyth, she would take his throne.

He was the Lord of the Heavens and could only have a goddess sit by his side at the throne and Elena was nothing but an angel. From the moment the words had left his mouth, vengeance had grown steadily in what remained of her heart.

Grinding her teeth and jerking the cover off the mirror that sat by the window, she stared into the green swirl of the River Styx. With a flick of her wrist, she tossed the jar into the mirror where she knew Charon was waiting for his payment. What better way was there to bring Gyth to his knees before her? Kill his son and daughter, take his throne, and end all humanity.

Chapter 28

Payne awoke and opened his eyes. Chanta was astride him leaning up on his chest on her palms. He started to reach for her face, but found he was chained to her bed. Her wings were laying on the bed and touched the floor. The pressure of her naked body sent shivers of pleasure through his rather extremely naked one. The soft smile on her lips brought one to his face.

"Did you do this?" he asked as he pulled on his chains.

She sat up and frowned. "I'm not sure. I waved my hand and the chains appeared and I wanted light and these candles appeared. I wanted you and then you appeared in the chains."

Payne grinned and laughed as he looked at the hundreds of candles that riddled her room. The light glowed on her skin, bringing out every single curve. She was beautiful and she was now his, whether she liked it or not. He knew he could easily break the chains, but he remained as she had placed him.

"I still burn inside. Why?"

"The Burning is not over yet. There is one more thing to be done," he replied as she ran her fingers up his chest and caressed the wound below his nipple.

"When it is done, will you leave?"

Payne frowned. "I have an obligation to fulfill."

"And Varick' promise of one wish? What will you wish for?"

Payne didn't answer her question. There had only been one thing he had desired since he could remember: Damon's death. "You must bond with a Destroyer and the Burning will cease."

Ignoring his statement, she asked again, "What will you wish for?"

"That is my concern."

She ran her fingers over the tattoos on his arms as she stretched over his body. "And these, what do they mean?"

"I am a Destroyer. They are the faces of the demons that I kill."

"And the scar on your back? Who put it there?"

"It was a long time ago and is best forgotten."

"Tell me Payne, who put it there?"

Payne gritted his teeth. "My mother."

Chanta leaned down to his lips and kissed him, running her tongue across his and grabbing his hair. She raised up and pulled his head back against the pillow. A sensual feeling filled his heart as she ran her fingers down his face and traced his lips. He arched under her as her hands traveled down his chest and her eyes took every inch of his body in. She slid her hips down from his stomach and pressed down on his erection.

"Are you in love with someone?"

Silence was her answer.

"Do you want me?"

"Yes."

"Do you want to be inside of me?"

"Yes."

She leaned forward and pressed her lips to his wound. Payne growled as her teeth sank into his skin and she sucked. He arched again and his shaft pulsed with pleasure as the wetness of her desire met his head. She pulled away and kissed the wound as she sat back onto his erection. Payne growled in pleasure as he went inside of her.

"Payne?"

His breath caught as she said his name. "Yes."

"I'm going to hurt you."

He smiled as she slammed down onto him. "I know."

She screamed in pleasure as she rocked against him. Her eyes glowed as her fingernails extended and fire covered their tips.

Payne closed his eyes as she scratched his chest. He was used to pain and he welcomed it as she rocked on his erection.

"Payne!" she screamed as she leaned forward. "There's something I must tell you."

He opened his eyes as his blood flowed from her lips and trailed down her neck. It trickled down her chest and dripped down her breasts. He effortlessly sat up and pulled free of the chains. She moaned as his tongue licked the blood from her nipples and he sucked until they ached. Her hands wrapped into his hair as flames danced up his arms. They licked at her as he grabbed her hips and pounded into her body.

Chanta threw her head back as her incisors grew. Payne turned his head baring his neck as she looked at him. He groaned as she clutched his shoulder and bit into his skin.

"Take it Chanta, take my blood and my body."

"I am part angel. My mother is an angel."

Payne growled nodding at her confession. "Take my blood."

Chanta pulled away and pulled him over on top of her. Her legs wrapped around his waist as he pushed back inside of her. She grabbed his hand and brought his wrist to her lips. She licked it slowly savoring the taste of his skin. She arched as he slammed into her and she bit down. Blood flowed down her face and dripped into her hair as Payne leaned his weight onto his left arm and rocked against her thighs.

Chanta licked at his wrist and ran her fingers through his blood, her blood! Their blood mixed and coursed through her body as he came down to her neck. She turned her head and closed her eyes as his teeth reopened the wound. She arched forward as he sucked and she bit into his wrist.

Chanta screamed in pain as he pulled away and pinned her wings to the bed. He buried his erection deep inside of her and she grabbed his waist with her fingernails. She sank them into his skin as the fire inside of her body entered his. She hissed and twisted as the smell of burning flesh filled his nostrils; his flesh was burning. She withdrew her fingernails and slid them to his chest.

He waited and kept himself buried inside of her as she claimed him for the bonding. She arched and moaned as her fingernails dug into his skin. Thin streams of smoke rose from his chest as she carved the symbol that she had been born with into the skin over his right nipple. He groaned as his skin burned and ached. She dug in deeper as she arched under him wanting more.

Payne gritted his teeth as she moved her fingers from his chest to the soft tender skin above his crotch. Her hand lingered there, hovered above his skin.

She looked up as the fire in her eyes dimmed. "Payne?"

"Yes."

"I won't mark you, but every instinct in me is screaming to do so."

He fell forward into her arms as he pulled out and pushed into her one last time. His seed released and she screamed in total pleasure as he claimed her lips.

His voice was barely a whisper as he replied, "I can never be yours."

"Is it because of Bastilla? Are you still in love with her?"

"It isn't because of her." Raising up, he stared into her eyes, saw the tears that made his heart ache. "I made a pact with Isten. I have a mission that I must face and odds are I won't survive it. If you mark me and completely bond yourself with me, you will be endlessly tormented by my death."

He wouldn't have let her mark him, but he was overwhelmed with her primal beauty and passion. But he knew that he could not have refused her if she had done so. And his heart, his heart had wanted it more than anything he had ever wanted.

She had somehow eased the burden he carried in his heart. And that was enough to pledge himself to her, but he wouldn't condemn her soul to torment if he died.

She drifted into a calm sleep as Payne held her to his chest. His heart thundered and an ache pounded inside him. In the little time he had been with her, he had lost a part of himself to her. His enchantress had defied all odds and won a piece of his heart and his soul.

Her father was Gyth, a god that Payne despised almost as much as his own father. Her brother, now a god, was his one and only friend. Not to mention that once this was said and done, he had no intentions of walking away from Damon alive. They both had to die, to end Damon's lust to create witches out of the members of the One Race and to end the torments that Payne lived with every single day.

A smile spread across his lips as she cuddled closer to him and whispered his name. "Please, don't die. I have just begun to know you, the real you."

"The Burning is over." Payne frowned, an ache building in his throat. "I have to leave soon."

"Will I ever see you again?" Her voice quivered as he felt tears drip onto his chest.

"Probably not." He pulled her closer to him. "When I made the pact with Isten, I had no intentions of coming out of it alive. I have lived a long time and the burdens I bear within my soul tire of the aching."

"Is there nothing I can do to ease your pain?" She looked up and took his chin, looked into his eyes. "Is there nothing I can do to make you want to come back? To make you stay?"

Payne closed his eyes and a lie fell from his tongue. "No."

There was something she could do, but he would never ask her for it. There was one thing in this life he wanted more than anything, to be loved. Just once, to be loved for who and what he was, to be cherished by someone, but that would never happen. He was the devil's son.

Chapter 29

Bastilla appeared in the late hours of the night in front of the apartment that Payne had been lurking around. She grinned as she thought of Payne; right now, she was so close to having him back, so very close to ending Damon's miserable life. Pushing the doorbell, she knew she would have to hurry before Payne showed up and ruined it all.

She smiled as Chanta answered the door. She was such a pretty little thing with her mop of white blonde curls and big gray eyes. Nonetheless, the sight of her made Bastilla want to vomit.

"I'm sorry to bother you, but I was wondering if we could talk a few minutes. It seems I'm in a bit of a pinch."

"How can I help?" Chanta smiled, which infuriated Bastilla, but she managed to keep her cool.

"I'm a member of the One Race, just like you and I need help."

Chanta smiled again as she stepped back and opened the door wide. "Of course, come on in. My name is Chanta. What's yours?"

Bastilla smiled back entering the doorway. "I'm Bastilla."

Seeing the downcast look on Chanta's face brightened Bastilla's heart. So, the little witch had heard of her it seemed. Several seconds passed as Chanta searched Bastilla's face before finally closing the door and offering her a seat.

"Payne isn't here." Chanta crossed her arms over her stomach clearly showing her defense. "He left this morning."

"I'm aware that he did." Bastilla smiled softly. "I just wanted to meet you."

Suspicion crossed Chanta's face. "Why?"

"Because Damon is still in love with you." Bastilla wanted to puke as soon as the words left her mouth. Damon and love? The two words should never be uttered in the same sentence. "I came to see if you still had feelings for Damon or if for some unknown illogical reason you have feelings for Payne."

"I have no need or desire to speak of Damon to you. If it's Payne you're after, you'll have to find him somewhere else. Like I said before, he isn't here."

Bastilla gritted her teeth. Chanta was everything she was not. But more importantly, she was standing in Bastilla's way. By killing her, Bastilla took care of two birds with one stone, a sweet little revenge against Damon and the means to pull Payne back into her arms.

"He still loves me. I don't want you to get caught up in the middle of this situation. I recently regained my freedom from Damon and I'm sure that you'll agree there's no sense in you getting hurt in the process of Payne and me getting back on track with one another." Bastilla let a fake tear slide down her cheek. "I have waited so many lifetimes to be in his arms again."

"I'm sure you have." Chanta went to the door. "I can't honestly say where you can find him."

"Do you mind if I sit for a while?" Bastilla looked at her couch. "I have not taken the time to get used to being back on earth." She slowly sat down before giving Chanta a chance to answer. "I am tired as I have been non-stop in my search for Payne."

• • •

Chanta swallowed harder than she ever had in her entire life. "I'm fixing a sandwich, do you want one?"

"No, I don't believe I do, but ... "

"Yes," answered Chanta over her shoulder as she stepped into the kitchen. "I have some left over pizza if you want."

Bastilla pulled a dagger from her hip as she stood and walked into the kitchen. "No, I just want you to know that I am Payne's lover and it's always been me that he loves."

Chanta turned and stepped back as Bastilla lunged forward with the dagger. The bread in her hand tumbled to the floor as she went to her knees and scrambled to her left. Bastilla caught her by the hair and pulled her back. Chanta screamed and tried to stand.

Cold laughter filled Chanta's ears as she grabbed the counter and pulled herself to her feet. She twisted and Bastilla let her hair go. Chanta bolted to the drawer below the breadbox and grabbed a knife. As she turned, out of the corner of her eye, she saw Payne appear. Bastilla lunged again and sliced into Chanta's arm as Payne grabbed her by the throat baring every inch of his glorious fangs.

Chanta ran towards the living room and glanced over her shoulder as Payne threw the woman into the wall by the refrigerator. Her arm was dripping and aching, but it still had not registered with her as she turned to face the battle in her kitchen. What the hell was going on?

With a deep breath, Chanta cursed. She was a demi-goddess now with powers, why hadn't she thought of that when the witch had attacked her?

Payne grabbed Bastilla and cursed as she shimmered and disappeared. Chanta went to her knees still holding the knife in her hand. She looked down and dropped the knife grabbing the cut on her arm.

She felt the wound healing, her skin prickling as it began to repair itself. Payne towered over her. "Are you hurt?"

She shook her head. "It's nothing, barely a scratch."

"What did she say to you?" When she looked up, his eyes were glowing blue.

Chanta stood, shoved past him, and went to the living room. "Nothing."

"Don't lie to me." Payne took a step towards her. "She wanted something and I need to know what it was. I won't have her coming after you."

Turning on her heel, she replied, "She said Damon was still in love with me and she wanted to talk … about you."

Payne simply stared at her, his lips forming a thin line as he narrowed his eyes. "Are you still in love with him? After what he did to you, is that why you refuse to stay at the sanctuary? Hopeful that he will show up on your doorstep?"

"How dare you?" Chanta clenched her fists, felt the blood trickling down her injured arm. "You made it perfectly clear that you could care less about my life. After all, the only reason you were even here was to get your stupid wish from Varick." She paused, too many thoughts running through her mind at once to concentrate. "Why are you even back?"

When he spoke, she almost cowered, his voice so rough and full of male energy her knees quivered. "I came back to fucking apologize for making you feel like a piece of meat! I know the feeling all too well and I didn't want to leave you hating me."

"It doesn't change the fact that the only reason you slept with me was to get that wish." Determined not to back down, Chanta pointed at his chest. "And that woman was here for you. She's your lover and I don't blame her for being pissed. The only reason you slept with me was to get her back."

"You don't know what you're saying. She's Damon's whore and a witch." Payne took two steps towards her and she took three backwards.

"Whore? Is that what you're going to say about me, that I was once his whore too? After all, I slept with him for two years." Chanta laughed, a cold wind stirring around her, but she gave it little thought. "I was in love with him. Was, past tense. He lied to me and used me for his own perverse pleasure. And it makes perfect sense now, doesn't it? I'm his worst enemy's daughter. What better way to get some deep seated, reasons probably long ago forgotten, eternal revenge?"

Payne grunted as he ran his hand threw his thick black hair. "He used you. You didn't know who or what he was before you fell in love with him. I won't place the blame on you for that."

"You don't know what you're saying or even talking about. Damon wasn't like that at first. He wasn't … " she wasn't sure if she was trying to convince herself or Payne. Maybe both. "And why would you blame me? Other than because he is your father."

Chanta held her breath, almost regretted saying it. He remained silent as he dropped his head and turned his back to her. She stepped forward cautiously.

"You asked me if you could make me want to stay." He looked over his shoulder at her, his eyes swirling with the blue fire that she was beginning to love. "Did you mean that? Do you want me to stay? Or is your fascination with me only because I resemble my father?"

Her throat tightened. "I did want you to stay, but that was before your lover showed up and tried to kill me." With conviction, she let her emotions free, let them wrap around Payne's mind. "And no, my feelings for you have nothing to do with Damon."

"She isn't my lover." A growl ripped from his throat as he turned and stared straight into her eyes. "You're the only woman I've ever been with. You're the only reason I'm hesitating to do the very thing I have lived my entire life for."

Before Chanta could reply, Bastilla appeared between them, a broad smile on her face. "Time for a change of plans."

She turned to Payne as she grabbed Chanta's arm digging her poisonous fingernails into Chanta's flesh. The poison invaded Chanta's body, her muscles seizing as Bastilla shimmered and Chanta screamed Payne's name as she disappeared with her.

• • •

Breathing in through his nose, Charon closed his eyes and smelled the scents that floated around the isle that he had called home for so many centuries. Endless centuries. Endless, empty, and lonesome centuries until the *Book of Creation* had called out to him. Since that day, something had stirred inside Charon, something different, new, and unexplainable.

Opening his eyes, he stared at the books he had collected. He now had five of the fourteen books. Isten had ordered him to retrieve the books, but his orders mattered not to Charon although those orders should have. Charon was Isten's grandson, blood of his blood and part of Isten's pantheon.

And yet, Charon gathered the books because something inside him demanded it, needed it to be done. Frustration caused his fists to clench at his sides. He couldn't explain the need. He couldn't explain the desires, the wants, and the ideas that were popping in and out of his head since the book called on him.

Anger coursed through him, his arms trembling. He needed an explanation. And if it took defying Isten and all the other gods, he would do so without thought or question. A sound, eerie and deep echoed around him. He caught his breath and whirled around, searching the isle, searching the skyline ... to see nothing.

Speaking out loud, he tried to ground himself. "I am Charon. I have no free will, born of Isten's blood, I must do as he commands."

His hood lifted and slid from his forehead revealing his glowing red eyes as the books began to hum. Charon grabbed his chest as the same hum vibrated inside of him, grew more intense as the seconds ticked by. Disorientation surged through him as he fell to his knees, a scream ripping through him.

A power so intense and overwhelming seized him, he felt it from the tips of his toes to the top of his head. He fell forward onto his palms. Every inch of his body hurt, like white hot lightning had pierced through his skin and was doing a boot-scoot-and-boogie inside his body.

Fear rattled his brain. He had never experienced pain before or fear for that matter. A roar spilt the calmness of the isle and he realized it was his as his shoulders were jerked back with unseen tethers. On his knees, suspended there like a puppet, he saw the books' pages fluttering, the sound growing louder as a brilliant glow flared before him.

A tornado of molecules, shining and sparking, whirled faster and faster until they formed an apparition, a ghostly sight to behold. Charon's shoulders relaxed, released from their hold. And before him stood Jaiden, the lost god of prophecy.

Just as Charon remembered, Jaiden stood seven foot tall and was built like one of the Destroyers. After all, the Destroyers were fashioned after him. He was dressed in black, even the cane he leaned on was black. His hair was long, to his waist and as red as the blood of the humans. But it was his eyes that held Charon's attention. They were like looking into infinity, the past, the present, and the future combined.

Concentrating on the power swirling around the apparition, Charon spoke. "Jaiden? How?"

Electrifying pain split through Charon's skull. Charon grabbed his head, closed his suddenly burning eyes as Jaiden moved, and placed his ghostly hand on Charon's shoulder.

In a thousand voices, sharp and crystal clear, Jaiden proclaimed, "For this world to survive, I must be awoken. Gather my books. Seek and destroy all who dare to stand in your path."

Chapter 30

First, there were blue flames everywhere, surrounding Chanta, invading her thoughts and whipping through her soul. Second, the sound of Bastilla screaming profanities and swearing to whatever gods would listen to her filled Chanta's ears. And third, Chanta saw Damon.

"Damon." His name fell from her lips like a curse.

The flames held her still, immobile. She was standing on a large marble star in the center of a throne room, Damon's she was sure. In front of her, Damon had grabbed Bastilla by the hair and slapped her, hard. Blood splattered across the floor from her lips and nose.

Bastilla laughed. "I bring you a gift and this is what I get in return?"

He pointed towards a door and roared so loud the walls trembled. "Get out of my sight you worthless leach. How dare you make a bargain with Charon and bring this," he looked at Chanta. "This half-breed angel into my realm."

Bastilla jerked away. "I'm not a fool Damon. I know you have coveted this woman for a long time. I've seen the way you look upon her in your cauldron."

Chanta winced as Damon backhanded her sending her sprawling across the floor. "You'll be punished for this with blood and bone."

Bastilla stood, anger and humiliation on her face. "Aren't I always being punished for something? At least there will be a reason this time."

Before Bastilla could move, Damon had her in his arms, his lips on hers. Chanta closed her eyes, heard Bastilla moan and utter things Chanta never wanted to hear again for the reminder of her life.

"Bastard." Chanta opened her eyes to see Damon grabbing Bastilla's hands and a snake firmly attaching itself to both of her wrists.

A huge male, she assumed it was male, dressed in black leather came out of the shadows and took Bastilla out of the door to Chanta's left. Although she was kicking and screaming, the male pulled her along like a disobedient dog on a leash.

Damon circled the star Chanta was standing on, his hands behind his back. Memories tried to surface as she watched him. Forcing them aside, she wondered what the odds were that she would survive this encounter with Damon. He came to a standstill in front of her and the flames dissipated.

Swallowing back her disgust, Chanta glared at the snake god standing before her. She could smell the potent arousal erupting from him and even worse, it was written all over his face. She had the urge to spit in his face as his smile pulled at the corners of his black eyes. A cold chill went up her spine as his face contorted and twisted revealing the resemblance to Payne.

"Do you remember me, Chanta?" His voice was a barely above the sound of a fog horn and she caught her breath as her past slammed into her brain like a thousand piercing needles. "Of course you do, how could you possibly have forgotten the man you once wanted to marry?"

Anger ripped through her body and she lurched forward to attack. The heavy shackles on her wrists bit into her skin as hatred filled her heart. He was the reason she had lived so long in fear. He was the reason Gyth could never reveal he was her father. His cruel, cold laughter echoed in the room as the ground beneath her twisted under her feet.

She looked down and a gasp of horror escaped her mouth. Thousands of dead and decaying naked bodies littered the floor. No, they were the floor. She stepped back and tears filled her eyes as Damon waved his hand, making her face twist to the left. In the far corner, a tall, slender man with one arm and a black leather mask stood holding a large bloody axe.

"Watch him, my beautiful half-goddess, watch him. If you dare to disobey me, it'll be Payne on his chopping block." Damon's smile widened. "You wouldn't want that, now would you?"

Chanta closed her eyes as another lithe skinny man with a leather mask came forward with an unconscious human thrown over his shoulder. Her stomach roared and her heart thumped hard against her chest threatening to explode as her eyes were forced open. She bit her tongue and tears streamed down her face as the human was laid out onto the black chopping block. The human, a blond male, stirred and gasped in terror as he realized he was being chained to the marble.

"Daughter of mine enemy and now lover to my son, what shall we do about this little predicament we seem to be in?"

Chanta tried to speak, tried to beg for the human's life, and tried to jerk from Damon's hold. He laughed softly as he stepped closer and leaned forward as he smelled her hair. Her skin crawled as he hissed in her ear. He stared at her face as he nodded to the executioner. Her face twisted in pain as she watched the axe fall and slice through the human.

"I so wanted to seduce you my beauty, but alas I'm not known for my patience. Close your eyes beauty and remember me as we were before." Chanta's stomach lurched. "Remember when we had love between us? Remember when I lay between your legs and took what you offered me."

Chanta screamed, no sound came and she screamed again as she remembered how he had saved her and frightened her. She remembered how he had cut her hair, how he had ripped her clothes from her body the last night she had seen him. His sharp intake of breath made Chanta's body snap together and her brain went into overdrive.

She willed her power, her gift from the Burning, to her hands. Sweat beaded her forehead as she felt the energy fill her fingertips. Fire leapt up her hands and melted the shackles from her wrists. Her eyes glowed bright red as she turned to face Damon with an undeniable rage.

He never flinched, never batted an eyelash as she rushed forward and struck his cheek with her fist. Chanta shivered as a cold power surged around her and invaded her body. Damon's overwhelming evil took her to her knees before him. She looked up and her eyes widened as he threw his cloak back over his shoulders and his true form stepped through his human facade. He was nothing more than a hideous white skeleton with stretched ashen skin. Oh good god, and the snakes that scoured his body were those that crept into nightmares.

They surrounded her and bound her hands and feet. Twisting and jerking proved useless as the snakes slithered around her and pressed together. She was forced to stand as the snakes melted to her skin forming a long black leather-like dress with a tint of red at the edges of the hem that dragged on the embodied floor. On her hands appeared black fingerless gloves and on her head a crown of tiny hissing black serpents twisting through her white tresses.

Damon stepped closer and softly spoke. "Come, my beauty, is that all you remember of me? Don't you recall how I held you with gentleness and adored you?"

Chanta felt her body move even though she begged it not to.

Payne! Oh, god, Payne where are you? Don't let this happen to me! Gyth? Gyth? Please!

Damon laughed. "Gyth's powers cannot reach the Underworld. This is my domain and I am master here!"

Desperation and fear surfaced in her heart as she was led down a dark hallway and ushered into a large bedroom. Damon smiled as his face twisted and took the form of Payne. Chanta's eyes narrowed and her heart felt as if it had stopped.

"Will this make it easier for you, beauty? Will having my son's face and body make your stay here better?" His smile was sinister, Payne's face but not his heart or his soul.

Her lips still firmly sealed burned as she tried to speak. Tears rimmed her eyes as she wondered what he was going to do to her this time. Finish what he had started so long ago?

Damon led her to the bed with its red and black silk sheets and bleached bone bed frame. "Had things taken a different turn, this would have been our bed."

He stepped back as he waved his fingers towards the bed. Her legs obeyed as she tried to fight the persuasion to follow his lead.

"Tell me beauty what I want to hear. Say that you love me and you have never forgotten me. Tell me."

Her lips opened. His power over her slowly vanishing. "No! Never!"

Damon hissed as a serpent slithered across her shoulder. Chanta suddenly realized he hadn't touched her at all, not one slight touch. She stepped away from the bed and crossed her arms over her chest.

He looked at her, from the top of her head to her toes before his eyes rested on her stomach. She looked down and swallowed hard.

"So, you have made a bargain with Charon and you're carrying my child." Her stomach flipped as he smiled.

"I'd rather die than let an innocent child suffer."

He came at her, his face twisting back to his own. With her heart in her throat, she stood her ground. He stopped inches away from her, his eyes latched onto her belly.

"Swear to me that you'll raise him and tell him who his father is." For a split second, she thought she saw a flicker of sadness cross his face.

"I'll raise him as my own. I think it would be best if he never knew of you and for that matter that no one else does either."

Damon's eyes burned white hot, rage manifesting onto his face. "He's my son, my blood! I want him to know who I am."

"I'd tell you to go to hell, but wait, you're already here aren't you? Tell me Damon, what did you do to deserve being imprisoned down here in this stinking hole?"

Damon's anger reached a new level as he peered into her eyes. His upper lip twitched and curled up showing his sharp jagged teeth.

"I will enjoy killing the last good part of my other son. And then I'm going to rip Payne's head from his body and spit down his throat for touching you."

"Why does causing so much pain and heartbreak give you so much pleasure?" She tried not to scream the question but heard her voice bounce around the room. "Why do you hate Payne so much?"

"Pain and heartbreak are the only things real in this world." He shook his head. "I don't hate my son, I did what I had to do in order for him to survive. His pain and anger has been the backbone of his will to live." Chanta stared at Damon, reminding herself he was evil incarnate. "One day, I'll have my revenge and my sons will be my right hands."

"Revenge against what?" She spat out. "What happened to you that you hate so much, that you hurt so much that you inflict that same pain on whoever comes near you?"

He stopped, stood as still as a stone statue. "I've never had a choice but to be who and what I am." A mirror slid across the floor and stopped in front of her. "And this reflection of yourself is what I wanted from you, but like everything else in my life, I had to let that go and trade it for something else."

She stared at herself and didn't know what to say or to think. Damon had wanted her to be his queen? She ran her fingers across the serpents in her hair that formed the crown she was wearing. They leaned into her fingers as if they wanted to be petted, to be loved. He groaned softly as she ran her fingers down the front of the snake skin dress, like a glove it held her, molded to her body.

"What are you going to do with me, Damon?"

The dress and the crown vanished, leaving her naked and fearful. Damon didn't even look at her, his head turned and a soft growl echoed around the room.

"I'm going to use you as bait." He looked at her suddenly, a cruel expression stared back her. "But don't fear, I'll not harm one single hair on your head. How could I?"

"Why wouldn't you? You did before, so why not now?"

He laughed, the cruelty in his voice bouncing around the room. "Because dear little Chanta, I made a bargain with Charon as well. But trust me, if I had not made that bargain, I would be all over you licking up your pain and misery with every breath I took."

With those words, Chanta sat up in the bed she was on. As she threw her feet over the side of bed, Damon appeared at the bottom of the bed. Black rose petals fell from the ceilings, showering her in their dark fragrance. His smile made her skin crawl. With a wave of his clawed hand, he left her stunned, speechless, and naked.

Chapter 31

Payne reached for Chanta as she vanished, falling to his knees, his heart ripping from his chest, and hatred filling his soul. Damon would die!

"I will kill you with my bare hands! Do you hear me Father? I'm going to rip every inch of you apart and throw your bloody ass into the flame of the Underworld!"

Sharp pain exploded inside Payne's head. Damon's voice roared, "I'll be waiting for you my son … and your woman will be sitting at my feet begging me to pleasure her!"

Payne looked to the ceiling and closed his eyes. "Gyth! I beg of you! I beg like the snake I am! Give me the power to defeat him, give me the strength to rip his soul in half, and give me the birthright that I have so long denied!"

Gyth appeared, his white robes settling around his feet. "You do not know what you ask. The birthright may very well make you like him. There is not enough good in you to keep you as you are."

"It matters not as long as she is returned and Damon dies."

"If Damon dies, someone will have to take his place." Gyth's jaw flexed, his eyes swirling with the white glow Payne had seen in Chanta's eyes. "The Underworld will claim you if you kill him. You will become your father because the universe must remain balanced."

On his knees, Payne roared, his heart aching, his mind in turmoil. "And what happens to Chanta if she remains in the Underworld? She has a power unlike anything I have ever seen. What happens when Damon tortures her? Tries to convert her?"

"No one said we were going to leave her there." Gyth eyes glowed brighter. "Don't you think that I would have killed that abomination already if it weren't for keeping the balance?"

Varick appeared beside Gyth as Payne got to his feet. Clenching his fists, Payne manifested his weapons. Gearing up for the fight ahead, he loaded himself down with enough weapons the Army would have stared wide-eyed. He palmed a hunting knife, ran his thumb across the glistening blade.

"Give the power back to me that I gave you freely."

Payne stepped toward Gyth fully intent on going head to head with him when Varick grabbed his arm. "He can't."

Payne growled, the sound a low vibration growing louder with each passing second.

"He doesn't command the Destroyers anymore. He has no power over them or over you."

Not believing his ears, he turned to Varick, all too aware that Gyth's eyes were hard set on Varick's face. "What the hell do you mean?"

The air in the room dropped twenty degrees, Gyth's hair fanning out and tinging with red. When Varick spoke again, Gyth vanished. "It's the reason I've had such a hard time controlling these god powers. It isn't just mine that I have. When Isten reset my destiny, I became the leader of the Destroyers and every power that Gyth took is now mine." Varick stepped back, his topaz eyes glowing with a soft light. "I owe you a wish."

Payne had wanted his complete revenge on Damon; he had wanted him begging for Payne's forgiveness and he had wanted to see him die a painful death. But now, Chanta was in trouble and he wanted his birthright, the one thing that was powerful enough to destroy Damon, and the one thing that could send him straight to the Underworld to get Chanta back.

• • •

Damian snuck through the cave and waved for Bastilla to follow. The boyish grin on his face appeared as she glided up behind him and they made their escape out into the sunlight as the coven slept. The sand beneath his feet scratched at his heels as they raced along the riverbank.

Out of breath and safely out of the hearing distance of the coven, they burst out into laughter. They held hands as they raced to the river. Plunging in headfirst they swam across the great water to the other side.

Damian lay looking at the bright white sky as Bastilla took his hand. "I love you."

"I love you too," he whispered as he turned his head to look at her. "I have a secret I want to share with you. Someday, when I learn how to control it, it will be able to free us from this hell."

Bastilla sat up and her eyes widened as Damian summoned his powers. Purple flames leapt to his fingers and danced up his arms. She knew the nature of the flame, it was the flame of the Underworld, Damon's flame. She bit her lip as he stood and held his arms out. His body lifted as the flames completely engulfed him.

His body twisted as it transformed, as the skin melted and reshaped over his bones. His black hair grew and fell to the ground under his feet as muscles bulged under his new skin. Flames leapt from his mouth as asps slithered around his waist forming his clothes. The clothes shined as they covered his body and hissed as a crown of blood formed above his brow.

His fangs extended and he threw his head back in pleasure as the asps settled over his skin. Long sharp spikes protruded through his snake cloths at his elbows, his shoulders, and his forehead. Opening his clenched fists, four long sharp eight-inch metal-like spears ripped through his knuckles.

He floated to the ground and smiled triumphant at Bastilla. His triumph did not last. Her thoughts and emotions poured into him.

Bastilla groaned as she looked upon him from head to toe. He was dark, dangerous, and powerful. She covered her mouth as she realized the snakes were poisonous, that Damon's were not, and that Damon did not know of Damian's power. Her eyes narrowed and her heart tightened in her chest. A cold blast of jealousy ran up her spine as she looked upon him.

Everyone in the coven thought he was human, even his mother. Bastilla had always thought that Damian was weak and inferior. She not only had tried to protect him, she had coveted the fact that he had needed her. She had often dreamt that Damian would fall at her feet when she became Damon's bride. That she would be worshipped as queen of the Underworld, that Damian would one day be her slave and hers alone, and .

"Why do you stare at me like that?" But he knew the answer before asking the question.

Bastilla inched away. "You must get rid of that power. You must not ever use it again. Lord Damon will kill you! You have lied to us all … your mother will not be pleased!"

"But … Bastilla I hid this for us, that someday we could be free … " His words were lost, his heart breaking.

Bastilla turned her back and ran to the river. Damian knew where she would go and knew she would tell them all. His heart grew cold and bitterness swelled in its place. In that second as she reached the other side of the river he knew he was alone in the world, completely alone.

Damian, son of Damon, looked down at his hands and clenched his fists. He willed the power to hide and the flames died slowly. His feet touched the ground as his body transformed back into the child he was. But now he was different, a dark spark twinkled in his eyes where once there had been a sparkle of hope. But there was no more hope in his soul, only darkness.

Ten minutes later, he walked back into the coven's lair and leaned against the cave wall. He watched as his mother looked upon Bastilla in horror and rage as the girl told her in detail of Damian's power. A slow steady growl erupted from Damian's chest as the coven turned to look at him. He knew what was coming and he wasn't going to fight.

He stood perfectly still and his heart never once sped as they surrounded him and slammed him to the ground before their mistress's feet. The pain felt good, it felt right, as if it was meant to be. With every ounce of his soul he forced the power of his father deep down inside of him. He sealed it inside so tight that even he was no longer sure that it had existed. He pushed its memory to the farthest recesses of his mind and latched onto the wall of hate that was forming around his heart.

Chapter 32

Pain. Misery. These were the things that called out to Ania. Not by her choice, but by fate's. She silently craved for peace from her ordained duty, but the reality always kept her at a bitter distance and her dreams full of nightmares.

She cast an eye over the darkness, hoping that she had somehow mistook what her senses were telling her, yet she knew she hadn't. Damon was here, somewhere in the black dense forest, alone and suffering. And she had to find him, Terror Sky insisted that she deliver a message in fear of what was transpiring in Damon's black heart.

Through the years, Ania had managed to keep her distance from Damon even though he yielded such great miseries, not only from himself, but from others around him. Something about him intimidated her, his name a cold living thing burying into her chest.

Damon was a master of misery and even though Ania had never met him, she had dreamed of him, had felt his pain and misery. Part of her was fascinated and had longed for this moment, the other part of her was wary, equally petrified.

The forest in which she stood was dark, no noise and no movement. It would have been damn eerie if she had of been a human. As she walked through the branches, the only sound were her light footsteps. She knew she was getting closer because her skin starting tingling, her body buzzing, and her lithe muscles jerked.

Her heartbeat quickened as she stepped out into a clearing. Nestled in the center of the flat clearing, a standard issue cabin stood. From the windows, flickering light jumped up and down casting an eerie glow across the steps that led to the porch.

Ania walked onto the porch and looked through one of the windows at Damon who stood before a fireplace, his head downcast, his shoulders sagging. Who would have ever thought he could look so downtrodden?

Summoning her powers, she slipped into the black smoke and stepped out of it behind him. The flame in the fireplace crackled, his head lifting slowly, but he remained as he was. One hand was on the mantle, the other hanging at his side. In human form, shirtless and in leather pants, Damon laughed.

"This," he held out his hands indicating the cabin. "This is my reprieve. A sanctuary away from the Underworld in which I must rule."

"A hiding place, nothing more." Ania tried to look away from his back, from the tight hard muscles that bunched as he moved. "I can feel the burdens you carry."

"Ah, yes." He turned slightly, his profile silhouetted by the fire. "You must be the goddess of misery I have heard so much about."

"I am Ania." She took a step closer, cautiously. "I came here for two reasons."

Before she could blink, he was in her face, his hands clutching her shoulders. "And what might that be?"

The instant he touched her, she groaned, his words lost. The integration with his mind happened so suddenly, she found herself in his arms, against his chest. She knew that sex and pain were releases for him, but what she was seeing was so beyond that. It was a curse, a drug he had to have to survive.

"You must release me." Her hoarse whisper rattled the ceiling, the wrought iron and candle chandelier swaying. "I will not be responsible for my actions if you don't do as I insist."

The second he released her, she wanted to protest. But she was here for a reason and it didn't have to do with her needs or desires. Nor was it about Damon. This was about Payne.

"What do you want?" He turned his back to her, going back to the fireplace, staring into the flames.

"I come with a message from Terror Sky." Ania watched his muscles bunch as he rolled his shoulders, stretching his neck. "You must take cautious steps during the next few days. The events happening around you are leading to your demise."

"My demise?" Damon swirled around, his face twisting in rage. "Now, why would Terror Sky care about my demise?"

Ania stepped back, her face burning. "As you know, balances must be maintained. Now is not the time for evil to be triumphant over good. If you die, Payne will rise from your ashes and destroy this world as the Heavens will fall and all mankind will suffer."

He laughed, the sound a symphony of misery and aching. "Didn't Terror Sky tell you? I would just as soon watch this world destroy itself than take another breath of this putrid air around me."

He came at her and she held her hand up, stopping him in his tracks. Enough was enough. She was one of the oldest goddesses in this realm and no one was going to threaten her, least of all a snake god that clutched his past to his chest and used it to justify the things he did.

"Regardless of how you may or may not feel, if you want to live you will listen. Regardless of the emotions running amuck through what's left of your heart, you will take heed to this warning." She turned on her heel, her own anger rising up her throat. "Payne will kill you, Chanta will die, and your unborn fetus will never know his first breath. Change the game, Damon, Lord of the Underworld, or watch as everything burns down around you."

Before he could reach her, she vanished, but not before he spoke.

"My son will stand before the rivers of blood he creates and it will all be in my name."

• • •

Payne's insides quivered, his spine tingling.

"Give me the damn power back so I can save her!" Payne gripped his swords until his knuckles turned blue. "I need to save her."

Payne's spine tingled, alerting his honed senses to the impending danger that had grown closer. Without a word spoken, they both nodded as Damon's presence on earth sent their spidey senses into overdrive. He and Varick both dematerialized and reappeared in front of Tortured Souls.

Crouching, Payne drew in a long breath and let his feral instincts override his emotions. The proverbial line had been drawn and Damon would pay. He would pay a thousand times over if he so much as harmed a single hair on Chanta's head.

Payne grimaced as he looked down the street and out of the corner of his eye, he saw Varick take his defensive stance. Eighty Destroyers were taking the same stance as he pulled himself together for the fight that lay ahead. With the sanctuary they had all come to know as home behind him, he withdrew his scimitars. Mentally, he was tense and his thoughts were preoccupied with Chanta—the woman he had fallen for.

Hell, fallen for was not even close to describing what he felt. He was head over heels in love with her. Love! Did he dare to love anyone? Could he? Regardless of the conflict his emotions were going through, he knew beyond a shadow of a doubt that he would die for her a thousand times over if need be.

As he stood with the other Destroyers, Payne looked at their faces, knew them, fought with them, and would die for any of them in heartbeat. He had always saw being a Destroyer as a job, nothing more. But now, he realized that this was his family. This was what he should have been fighting for, not the revenge that had always laid upon his soul.

The years behind him flashed through his mind. The fights, the uncountable confrontations with the vermin that spewed out of the Underworld were necessary to keep them spreading their disease and chaos. But this night was different.

A war was coming and this night was the first of many to come, of that, he was sure. The stakes were high, not only the lives of his family, but of everyone on Earth, in the Heavens, and in the Underworld. Gyth may not be the best choice of Lord of the Heavens, but he sure was a better one than Damon would ever be.

And then there was Charon, Isten, and the missing Jaiden. He wasn't sure where they bled into all this, but he was damn sure it couldn't mean anything good.

As the street lights faded and the sinister darkness emerged from the shadows, Payne as well as Varick started counting. Twenty, thirty, forty, fifty … .and even more vermin poured from the blackness. Deep rooted growls and hisses split into the night air as ominous clouds covered the moon. From a distance, a resonating howl splintered through the streets.

"What in the nine hells is going on?" Payne turned to Varick. "They never gather like this." He watched as werewolves, vampires, and witches slithered out of the darkness.

Six of Payne's brother Destroyers appeared alongside Varick. Dressed to kill, they nodded at each other and readied themselves for the battle. Grim faces and weapons in hand, they waited for the enemies to make the first move.

On the ledge of Tortured Souls, three gods appeared and simultaneously four appeared on the building across the street. The Destroyers felt the powerful forces appear and their growls deepened. So, the bastards had come to watch! Well, far be it from the Destroyers to deprive the gods from their entertainment.

Payne and Varick shared an odd look. Seemed the ruling powers of the Heavens and the Underworld all had a stake in this battle.

"Where the hell is Gyth?" Payne muttered flexing his wrists.

The wind gushed angrily over the scene rattling the loose signs and banging the doors on the sanctuary behind them. Thunder crashed overhead as the doors of Tortured Souls flung open and a leather clad woman glided out to take her position amongst the warriors.

"Gyth? It's untelling. You have me and be thankful that I am on your side." Varick winked at Payne as Angelica, his mate, took her place at his side.

Payne chuckled, winked at Angelica. "I'm glad Angelica is on our side. She looks more dangerous than you ever have."

Angelica bowed and grinned as she stretched the black wings that unfurled from her back. "Well boys, better call some reinforcements, looks like we're going to have our hands full."

Above, thunder boomed and lightning flashed as dark clouds dumped rain on the scene below.

Above the rain, above the growls, and above the adrenaline that was pumping like mad, Angelica's voice boomed as her body levitated, "Victory will be ours!"

As if on cue, the two armies crashed together like a hundred car pileup, the noise as deafening as if a flaming meteor had landed around them. Hard core military style jack hammering fists and swords danced in time to the now down pouring rain. Left and right, bodies were flung from the fight, but as quickly as they were flung away, they got up and returned to battle.

Angelica, jacked up on some major adrenaline, swore under her breath as a vampire latched onto her arm, "Why don't you … just die all frigging ready?"

Varick pulled back from the werewolves that kept stalking around him and grinned at Angelica. "Try sticking that sai of yours through his chest. You got to get that little black ball out of his ribcage before he'll kill over and turn to ash."

Angelica flipped backwards and landed on her hands as the vampire tried to grab her forearm. On the return to her feet, she pulled out her sais and swung first to the left getting the vampires attention so that he would draw to the right. She smiled and winked at him as her other hand came around and stabbed him in the middle of his pasty back. Grinding through bone, the orb was forced out as the sai penetrated his spongy body.

Ashes filtered to the ground around her feet as she took a slight bow to Varick. "Thank you my darling Stud Muffin."

Varick grinned as the werewolves attacked in three different directions. "We seriously have … " Stepping to the right avoiding a clawed paw and a pair of especially nasty fangs, he frowned as he continued, "to discuss these pet names you insist on using."

Angelica rolled her eyes and aimed and threw one of her chakrams to the third of the werewolves attacking Varick. "Okay, Mr. Sexy in Leather, but I'm warning you that I'm not easily persuaded."

Varick laughed as his boot contacted an unsuspecting werewolf jaw. "That I am all too well aware of."

Chapter 33

Payne shook his head as his scimitars sliced his way through the mass of witches that seemed to keep coming non-stop. His attention however was on Varick and Angelica. Who the hell would have ever thought that Varick, yeah, Varick Ta Farg, man of no emotion, would be consumed with a female?

"Payne!" The sound of his name swung his body around.

"What the fuck?"

Payne looked up to the ledge, saw Damon dressed in black leather. Isten's eerie presence in Payne's mind was a cold jerk on his nerves. The god had delivered his promise it seemed.

"Payne … son of mine."

A smug smile tugged at the corners of Payne's mouth. "Fuck you daddy!"

"Join me and I shall let your friends live … for now."

"Why don't you bring your sorry ass down here and face me?"

"I have a much better idea." Chanta appeared at Damon's side. "Why don't I just kill her instead?"

Without thinking, Payne spun and hurled his left scimitar at the rooftop towards Damon's head. The blade sung through the air like a true instrument of death. Damon hissed and tried to sidestep the blade. He hissed louder realizing he was immobile and his true form writhed from his human body. Straining to move, Damon met Chanta's eyes.

She was protecting Payne. Her emotions were lit up like fireflies dancing in the night. Payne held his breath, she was protecting him.

"You're in my domain now you lecherous black hearted bastard and I say you can fuck yourself!"

"Release me or I will kill them all." Damon grinned and Payne knew Damon could break free from her hold. "Release me."

"You're in no position to make demands." Chanta crossed her arms over her chest. Defiant and beautiful. "Leave Payne alone, you've done enough to him already."

Damon threw his arms back and black serpents slithered from his mouth as Chanta's hold was broken and Payne's scimitar sliced through the tendons of his neck. Damon grabbed at the hideous wound, several snakes pulling back to his body and wrapping around his neck covering the wound. Blood spurted as his skin healed instantly, the snakes disappearing under the new flesh.

The earth trembled as his voice screamed out across the universe, "I am the god of the Underworld! You pathetic creatures cannot kill me. Enough of these games! I will kill you all and devour your souls!"

The demons, werewolves, witches, and vampires alike, pulled back from the fight cowering under the voice of their master. Slinking back into the shadows, they watched warily as Damon levitated to the street before the Destroyers. His horns glistened as the moon peeped out from the dark clouds.

Writhing, his body twisted and the serpents uncurled from his arms and waist as his eyes fired and blazed. The Destroyers looked upon him as if he were scum of the earth and a few laughed as Payne stepped forward with a grin that told of his eagerness.

"Well, Dad isn't this what you really wanted? Here I am. Now, what are you going to do about it?"

Damon held out one long pointed skeletal finger and said, "This."

White-hot lightning poured into Payne's chest taking him to his knees in an agonizing scream. The next few seconds blurred together. Payne tried to stand, his knees defying his orders. His heart stopped as Chanta dematerialized and rushed forward to be knocked into a parked car by a blast of energy from her left. From the corner of his eye, he saw Bastilla in the shadows.

Varick attacked Damon grazing his left arm with his sword as Angelica stabbed her sai into Damon's side. Damon's snakes struck, biting into their flesh. Payne could only watch.

Damon roared and stomped his foot, the blast sending Varick and Angelica flying backwards. Two more Destroyers leapt forward howling viciously as he turned to face them. With a wave of his hand, the two warriors were taken to their knees and pinned down by an unseen force.

Deep sinister laughter echoed down the street as the other warriors were all flung backwards away from Payne's body. Stepping in front of his son, Damon went to one knee and grabbed Payne's chin. A snake slithered out of Damon's mouth and attached itself to Payne's chest. Instantly, Payne felt his powers draining, slipping away from him.

Was this what it had come down to? Dying in his father's grasp again? With the last of his strength, he forced his head to turn and looked at Chanta's still body. He would have done anything to keep her from harm. He hated that he had fallen for her, hated that she had that something that he couldn't resist nor did he want to.

His vision blurred, his life teetering on the edge. At this moment, he would have traded his entire existence to have saved Chanta. He would have suffered a thousand lifetimes over just to get to tell her one time he loved her.

Varick whistled grabbing Payne's attention. "I have a gift for you. The power that Gyth took from you, I now return."

Slumping forward into his father's arms, Payne's scream reached beyond the heavens, beyond the universe's unfathomable distance. He felt the powers that he had once hidden flow into his very being. His insides churned and twisted under his skin as the power spread to every fiber of his body. Every feral instinct fired, every hate and longing surfaced, and worst of all, his heart blackened almost to the point of no return.

He was his father's son! Nothing short of being a devil, he rose to his full height pulling away from the cold embrace of the bastard that dared to sire him, he embraced the power he had been born with. Purple and blue flames danced up his arms and engulfed his shoulders as horns split through the skin on his forehead.

This was who he was, who he had been born to be. And he accepted it. Embraced it.

Rearing his head back and staring at the moon, he released his inner demons, every single last one of the freaking bastards. He felt the power inside of him gush out, felt the snakes he had been born with slither over his skin. Grinning, he watched his body transform as his black hair fanned out from his shoulders and trailed down his back to the ground at his feet. His already huge muscles bunched and pumped higher as his blood veins popped up. The poisonous asps wrapped around him creating a layer of impenetrable armor, as horns spiked from his elbows and shoulders.

He had been conceived in the Underworld, the flames of the abyss melding with his very soul. The Underworld wanted him, longed for him to return to that domain and rule. After all, the Underworld had longed for a true master and with Payne's unique power, he alone could control the flames and conquer the world. The limitless demons and evil that had been captured and imprisoned within the Underworld's confines would be at his command.

His. Payne's command. Rearing his head back, he opened his mouth and roared, his arms swinging back, his chest expanding with the awesome power. Damon slid back, his claws grasping into the pavement to stop his slide.

Looking down at his hands, which now were framed with long black fingernails, he knew what lay underneath the skin of his knuckles. He flexed his hands, growling in absolute enthrallment, and looked down into his father's yellow eyes. A grunt of self-satisfaction rasped from his mouth, hell, he had grown some seven inches or better. Yeah, he was so his father's son and then some.

• • •

Varick turned to Payne as a blinding pain took him to his knees. A Destroyer's face appeared before his eyes and he watched helplessly as his soul was sucked from his body by a giant horned vampire. Rage and sadness enveloped him as he saw the life leave the Destroyer's eyes. How could this be happening? How could a vampire that strong be so close and Varick not notice?

Pulling himself to his feet, Varick trembled as Payne threw back his head letting the powers take over. So, it had come down to this? He silently prayed that Payne would not go over to the other side. Shaking himself, he stumbled to Angelica who was trying, without much luck, to unwrap a light pole from her legs.

He would have to let Payne deal with Damon, not that he wanted to, but everything in him screamed it had to be done, that this was the crossroads where Payne was meant to be. He had to be the one to make this choice.

Angelica kicked at the wooden pole and frowned as pain shot up her legs. Tons of splinters bit into her flesh as she jerked trying to free herself from its clutches. She watched breathlessly as Varick snapped the pole in pieces as if it were a toothpick.

Pulling her to her feet, Varick turned to Chanta. She was lifeless, bones apparently broken and blood everywhere. Rushing to her, he carefully lifted her head.

Sadness enveloped him, rage festered in his heart. This was his fault, she wouldn't have been hurt if he had control of his powers.

Looking to the Heavens, he swore to their father, "If anything happens to her, I will find you and I will rip out your heart."

Chanta groaned, her body jerking as it began healing. Varick held his breath as she twisted in his arms.

He smoothed her blood soaked hair from her face. "Chanta?" Varick's voice cracked. Tears of blood fell from his white eyes. "Sister mine?"

Chapter 34

Chanta's blurry vision tried to clear. She could hear Varick's voice over the thunderous noise in her brain, could make out his outline silhouetted by unearthly blue and green light, and sense his destructive emotions. Slowly, she tried to sit up, her bones and flesh mending. The relief that washed over Varick's face almost stunned her. Not many people had honestly cared about her and it made her heart bloom.

Darkness closed in, her mother's voice bouncing around her head like acid on metal. Unable to make out what she was saying, Chanta refused to give in to the inky dark depths that were trying to pull her under. Reaching out, she grabbed Varick's shirt and turned her head trying to find Payne. He had to be okay.

"It's time." Lysander's voice grabbed her attention as he appeared behind Varick. Angelica was crouched next to Varick, the Angel's appearance going unnoticed.

Lysander was poised with sword in hand, pointed the thing straight at Chanta's head. "This death will not be wasted. Your mother wants to take the throne, wants your father dead."

Before Chanta could scream or even move, Gyth appeared, his long white hair fanning out as red streaks ran down its length. Death was in his eyes as he tackled Lysander and the sword went flying across the parking lot.

Gyth moved so fast, she couldn't keep up. Their bodies became blurs as they rolled around, fists thundering into one another's faces. One second Lysander was on his feet, the next he was flung against Tortured Soul's wall with Gyth all up in his grill.

Varick pulled her to her feet just as Lysander fell to his knees before Gyth. Pointing to the display, Chanta heard herself say. "Someone help him."

Varick turned, his eyes widening as Gyth bent down and retrieved Lysander's sword. Chanta stepped forward, intent on stopping her father until Lysander spoke. Gold blood dripped from the Angel's mouth and nose, his eyes glowing with an illuminating light.

"There will be consequences for killing an Angel." Lysander bowed his head, his eyes peering at Chanta. "But I release you from blame or guilt, I knew my death was but a moment away when I materialized on this earth."

Lysander spoke again, softly and Chanta's heart chilled in her chest. "Your mother erased yours and Payne's destinies from Jaiden's books. She wanted you to die, knew it would cause Varick to destroy Gyth so that she could take your father's throne and condemn all humanity. All because your father refused to have her as his queen."

Chanta screamed as Gyth raised Lysander's sword and brought it down, slicing the angel through his neck. She turned to her father as Lysander's head rolled toward her. "Why did you kill him?" Her voice rumbled inside her head as she rushed forward and beat her fists into Gyth's chest. "He didn't deserve to die."

"He tried to kill you." Gyth turned on his heel, his body dematerializing. "And your mother will pay the price also."

Varick grabbed Chanta's arms and turned her around to face him. "I would have done the same."

"No." Chanta pulled away as she heard a growl erupt from Payne's throat. "This isn't happening." She grabbed her head as a dull roar echoed around her brain, Payne's emotions ripping through her. "Make them stop, Varick."

"He needs to do this, Chanta. He has to. This is where his destiny has been leading him his entire life."

"You don't understand." She grabbed her chest, felt Payne's misery and rage. "He's standing on the edge of good and evil."

He shook his head. "We all know this is what Payne needs. He has to face his father."

"We?" She looked around, countless Destroyers emerged from the buildings, the dark streets, and some appeared out of thin air.

"Yes, we all have been waiting for Payne to face Damon." Varick pointed to Payne. "Let him make his own destiny."

Payne and Damon were fighting, each holding their own. The air was cold, the temperature dropping the longer she stood there with the Destroyers and Varick all lining up behind her. The rumble inside her head grew louder, like a train in the distance getting closer with each passing second.

With each impact of fists, Chanta's heart thundered louder and louder. She watched, not because she wanted to, but because she couldn't tear her eyes away from Payne. Somehow, he had become more than just important to her, he had stolen her heart, her very soul. And as she watched the man she loved fight with such vengeance and menace, his agony became hers.

Payne landed on his back, his roar filled with anger, menace, and vengeance. Damon towered over him, laughing as Bastilla came out of the shadows at a sprinters pace. In her hand, Chanta saw the dagger, saw the evil twist of her full lips as Bastilla came right straight at her.

Chanta felt Payne look at her, felt his sudden fear, something she knew Payne had never experienced. Chanta understood in that moment what Bastilla had wanted from Payne, not his love, but his power. She had used Payne all those years ago and was trying to do it again.

And then the air stilled. The roar in Chanta's mind overtook her thoughts and actions. There was only one thing she knew she had to do, protect Payne.

Bastilla launched herself at Chanta, the knife coming up and slicing downwards. Chanta stood still, her eyes narrowing as time seemed to slow. She watched as if she alone held the remote,

Bastilla's face twisted in rage, her eyes so full of hate. From the corner of her eye, she saw Varick step forward, but with a slight push of her hand, Chanta sent him sprawling backwards.

She felt her powers rise, they pulled together in the center of her chest as her wings split out from her back. Tiny black flames danced along her skin as her body lifted into the air.

Looking down at Payne, Chanta smiled as she raised her hands and lightning streaked across the sky, came together and blasted the ground in front of Bastilla. Bastilla's body flew backwards landing with a thump against a parked bus. On her hands and knees, she screamed in anger.

"You're no match for me." Bastilla stood, her eyes glowing green as she reached to the sky and started chanting.

Chanta gritted her teeth as Bastilla lunged forward again, this time with clawed hands held out and glittering sharp teeth emerging from her lips. With a bitter laugh, Chanta crouched and leapt forward meeting her head on.

Between blows and curses, Chanta calmly said, "All you need is a pointed hat and a broom."

"And all you need to do is die." Bastilla punched Chanta in the stomach. "And when you die, Payne will once more be mine."

Doubled over, Chanta saw red. Literally. Her vision hazed over. When she spoke, Chanta didn't recognize her own voice. It was warped and twisted.

"FYI, I'm a demi-goddess, you two-bit worthless bitch. And not just any demi-goddess." Chanta raised up and grabbed Bastilla by the throat. "And Payne is mine."

With all she had, Chanta flung Bastilla backwards. Charon stepped out of the shadows and swung his scythe as Bastilla landed in front of him on her stomach. Chanta didn't turn away as his scythe cut deep and to the bone.

Bastilla's screams caught Damon's attention and he turned with a grin. Charon nodded at him as he vanished. Chanta didn't think, she ran toward Payne.

• • •

Damon's snakes poured from his body and attacked Chanta taking her to the ground. Payne breathed in deep as Chanta blasted the snakes away and was on her feet in the blink of an eye. Varick was grabbing her and pulling her away as Payne turned his attention back to his father.

Payne rolled to his left as Damon manifested a pair of swords and swung down at him. With a vicious kick, he knocked Damon backwards, the swords clattering to the asphalt. In a blur of black leather, Damon charged at him. They battered and rammed each other, banging into parked cars, shattering windshields, and knocking down light poles.

On one knee, Payne struggled to stand when something hot pierced his stomach. Looking down, he saw blood and lots of it as well as a dagger protruding from his stomach. Damon was laughing as he circled him.

"Son of mine." Damon stopped in front of him as a wall of blue fire encircled them both blocking out the Destroyers. Blocking out Chanta. "Join me. Come to the Underworld and rule at my side."

Payne shook his head as he stood and pulled the dagger out. "Why don't you go back down there and rot for two thousand more years?"

Damon threw his head back and laughed. "Come with me. Accept that power inside of you, feel the desire that courses through your soul to be my true son. Rule the Underworld with me as you were meant to."

"Why would I rule with you when I could rule alone?" Payne snarled, his thoughts bending and twisting. "There's only one thing I have desired most of my life."

"Tell me what it is and we can make it happen. Together, we can rule this pathetic world." He paced back and forth. "We can conquer Gyth and take the Heavens to its knees."

"Your death. I have wanted it for so long, it's all I have ever known." Payne saw Chanta through the flames, the worry and the fear written on her face as she tried to see him. "But no longer do I desire it. I no longer wish for those things."

Damon stilled. "I can give you anything you desire or wish for." He stepped toe to toe with Payne. "Look deeper into that black mass of a heart. We both know what you truly want. Power, more and more power to conquer your fears, to get everything you ever wanted."

Payne stepped back, his powers and the Underworld pulling at him from every emotion he had ever felt. He could rule, he could destroy both his father and Gyth. He could stop the insanity by losing his own. And lose Chanta in the process.

Payne shook his head in an attempt to clear the thought his god powers were conjuring up. "No, father. There is one thing that I want, that I desire, that I need that you can never give me."

Blue flames raced up Payne's arms as he lunged at Damon. Burying the dagger to the hilt in Damon's chest, Payne watched his father's surprised expression. The flames on his arms covered Damon and swirled around them both.

Jerking backwards, Damon jerked the dagger out. "There is nothing I can't give you."

With a mighty roar, Payne slammed his fist into Damon's wound. "You can never love me. Now, go back to hell and stay there."

Damon fell forward and grabbed Payne's arms, disbelief filling his eyes as blood spurted from his mouth. "Then why not kill me, son of mine?"

"Because you're my father." Payne pulled out of Damon's grasp. "And because I'm nothing like you."

The flames burned brighter and swirled out of control as Damon vanished with a roar. As the circle of blue flames died, Payne's eyes sought out Chanta, found her, and devoured her. Without doubt, she was the only thing that had kept him from destroying his father, kept him from becoming his father.

Epilogue

Charon stood before the Tree of Life, his thoughts scattered and confused. The instant he had crossed the threshold of disobeying Isten's orders, he had become a traitor … to his own grandfather, his own blood. And now, there was no turning back. Not that he wanted to.

No, he didn't want to turn back to that pantheon and watch as the universe imploded around him. No, he didn't want to be on the losing side of any battle that may loom in the future. And most of all, he didn't want to be subservient to a god that was imprisoned on an Isle dependent on others. He wanted emotions, free will, and the ability to refuse any bargain. What Charon wanted was his freedom.

In human form, with his black robes covering his entire body, the only thing that stood out were his eyes, which he knew were glowing with his reaper powers. Odd that the red tint to his vision plagued him now, after all the countless centuries he had been looking through these eyes.

Without warning, the hair on Charon's neck stood to attention, his senses suddenly on high alert. Then the smell of earth after a thunderstorm curled inside his nose, instantly relaxing his muscles. Like a cobra swaying to hypnotize its prey before it struck. Jaiden was here. Or more appropriately, Jaiden's apparition.

At one time, Jaiden had been the top of the food chain, his powers almost unstoppable, his presence leaving one awestruck for days. Perhaps, those powers were unstoppable, after all Jaiden was here in visual yet incorporeal form, his power growing with each passing visit.

"How many souls do you require?" Charon tried not to bite out the question.

Staring at the books he had collected, he held out his large hand. A small glass jar appeared in his palm, Bastilla's soul swirling inside its temporary prison.

Jaiden's form stepped between Charon and the Tree of Life. No longer was his hair flaming red, now it was the color of the deepest ocean, and his eerie eyes as green as emeralds. Those eyes, changing from green to purple watched as Charon lifted the lid of the jar.

"Enough to harness the energy I require." Jaiden's eyebrow rose as Bastilla's soul darted across the Isle and screeched. He glanced at Charon as he took out Lysander's jar. "I sense your frustration. Explain."

Jaiden's wraith, yes, his wraith Charon thought because his very presence screamed war, threatened the very air surrounding him. And there was only one option when in his presence, bow down to him because he was the higher power. But that was the way with Jaiden; he ordered and you simply obeyed.

Charon gritted his teeth, felt his fangs scraping against his lips. "I do not enjoy killing nor do I enjoy these bargains." He paused as Bastilla's soul careened about the Isle realizing it was in yet another prison surrounded by the invisible waters of the River Styx. "I want freedom, free will, and to be able to make my own destiny."

"Think of it in its simplest form according to your grandfather's, Isten's greater plans. Everything must remain balanced." Jaiden's lips twisted into a cynical smile as he held out his hand and Bastilla's soul suddenly stopped in its tracks. "The souls I need you to collect have all been fated to be forever tormented, forever lost in the abyss of the Underworld. These bargains ensure that doesn't happen to them."

Bastilla's soul swirled into a ball, slowly made its way to Jaiden's hand. Long black nails emerged from his fingertips. Jaiden grabbed her soul, those black claws digging into the soft mist until it solidified into his palm. His eerie eyes darkened, his black pupils eating up all the color and then the whites of his eyes until nothing remained except two black fathomless holes.

He spoke and a million voices echoed around the isle. "I am simply relieving these souls of a tormented future."

"I know not what you are planning but in exchange for my free will, I will pledge my allegiance to you."

Jaiden's smile lifted one corner of his mouth as he held out his free hand and pointed to Lysander's jar. "An angel's soul?"

Charon nodded as he lifted the lid and watched the soul float to Jaiden's free hand. "One witch and one angel just as the *Book of Creation* demanded."

Jaiden's smile widened. "No, Charon, not as the book commanded, as I commanded."

Charon bowed his head as Jaiden absorbed the souls. It wasn't something he wanted to witness. When he looked up again, Jaiden was standing by the books of knowledge, his black fingernails softly tapping on the *Book of Light's* cover.

"I will need all of my books." Jaiden's voice had returned to normal, yet now it sounded more grounded. "First, find the remainder of them that are on earth."

"It would be most helpful to know who has them or at least where they are located."

Jaiden closed his eyes, his head tilting to the right. "Seek out the one called Alexander, a descendant of Amay. He will lead you to the next book and to the next soul I will require. "

"The Destroyer?" Charon bowed his head as Jaiden nodded. "And if he stands in my way?"

Jaiden's eyes flashed. "Persuasion will go a long way and if he refuses, do whatever you need to do to retrieve the book and the soul of someone lost, but never forgotten."

Charon bowed his head. "As you command."

• • •

Payne materialized inside Isten's throne room to a thunderous roar. The walls shook, a fine shower of dust and small pieces of black marble cluttering the air. In front of the throne, Gyth stood with his hand firmly on Elena's shoulder, holding her in place on her knees before Isten. Varick stood to the right of Gyth, his head bowed, but with his fists clenched behind his back. Payne couldn't help but notice his knuckles were white and his jaw was jerking.

Isten stood as Payne cleared his throat to announce his presence. Isten's hand tightened around the hilt of the sword hanging at his side as he descended from the steps to stand before Elena.

"Where are Jaiden's bones?"

Elena laughed, her lip dripping with gold blood. Her wings fluttered, their soft glow shedding light on Isten's cold, dark throne room. Anyone would have taken the situation at hand differently than it actually was. She looked the saintly victim.

Without pause, Isten drew his sword, pointed it at her throat. "Speak the truth, Angel. Tell me where his bones are and tell me where that forsaken book is."

"Which book are you referring to?" Elena spat out as Gyth shoved her down, pinning her shoulders to the floor.

"Tell him, Elena. You have done far too much damage as it is." Gyth eased his hold. "Where are the books that were in your possession?"

Slowly, she sat up, her arms shaking. Isten walked in a circle around her as she tried to regain her composure pulling her wings closer to her body.

When she spoke, there was venom dripping from her words. "You shall all reap what has been sowed."

Isten kicked her forward, stepped onto her spine, and grabbed both wings in one hand. With one swing of his sword, her wings were cut off at the shoulder blades. Elena screamed, the sound reverberating off of the walls. Her blood glittered as it spurted into the air, droplets splashing across Isten's armor. She scrambled and jerked, her body contorting with pain.

Gyth grabbed her, turned her onto her back as her blood pooled beneath her. Payne swallowed hard, regardless of what the Angel had done, this was torture and he knew what it felt like to be on the receiving end of it.

"Where are those books?" Gyth's face was emotionless. "Where are they?"

"In hell." She spit in Gyth's face. "Kill me now."

"No." Isten replaced his sword. "What say you, Gyth? What fate should she receive?"

Gyth jerked Elena up as Isten turned to Payne and motioned him forward. Gritting his teeth, Payne stepped forward trying to keep the pity he felt for Chanta's mother smothered in his chest. Regardless of the fact that Isten and Gyth were gods, the ruling powers that be, wrong was still wrong.

"Life renewed." Gyth ushered her toward Isten. "As human. To live as one who she would have condemned."

"No." Elena twisted, tried to break free of Gyth's grasp. "I cannot live as those mongrels do."

Isten grabbed her mop of sunny blonde curls and brought her to his chest. In a blur, Isten buried his fingers into her ribs. Instantly, she slumped into his arms, her scream fading as he took her powers. Payne watched as her dripping blood lost its glitter, turned orange, and then ran red.

Tightening his fists, Payne put a leash on his emotions. "Jaiden's bones and the books are in Charon's possession. He is your traitor."

Isten released Elena, her body slumping to the floor as her tears streaked her face. "Charon? Are you sure of this?"

Payne nodded. "Elena made a bargain with him for those bones and one of his books."

The other book, the one Elena had given Chanta was also in Charon's possession. Payne was all too well aware of that, he had been completely aware of the bargain Charon had made with Chanta, just unable to stop it or interfere.

Isten turned on his heel. "What did she receive in exchange?"

"That Damon would have no physical contact with her daughter."

Payne flexed his jaw. Chanta was carrying Damon's child, Payne's brother, but no one needed to know that. Let them think the child belonged to him. He would be loved and treated well. He would have the life that Payne never had.

Isten laughed, a deep roar echoing off the marble walls. He stared at Elena, his tangible fury mocking his laughter.

"In hopes that Chanta would not give birth to a son fated to kill his grandmother." Isten paused and met Gyth's topaz stare. "Funny thing about fates, they tend to work themselves out in the end no matter what you do to stop it."

Gyth stiffened visibly. "If Charon made that bargain, he will ensure Damon never touches her."

"We shall see." Isten turned back to Elena briefly. "Get this wench off my marble, deposit her on earth, and find Charon."

Gyth dematerialized with Elena as Isten spoke again. "Varick, you seem to owe Payne a wish."

Varick nodded. "What is your heart's desire?"

Payne stood there, couldn't find the words. His heart's desire? There was only one thing he wished for at that moment, one little thing with white hair and big gray warrior eyes. Chanta was his only desire. And she was Varick's sister. He was sure that was going to go over real well.

Cold steel eyes met his. "Speak, Payne. You have kept your end of the bargain and we shall keep ours."

Payne shook his head. "I want nothing from either of you."

There was only one place he wanted to be, one thing he desired above all else, and one thing he wanted to embrace. His last sight was of Varick looking confused as Payne dematerialized and reappeared inside Chanta's small apartment.

• • •

As Chanta walked out of her tiny kitchen with her steaming mug of hot chocolate in her hand, his heart melted. Her blinding smile welcomed him as she quickly sat the mug on an end table and threw herself into his arms.

"There's something I need to tell you." Chanta whispered.

"There's no need." Payne wrapped his arms around her, embraced her. "I was aware of the entire conversation you and Charon had."

Placing his hand on her belly, he bowed his head closing his eyes. "My brother will have a life I never had. He will know love, family, and friends."

"Payne?" Chanta ran her fingers down his cheeks.

"You once asked me if there was anything you could do to make me want to stay."

He knew she was nodding without looking, felt her body stiffen. But it was now or never, he had a confession to make.

She tried to step back, but he held her against his body, her tiny frame suddenly becoming his anchor. "There's something I need to tell you though."

"What's that?"

"Can you handle the devil's son being in love with you?"

A small laugh escaped her. "Only if you can handle being in love with Gyth's daughter and at this point I don't think that's much better of an option."

Releasing her waist, he took her face in his hands and kissed her lips. "Oh, I think I can see past my differences with your father."

"Well, it's a good thing because I'm afraid I might actually, kind of, sort of have a thing for the devil's son."

"Kind of, sort of?"

Chanta smiled. "Yeah, just a little bit of possessiveness has been showing through."

He laughed, his smile threatening to overtake his face. "Yeah, I kind of heard you tell this poor woman that he belonged to you."

"Heard that, did you?"

He nodded as he kissed her again. "I think we need to make this official or something."

"I think that can wait." She looked down the hall. "I have other plans for you right now."

"What plans are those?"

"I want to make love to you." Her eyes twinkled as the red streaks appeared in her hair. "And I want you to know exactly how you make me feel."

As she took his hand and pulled him behind her, he had to fight back the tears. The world was always going to be threatened by some kind of impending doom, but as long as Chanta was by his side, he could face anything. He could even defy the odds and rewrite his own destiny.

"I love you, Payne."

With a quick swoop, he lifted her from the floor and carried her over the threshold into her bedroom. "My little enchantress, you had me wrapped around your finger since the first time I met you and I was too blinded by vengeance to see it."

She laughed as he eased her onto the bed. "Then perhaps, we should be thanking my father for sending you to Kentucky."

"Indeed." His god powers shifted inside of him, but there was no need or desire to hide them. For the first time in his life, he was content with who and what he was.

As he stretched out on top of Chanta, he smiled. "This is my destiny. In your arms, I have finally found what I have desired my entire life and never had."

Chanta bit her lip. "What's that?"

She was smiling, her gray eyes shining. Payne's chest ached, his heart burning with passion. "Love."

More from This Author

(From *Embrace the Fire* by Spring Stevens)

Varick rarely ever dreamed, but as the first rays of the sun peeked over the horizon, images of people he had never known swam to his unconscious mind's eye. Their skin glowed iridescently, transparent right down to their souls. Smoky balls of shadow swirled inside the glow and clawed at their transparent prisons and screamed for release. Their sorrows and pains were magnified by the predominance of unrequited fury and unobtainable justice of their ills.

Dancing and swirling around those unfamiliar faces were black flames and daggers, the same daggers that graced his skin as trademarks of his immortal profession. He was a Destroyer, protector of the One Race and the humans, and bringer of death to the demon spawn of the Underworld. He was one of many but here, in this dream turned nightmare, he was bitterly and utterly alone.

The swirling images settled, the landscape in the mist manifesting under his feet, glowing with the vivid greens and blues of some lost jungle. Swathed in white silk and flowing robes, his form appeared atop a towering mountain minutes before dawn. Known for his unshakable logic and meticulous approach to any situation, he swallowed hard, realizing his insides trembled and his hands shook.

Directly below the peak, hundreds of writhing vampires screamed in agony as the sun rose without mercy, slowly spreading the deadly golden hue. Their dead eyes looked up to him as they tried to claw their way into the ground. And those empty, dead eyes seemed to beg him for deliverance, even if it was at the end of his sword. A quick death by sword was degrees better than suffering the flaming torch of the sun.

And he stood as stone, watching and uncaring.

He twisted violently in his bed of black satin sheets. His mouth opened as if to scream. His long incisors gleamed in the darkness of his chambers as his back arched up from the bed. Still deep in the dream, he watched helplessly as his own skin began to melt and drip from his bleached-white bones. His ashes flew into the four winds and disappeared with the blinding sun's rays.

His eyes flew open, thankful they were looking into the blackness of his chambers. He clutched at his chest, his heart racing wildly.

Jackknifing off of the bed, Varick ran his shaking hands through his long, white hair. He strode across the windowless room, his topaz eyes seeing clearly in the pitch black. He reached for a glass and a bottle of brandy as he tried to collect himself. He swallowed hard, much harder than he had in the dream. Brandy was his preferred drink, blood was his necessary nutrient, and death was but a bittersweet dream.

Laughter rang out as he settled his thoughts. Death? Indeed!

He had experienced it once, and now he wondered when he would experience it again—even immortality had its end. Would his soul ever know peace? Or would Gyth capture it again, as he had so many years ago, when Varick had met his first death?

"Your dreams plague you," a detached voice echoed around his room.

Cursing profusely, Varick spun around, barely managing to keep the glass in his hand. With a soft growl, he bowed slightly as Gyth appeared in the same long, white robes Varick had been wearing in the dreams. Suspicion crept up his spine as the god raised his hand and the overhead lights flooded the concrete and steel dwelling.

This was his sanctuary. It was deep underground and almost out of everyone's radars. All except for Gyth, of course.

"You're shaking," Gyth stated flatly as he turned and inspected the chambers where Varick slept. "Do your dreams often plague you?"

The only time they didn't plague him was when he was blissfully intoxicated. Currently, he was extremely sober, but as soon as Gyth was gone, he was going to remedy that.

Gods, how many years had he been a Destroyer?

Two thousand, almost to the day. He thought back to the time when there had been ten Destroyers, ten who hunted the vampire, the witch, and the werewolf. For over a thousand years, the ten of them had killed without mercy, without pause, and without regret. Humanity had flourished easily with the decline of the demons, their sightings diminishing so much so that the humans had eventually considered the demons myths.

"What do you want?"

"Destroyer," Gyth grunted. "You're not your usual self. I'll forgive you this one insolence, but dare not to make another."

Trying to keep from rolling his eyes, Varick set the glass down. "Alexander is our leader—why come to me? I'm just a Destroyer, and I follow his orders."

"He is only because you refused to accept leadership." Gyth sat on the edge of Varick's bed, looking completely out of place. "Tell me, Varick—being part vampire, does that bother you? Does destroying other vampires plague you?"

A slow burn of bitterness welled up inside his heart. "How do you refuse to answer a god?"

"You don't."

Gritting his teeth, Varick brought the glass to his lips and swallowed. "There's not one day that passes in my long life that I regret slaughtering any of them—not vampire, not werewolf, and not witch. And until I meet my end, I'll continue doing so."

"Why, then, do you have these dreams that make your hands shake? You're a meticulous, calculating Destroyer, eager for battle and eager for the hunt of my enemies, yet when in the confines of your privacy, you have trouble sleeping." Gyth stood, his robes pooling at his feet. "It seems highly illogical."

Biting back his pride, Varick took a deep breath and nodded. "Seems that way."

"I'll leave you with some advice, wanted or not."

Perhaps he had not heard the god correctly, or maybe he was still dreaming.

"Advice?" Varick laughed bitterly. "I don't need your advice!"

"Careful, Destroyer. You threaten to step across a line that will lead you down a paved road to punishment."

"Don't you mean pain? Because that is, after all, what you do when we defy you or threaten your tyranny." Varick stepped toe-to-toe with the white-haired god. "I already kill for you—what else you want? My blood? Oh, wait, you got that already when you let me drain dry before I was reborn. My sworn oath? Oh no, you got that too. Let me guess—my skin hanging in your bedroom?"

A rumble of power echoed around the room as the Destroyer was lifted from his feet and slammed into the concrete and steel wall with unseen hands. Gyth grunted and held him against the wall with his powers.

Releasing him, Gyth announced nonchalantly. "For the next several weeks, perhaps months, you'll find yourself under distress as the Mating Rite lays siege upon your body."

As his backside hit the floor, Varick groaned, letting his head fall back against the wall with a thump. "What? No, I can't go through that."

With a smirk and a quick laugh, Gyth answered. "You already are. Accept it as it is and don't fight it. The more you fight it, the worse it will be."

The Mating Rite was every Destroyer's eventual torture. It was nature's simple way of taking them down a notch or two. The need to mate would overwhelm him, and his control would slowly melt away and leave him depressingly needful of a woman. According to Gyth, the Mating Rite was a necessary evil, the consequence of being reborn.

Must not be his lucky century.

"Why?" he grumbled under his breath. "Why did you come here?"

The god shrugged. "Morbid curiosity."

Slowly, Varick stood. "Curiosity about what?"

Facing the Destroyer, Gyth narrowed his golden eyes. "Why do you not want to be the leader of my Destroyers?"

Destroyers. They were created by Gyth to protect the One Race, a race of people who resided on earth that were descendants of the gods. Members of the One Race were not considered true gods because they had only one parent that was. They were not allowed in the Heavens or in the Underworld. And there was always someone or something trying to eradicate the One Race. The Destroyers eliminated those threats.

Above protecting the One Race, the Destroyers were to obey Gyth, the king of the heavenly gods, in all things, no matter if those orders conflicted with protecting the One Race or not.

Of course, several pointed laws adhered to being a Destroyer. Do not stray into evil. Do not kill humans. Do not reveal your true nature to the humans. Do not rise against Gyth. Follow orders without pause.

"I'm not a leader. I'm a killer now, just as I was when you found me."

An odd expression lingered on the god's face. "Your hatred of your mother's race intrigues me."

"Does it? Then perhaps you should know that my hatred extends far beyond just the vampires. I hate everyone equally." A muscle ticked in his strong jaw. "It keeps me indifferent and makes me a better killer."

"And this hatred," Gyth whispered. "Is eating at your soul."

Varick turned and spat out, "My soul? I lost my soul when I watched my mother … "

The words stuck in the back of his throat, his eyes burning. He wondered what in the nine hells was wrong with him as memories flooded his mind. Shaking his head, he turned back to the desk where he had set the glass and suddenly needed more of the potent sting of alcohol against the back of his throat.

Gyth, the Great Infallible One—not only was he a god; he was the head god, lord and king of the Heavens and Earth. He was an all-powerful, all-seeing, and all kinds of pain in the backside kind of guy. Yeah, well, the way Varick saw it, if Gyth was so all-powerful and lordly, why couldn't he take out all the demons himself?

He paused in his thoughts as Gyth vanished, blackness closing in, and for a mere breath of a second he wondered why Gyth had come to visit him and why he had announced that the Mating Rite was on his heels.

Who was he to try to understand a god? And why should he care to begin with? It was not in his preordained position to question the whys and how comes. He knew his path. He was a killer—always had been and always would be.

Looking down at his still-shaking hands, he cursed. He was out of his element, out of his usual demeanor, and he damn sure didn't like it. After all, why would a dream and an unusual visit from Gyth affect him this way? It shouldn't have. Yet it did.

Or perhaps it was the Mating Rite closing in? It had nothing to do with his vampire half, nor did it have anything to do with the memories of his long-dead mother. And it sure didn't have a damn thing to do with his past, his present, or his future.

He was what he was. Easy as that.

Agreeing to disagree with himself, he shelved his emotions and forced himself to get a grip. He was a Destroyer, well known for his flawless accuracy and unbending logic and control. He was not going to allow the Mating Rite or anything else to interfere with his life.

Turning on his heel, he grabbed the bottle from the desk and stretched his six-foot-six frame out onto his bed. His rebirth, the day he had become a Destroyer, lay in the back of his thoughts, and that was just where the hell he wanted it to stay. His life before his rebirth was not something he spoke of, nor did he want to rehash those bitter, burning memories.

Closing his eyes, he yawned, his incisors slipping back into their sheaths as sleep once again demanded his attention. The dawn did that to a Destroyer and, unfortunately, it did that to a half-breed vampire as well.

• • •

The *Book of Creation* lay at the Tree of Life's deeply rooted trunk. The book's silver cover had been inscribed with the eight signs of the true zodiac in a perfect figure eight. The eight symbols depicted the original gods of Creation. Within the book's pages lay ancient knowledge that legions upon legions had fought and died for, that many a soul had given up home, family, and love for.

But the book was just one of many. Many that now needed to be found and brought together with the *Book of Creation*.

The book's caretaker stood on the edge of the small island, his black and silver robe softly fluttering against his long, powerful legs. Shrouded within his robes, his face was hidden, his emotions as unreadable as the wind. His demeanor was indifferent; his stance was that of a seasoned warrior, ever ready, ever deadly. There was but one purpose at all times, to protect and obey the written word of the *Book of Creation* at all costs and protect the Tree of Life.

The book's original owner and creator, an ancient god called Jaiden, was inconceivably missing and thought dead. He alone had protected the sacred words; he alone would have massacred the entire human and god-born races if the book so commanded.

Except now, the books were demanding Charon's attention.

Charon had lived on this island hidden in the translucent waters of the River Styx many years before the book had suddenly appeared. His only true companions were the Tree of Life, the book, and the River Styx. And here he had remained since the downfall of the Olympian gods, waiting, preparing, and watching until recently when he had felt the pull of Jaiden's soul.

The island floated in the invisible river that separated the Heavens, the Earth, and the Underworld; there was no better hiding place. He turned and stared at the silver palace towering above the granite hillside as his mind wandered with thoughts he had never had before. Thoughts that now puzzled him.

The robe covering his face fell away, his red eyes glowing in an ashen, yet beautiful face. With one hand curled around a red-and-black bone scythe, he held out the other and called forth the book. Hundreds of years had passed since he had read from the pages he so precariously protected.

One corner of his lip lifted as the book appeared open in his palm, eager for him to read. He watched the pages turn until midway a page fluttered, its soft glow shimmering as words appeared before his eyes. The translucent waters of the River Styx bubbled and whispered to him, a vortex of water opening at the edge of the island.

The page turned, the words churning in his mind as he slowly closed the book. The fate of the Universe hung in the balance of good and evil, dangled on many single choices, and Charon managed a cold laugh. And now the world's hope lay within the Destroyers' choices, as they had free will if they chose to use it.

He paused before turning to Styx.

Styx bubbled and gurgled around him announcing a visitor. Charon's eyebrow rose. No one had ever visited this place.

With a purple flash and a wisp of smoke, Terror Sky of the Elemental gods appeared before Charon in full dragon glory. Large red scales melted and molded into human flesh. His body contorted and decreased in size until standing before him was a man with long black hair and a single red braid hanging from his temple.

"What brings you to my world?" Charon asked suspiciously.

"As much as I don't want to trust you, Isten informs me that I must do so. He has seen a vision of a new age, insists that you be made aware of the importance of a male known as Varick. His destiny is uncertain, leaving the future uncertain as well."

"Yes, a new age is approaching, and soon these prison walls will crumble around us and the doorways will once again be opened." Charon's face shimmered, leaving behind the bleached white bones of a skull with red eyes. "Soon the tides will be set in motion, and the game shall begin. Only destinies chosen wisely will lead the sun to set on a new era."

"I have kept watch over Varick for many years." Terror Sky ran his hand through his long, dark hair. "He must be protected until the time comes for his decision."

Charon grinned under his hood. "A game of life and death. No doubt you're aware of his former life and what he'll become if the wrong decision is made."

Terror Sky narrowed his swirling eyes. "We must set things right and force the right decisions on these Destroyers if Isten's intended future is to be realized."

The book opened in Charon's hand as Terror Sky said, "Now is the perfect time to push Varick toward the life Isten intended for him."

Pointing a long talon at the words that had appeared in the book, Charon whispered, "This Varick Ta Farg, a half-breed vampire, must rise from his own ashes, choose a destiny that lies before him, and … " He paused as Styx rushed around him, causing small whirlpools to appear chaotically across the island. "And he will pave the road that will lead to salvation or destruction."

Terror Sky replied, "The fate of the world rests on a half-breed vampire's head. Are you prepared for that, Charon?"

Charon laughed. "The book has commanded, and I must obey."

"Someone is changing the words of Jaiden's books. I don't know how or why they do so, but they must be stopped before more harm befalls this universe."

"If the books are to be found, the *Book of Creation* will guide me to them," Charon stated.

Terror Sky paused, listening to the River Styx gurgling and swirling faster around the island. "Varick will have the power to restore the wrongs, but he must choose to do so freely."

Charon shook his head. "Perhaps his death will set things on the proper course."

"With my life, I'll protect him and his power even against the strongest of the gods." The Elemental's voice dropped dangerously low. "Even from that book and from you."

"I will not harm Varick at this time unless the book commands it—you can bet your immortality upon that."

"Or ever. Do we understand each other?" His silent threat hung in the air. "Or do I need to make myself perfectly clear on the subject?"

"Don't threaten me, Terror Sky."

"Harm one single thread of hair on his head, and you'll have no need to worry about your precious book!"

Abruptly the Elemental vanished, his telltale purple flash the only reminder of his presence. Charon laughed. Terror Sky's visit could only mean one thing. Whoever was meddling with Jaiden's books had to be found and stopped.

Styx churned with power as Charon stepped into the vortex of translucent water. Styx swept him up and cradled him as the Tree of Life groaned and settled deeper into the island's core, preparing itself for whatever might come.